I0535661

CATSKILLS TANGO

Third of CatSkill Trilogy

By
Lisa Annette Powell

ISBN: 978-0-9906428-3-1

Cover art design by author; graphics by Brian Busse

With grateful acknowledgement to Emily, Terri, and Tiger Creek Wildlife Refuge for allowing me the use of their beautiful photos and for all the great things they do for the big cats. Please check out and support their efforts at tigercreek.org

---

With gratitude to Joshua Tree National Park
for posting this beauty

TO THE WILD

May we appreciate your beauty

The origins of the Tuatha d' DaNaan (talented Gods and Goddesses revered by the ancient Celts) are shrouded in the darkness of time. Or do they reside in light?

1

"I should be court-martialed," thoroughly ashamed, I mumbled into Riordan's armpit.

The fragrance of resurrected wooly mammoth still lingered. Ah, this was the scent I detected on my husband upon his return from parts blocked to me. Not unpleasant, simply different. The natural scents of wild animals aren't anathema to my wild nature, even when I'm in human form. Other humans would not agree, I idly reflected, seeking to put off the inevitable remonstrance I deserved.

A reverberation orienting in Riordan's gut effused my way as he held my exhausted body in his arms.

The rumbles broke out, he laughed uproariously- surrendering completely to tension-relieving guffaws, jostling me like a ship in the wake of a storm's turbulence.

"Court-martialed!" He managed to gasp, in-between his raucous amusement.

"Whatever for? Wife, my Lioness, you were amazing! I wish there had been a camera on so you could see yourself. Never in history has such a young shaman, yet alone a female, had a more difficult trial-training by fire. Speaking of fire, you've added a third element to your repertoire. Bonnie, you are magnificent! I'm extremely proud of you. . ."

"But, I nearly got everyone killed! If you'd not come back. . . Gunne suffered two mortal injuries. Handsome! What was he doing here? My dad, Rick. . . Oh, my God! Were they watching? And you. . . The last I saw of you, you were slumped over Handsome's back stuck full of arrows! If I lost you. . ."

"Ssh, Wife, ssh," Riordan shook his head. He actually seemed puzzled at my distress.

We were out of sight of the battleground, thankfully. He could have transported us anywhere in the world, but here we were in a nearby, secluded pine tree enclosed spot, resting against a boulder, me in his arms.

"Look at me, Bonnie."

Tears started, accompanied by trembling. The aftermath. Realization of my inadequacies. Shock.

"Look at me," he demanded. "If you don't, I will cast a spell on you," he threatened with a quirky smile.

"You can't put a spell on me," I quibbled. "I've been under your sway ever since we met."

All too true. From the moment he'd instituted the English instructor's question into my fogged brain, watched me sleep through lunch-protectively hovering as if I'd not wake on time-the wonder of my body's every cell recognized its other half, my heart and soul. Even though I couldn't rationally accept any of it for a time, my spirit knew where it belonged and to whom.

"Wife," he lightly bussed my lips with his as my eyes rose to meet those glorious, gold cat eyes. "I forget how young. . ."

This roused me to indignant protest, as I'm sure he knew it would, but he caught and bound me closer to his chest, silenced my objections with a more fervent kiss. I didn't understand how. . .

"I see the list of questions getting longer and longer- sort of like a kid's wish list for Santa. I've something to say and then I'll allow you one question. The other 1000 can wait until you've eaten and rested. No one shaman with as little experience as you have could have frozen Chac in place for as long as you did, if at all. Raining that ice on the wraiths and the lightening and wind- ingenious! I hoped the stone would come into play; I assume it was the prophecy- 'It will save the life of all I hold dear.' Certainly, that came through today.

The superstitions the wraiths held as humans- well, they were struck dumb by your talents. As for Chac, I'm sure he regretted not having a snowball's chance, no pun intended, of winning you to his side. He must have rued the day he ever envisioned you. The fire that destroyed his flung spear- ah, Wife, I repeat, you are amazing! I know you're curious about a lot of things right now. Please suffice it to say, you were EXTRA-ORDINARY. When you reach your full capacity, I'm in trouble." An engaging grin sparked his eyes, so full of love for me.

"But. . ."

"If you insist upon punishment, it's because you just don't understand. In your intransigence, though, I'll oblige."

He really did think I had failed- his words were solely a balm poured on my shamed self! I hung my head again, felt tears dribbling, chin quaking.

"Bonnie, I'm kidding! If you feel you must pay for being amazing, may I suggest a few dozen of your cookies?"

He started to chortle all over again. Couldn't stop. His succumbing whole-heartedly, giving way to riotous laughter, made me pause and reflect.

Was it simply a matter of being inexperienced? Red Hawk, himself, had said Chac would most likely defeat him- a shaman of hundreds of years. In the violent sweep of the encounter I'd lost my focus for worrying about Riordan. . .

"I must remember in the future to always keep you informed that I'm all right, Wife. Now, to get you home, nourished and put to. . .bed," he winked provocatively as he tilted my chin up and enticed me with his expertise.

"The question you promised," I pulled away, regretfully.

"One," he agreed.

"Is it all over?"

Eyes full of merriment, he savored his reply. "I stomped that jaguar to smithereens, Wife, and those smithereens, as we speak, are being raked together for a lovely bonfire. Now, you have to rest. Tomorrow night the Lakota are staging a celebratory ritual, and we must attend, as ourselves."

"My dad, Rick, Handsome, Gunne, is everyone safe and well?"

"You're cheating, Wife," Riordan warned.

"Riordan, I couldn't possibly sleep without knowing," I refused to give in.

"Handsome is being treated for a very slight wound, although he'll probably present it to you. . . Never mind, he played a major role in the whole business. I'll tell you more, later. Better yet, I'll let him tell you. As for your father and Rick, they are unharmed, and were enthusiastically instrumental in efficiently dispatching many phantoms. You'll hear all the coup-counting stories tomorrow night. As for their witnessing the very end, well," Riordan paused, lips twitching, "Grandfather and Gunne are trying to convince Rick and Jim that I'm the new David Copperfield- master of illusions. Not sure if that's going to work or not. . ." Riordan mulled.

My jaw fell of its own accord, "Oh, my goodness!"

2

'Dragon,' I telepathically called.

'What now, CatSkill?'

'Would you remove your trance from the animals here? I don't want Bonnie to see them as 'dead'.'

The dragon harrumphed, loudly. 'That black beast of a horse refused to be seduced for his own protection. In fact, I've never encountered such a hard-to-guard crew of creatures. I couldn't find the cats. . .'

'Yeah, I expect Irusan had already provided for their safety. By the way, how are you feeling?'

'Thanks to Grace, pretty much myself. Luckily, my life is tied to. . .'

'Can it! I don't care to hear about your continued passion for my Wife,' I seethed.

'No other woman can ever compare to. . .'

'Dragon,' I snarled an admonishment.

'That elephant dance step of yours was certainly effectual. We'll be picking up jaguar bits all night, for cryin' out loud! You know Chac's demise invalidated the few remaining wraiths- skulking, struck dumb and dead, they simply vanished. I must admit. . .'

I let him rattle on to himself.

'CatSkill, you owe me a shirt!'

But I'd already blocked him. There were more important things to do- like get my Wife to bed. . .

"Riordan, I'm starving."

"You're not the only one. I've the appetite of an elephant- one who hasn't eaten in a very long time," I grinned at her enchanting form sitting up in our bed. "What would you like to eat, Lioness?"

"A pizza. A big cheese pizza with extra, extra cheese." I heard her stomach charivari its approval.

"Hmm, that does sound good. Phone it in, and I'll pop into town to pick it up."

"Pop into town?"

"Yeah, I think I know of a dark, quiet corner. Beats driving and you'll receive your pizza fresh and piping hot from the oven, Wife."

She reached for the phone while I showered and threw on some clothes sans 'eau de elephant'.

Bonnie wasn't kidding when she said she was starving. I paid for an extra-large and a large pizza from Rizzoli's, and hastened to my transport spot.

"Hey, Chief! Where you rushing off to?"

To ignore this invited their diligently dogging me- not sure of the cast of those words. However, wouldn't do, I was too close to where I'd hoped to disappear from.

Before confronting my fans, my wild senses informed me of how many contenders awaited my attention, and their exact positions in the alley schematics. Six intoxicated graduates looking for trouble. Sam, last year's basketball punk, acted as the leader.

"You'll have to excuse me this time, friends. I've had a long day, as has my Wife. We're both extremely hungry, and Bonnie gets especially riled when she doesn't eat on time, and our dinner is cooling as we chat. How about a rain check?" I offered a good-natured alternative.

Sam sneered, indicated for two of his buddies to flank me.

Oh, well, I tried. So much for fresh, hot pizza.

"May I at least set these boxes down in a safety zone?"

The idiots thought this was hilarious. I deftly ascended a stack of pallets and set the pizza boxes atop.

Briefly, I wondered how they'd respond to a wooly mammoth in their midst. Overkill, CatSkill, overkill. Just a thought, I quipped to my own censure.

The uncoordinated fist of one intoxicated, unsportsmanlike bully whooshed from behind me. I spun and kicked out- bowling all over again, only with drunks this time instead of football players.

Sam and two others rushed me. I Kung Fu sidestepped and spanked them on their way to sprawling in the fragrant, trash-strewn alleyway.

The last two swaying attempted to jump me. Attempted. Awkward, vain undertakings. Alas, the poor judgment of the inebriated. . .

'Riordan?' Bonnie's silent communiqué reached me. 'Where's my pizza?'

'A slight delay, Wife.' Uh oh, I'd said the wrong words.

Bonnie's wild cat sense had urgently implored to be let out this afternoon. In being denied its presence, the tiniest excuse provided an outlet. The cat was about to come out of the bag.

I heard her snarl of disapproval in the darkness. Flustered humans heard it, too. The strident pique nearly echoed in the brick-walled confines. Lovely.

"What was that?" Befuddled, they peered around, tried to regain their feet, groped for hand-ups from each stumbling other, startled, unhurt, not so sure about continuing the fracas.

The snarl railed again, followed by hissing and spitting.

'Easy, Lioness,' I cautioned.

"Gentlemen, I see my Wife has come to object to your holding up her supper," I thoughtfully clued them into the mystery. "I did warn you. . ."

Bonnie's long, drawn out snarl trilled eerily in what now sufficed as a twilight zone to my odious groupies. Pretty funny, except, I was hungry, too.

"Wh. . . What?" A smattering of brain cells must have remained unimpaired, for faces quickly endeavored to sober as they searched for the source of my love's objections.

"C'mon! He's just making those noises to scare us. He thinks we're stupid."

I didn't have to waste a split second ruminating on their IQ's; it was an absolute given the lowest ranks prevailed.

Bonnie accessed the cover of the myriad articles lining the darkened strip, and swatted at the seat of one of the brain-deficient.

A swath of jean material went flying. Such nice sharp claws- I leaned against a brick wall, and duly admired the proceedings.

'Careful, Wife, of their hide. Not sure it's beneficial to leave evidence of a cougar in downtown Cody.'

She hissed again.

"M…my pants!" The dismantled jeans of the recipient slumped about his ankles.

'Don't look, Bonnie, a potential streaker is in our midst!' I hooted at the spectacle- literally, owls are part of my repertoire.

Grasping pants with one hand, he tried to run as the others frantically searched for the assailant, yet not at all sure they should linger for the privilege.

No one was paying any attention to me anymore. I considered picking up the pizzas and going home.

But Sam had a last go in him, and came at me arms flying in a most un-boxer-like maneuver. I simply swept his feet out from under him.

Bonnie, my elegant Lioness, removed a few more articles of clothing in tattered streamers, and the idiots gunned their motors, floundering in various stages of undress in escalated efforts to exit- stage right.

My soul mate stepped from the shadows and transformed back to her lovely human self, after licking her paws.

I picked up our dinner and we traveled home.

"Think you could use a little bit of that fire and reheat these, Wife?"

3

"Aaah!" A shriek of monumental proportions hit the air waves.

I'd just settled into a sweet nap after a sweeter tango with my Wife. As my sensitive ears fought to live through the high-pitched scream, I bounded from the comfort of our bed only to be struck in the head by at least two kittens flying off in various directions seeking safer, quieter quarters.

Amore and the rest of her brood were jet propelled from their section of our king size bed and hurled out like a backwash. What a circus! And what the devil was all the racket?

Where was Bonnie? Chac had met his maker. Surely no wraiths hid under the bed or in closets. My head swiveled; my senses honed in on. . .

"Bonnie, my love, don't you think it's slightly beneath the dignity of such a powerful shaman to be screaming her head off about such a small spider? I'm sure he'd share the tub with you."

Half-naked, I stood in the bathroom entry, my gaze locked on a beautiful set of bare legs skipping about the tiled floor.

As the shrieks dwindled at her savior's approach, Bonnie pointed and I did my husbandly duty- softly scooped up the unwary trespasser, offered him a rueful grin. His ear drums didn't seem to be ringing. Briefly, I thought about setting him on Bonnie's head.

"Don't you dare," she warned, eyes glittering, trailing me to the nearest window. I blocked the thought- if it weren't so amusing I'd consider setting a no spiders' zone in place, and why hadn't she thought of that?

The old sepia photographs couldn't do justice to the colorful panorama gracefully adorning the meadow. Three tipis stood in a semi-circle on burgeoning prairie grass, bordered with evergreens to the west and newly leafed cottonwoods to the east. A gurgling stream provided background music as it happily tripped over rocks on its merry way.

Two of the tipis were painted with different designs using basic colors: red, black, yellow, blue. As Riordan and I drew closer, I discovered they were not canvas structures but real buffalo hide-bound lodges.

One of the structures obviously belonged to Grandfather. Simple wings were spread across the hide. Hawk eyes were painted above the opening as if to scrutinize potential entrants. The back side displayed the russet tail feathers of Grandfather's spirit guide. At the top flap opening, which was the escape route for the smoke from any fire within, constellations of the Milky Way were set against a near black background.

In front, near the open doorway, a feather-fringed shield portraying a Red Hawk was set on a tripod.

Another of the painted lodges, equally as large, had blue ripples painted near the smoke flap. Underneath, animals chased each other round the hide covering.

"Otters," Riordan broke into my musings.

Beneath the otters were black bands and wolf heads thrown back in a howling mode- four of them. The four directions, I knew.

"The water ripples represent the liminal area between worlds. This lodge belongs to. . . I'll introduce you later."

The buffalo hide walls had been raised from the ground to allow for air flow as it was rather warm for a Wyoming early June.

All tipi openings faced east and horses were staked near. Handsome was ardently investigating the female equine contingent, but he greeted me with a nicker of welcome before arching his neck and continuing his amorous pursuits.

"The Lakota were eager to rise again," Riordan leaned into me. I knew nothing of this- what my circumspect husband had planned on the sly. Puzzled, my brain tripped over which question to ask first, but before I could engage my voice. . .

"When we visited Cloud, I told him of what was coming. These warriors are our answer to Chac's phantom army. I described the odds- we expected near 300, but a good Lakota warrior is worth at least 30 aboriginals- at least, that's my understanding."

The corner of his mouth turned up in its beguiling fashion as he reminisced his secret planning.

"I used Crazy Horse's and Red Cloud's ruse, acting as if I were retreating, when in reality I was the well-planned, dangled bait. Drew those wraiths into a canyon. Gotta love a well-timed ambush! Those phantoms were dispatched like sitting ducks. Better than any carnival game."

I opened my mouth to protest the danger to my father and Rick, the arrows in Riordan's back. . .

"Cloud made sure Rick and Jim were at the far end of the action, well-protected. While the Lakota and Wolf Walker finished mopping up the ghosts, I hurried back to you as. . ."

I shivered with the revived frisson of those tumultuous moments.

"It was you, Bonnie. You were the key. Do you remember asking me what a jaguar would be afraid of? Other than humans carrying guns, an elephant would stand up to a jaguar. The maharajas used elephants to conduct them on their tiger hunts.

My absence was spent studying those great mammals. I took a side trip to Siberia to observe the unearthing of a mammoth. Figured a slight overkill never hurt."

A giggle bubbled up from my core. Riordan as a wooly mammoth! His great shaggy, musty body, flapping ears, tender, curious, impressively strong trunk, almost tiny eyes. . .

"Can you change into a mammoth, again?"

"You liked it, didn't you?" Gently, he elbowed me.

"I think I would like a ride."

He mulled this over. "I'll save it for a winter surprise. Too warm right now. Getting back to this," he nodded at the Native American panoply.

"Grandfather envisioned the army Chac would bring. No live human beings- too detectable and not as easy to control. Chac summoned ancient tribesmen and bound them to him- sort of like zombie ghosts- wraiths controlled by evil magic.

Chac had sold his soul to ensure my downfall and yours. Aboriginal warriors, wraith or not, would recognize bow and arrow weapons. That is how they lived and fought when alive.

Chac believed only iron could send them back to their graves, or his own death."

"That's why you asked my dad to make those arrow heads?"

"Yes, I wasn't going to put too much faith in flint arrows. Iron was known from its introduction by Europeans in a superstitious way. As being magical. Born out of fire and tempered with water, beat with iron into shape. We obviously could not use bullets. Can you imagine what the people of Cody would have thought, with all the shooting? Couldn't involve investigating minds. The trick, then, was to find Lakota men proficient in the old ways."

"The Lakota came to fight for you, Riordan." Emotions wracked my senses.

"They came to fight for Lakota. This includes you. Do you think the Lakota would allow another tribe to attack their shamans? I don't think so. Much pride went into this camp. You'll hear their stories tonight. Come, Wife, they're waiting."

I saw my dad step out of the hawk-embraced lodge. He had marks on his cheeks.

"Coup marks, Wife," Riordan explained. "Rather incongruous with flannel shirt and jeans, huh?"

Rick, Grandfather and several others exited behind him, ducking under the open, hide-flap tipi door.

The Native men were clad in leggings, breech clouts, moccasins, shields of bone and beads hanging down on their bare chests. Feathers hung from braided locks or tangled in loose, long black hair.

Except for one- I recognized BJ and his incongruous crew-cut.

I would never forget this sight.

"Riordan, there must be a way to show intelligent, interested people the beauty in the old ways."

Riordan turned his face to the sun, "Maybe, Wife, maybe."

My dad hurriedly made his way to Riordan and me.

"Honey, you all right?" He examined me carefully.

I threw my arms around my dad, hugged fiercely and then stepped back to admire him with teary eyes. The lines painted on his cheeks looked quite pronounced up close, and took on more significance as he blushed.

"Dad, you look great," I bit my lip to stem tear trickling. In no time, we were surrounded, and it wouldn't do to succumb to an overt sign of weakness- not in this gathering.

From the smaller, less decorated tipi, emerged Grace, Shadow and Singing Breeze. Instantly, I knew. . .

"Shadow fought?" There was a harsh redness on her left arm which I recognized as the leftover from a bowstring's sting. Self-consciously, she brushed aside short locks.

Riordan simply laughed.

Shadow's chin rose- she'd disdained my query as well as Riordan's sardonic grin.

"Shadow does well with bow and arrows, Wife. She has an eye for her target," Riordan nodded a greeting of respect to her.

"Men aren't the only one's who'll fight for their own. Greetings, Lady Shaman, Girl as Cat," Shadow said.

"Girl as Cat?" I questioned.

Riordan tilted his head. 'My Wife should have a Lakota name,' he silently informed me.

'So you picked the name the raven called me? Unbelievable!' I quickly glanced around, looking for that feisty flirt as Riordan chuckled beguilingly in my ear.

"Grace, how is Dr. Gunne?" How had I forgotten his sacrifice?

Her lively eyes spoke so much more than her terse reply of "he's resting."

Riordan smirked, "Enjoying all the female attention, is he?"

Shadow defensively broke in, "He did receive two lances in his. . ."

Riordan cautioned her- there were still some secrets to be kept from my dad and Rick.

"Singing Breeze, it is good to see you looking well," my husband welcomed a buckskin-clad woman whose fringed dress was decorated with colored quill designs and tiny shells.

"Someone had to cook for these warriors," she responded. The pride was evident in her voice as she looked upon the young men closed around us.

Shadow was also clad in a soft leather tunic and leggings. Her short sleeves bore fringes with shells tied on the ends. Quite becoming with its cream color against her dark skin. In her hair she sported an eagle feather- as did the male warriors.

Of the men gathered around us, I knew Cloud, Blue and BJ. Riordan introduced the others as Grace and Grandfather's eyes gleamed at me.

"Black Bull, Running Antelope, Standing Rock. Christopher- Standing Rock is attending Harvard," Riordan smiled at his protégés.

I wasn't sure how to properly greet these so-very-young saviors. But I did fit right in, at least age-wise. They stood so quietly proud. Only BJ couldn't seem to maintain that impassive Lakota demeanor- a beaming smile plastered his features.

'Just say hello, Wife. They are people and they have all heard of the legendary Girl as Cat.'

'They're all so young, Riordan,' I silently admired. And I graciously thanked each one in turn.

Aloud, Riordan complimented them. "Lakota warriors begin at an early age. BJ is 15. Black Bull, 14. Running Antelope, 15. Standing Rock, 18. As it was in the old ways, so it is now."

I shuddered. No one in my senior class could have filled these shoes, er, moccasins. Except for Rick. Rick, next to my dad, grinned from ear to ear. He seemed an integral part of the group even though he wore jeans and an orange and navy striped rugby shirt. My attention was quickly garnered at another's approach.

Walking with an easy, silent gait, a man near Dr. Gunne's age approached from the otter and wolf lodge. The others parted, according him respectful space. A man of importance.

Riordan's hand rested possessively at my waist. My wild senses stirred. This man was a powerful shaman, too.

Tall, lithe and virile with a powerful, hard-planed chest, and a beautiful bronze face which held black eyes that saw along every dimension. His dark visage contrasted sharply with white ermine tails hanging over one ear. An impressive eagle feather graced his extremely long, loose, blue-black hair.

On his broad, naked chest rested a wolf tooth, tied about his neck with a leather thong. He, too, wore buckskin leggings and breech clout.

Standing opposite my husband, the two assessed each other for a loaded minute.

"Man Who Walks as a Cat, I've heard of you," the shaman addressed Riordan, speaking in a Sioux dialect which, amazingly, I understood- shades of my honeymoon.

I guess it would always amaze me.

"Wolf Walker," Riordan replied. "We are honored."

The shaman turned his knowing eyes on me- eyes fathoms deep and something stirred in those depths.

"Girl as Cat, my friend, the raven, spoke highly of you."

The surprises kept on coming. He'd spoken with our wildlife safari guide- that insouciant raven?

The shaman's eyes glittered. Silently, he continued. 'You are called Girl as Cat, but you are more, much more.'

His hand rose as if to touch me. Riordan hissed, but Wolf Walker took it in stride.

'You are also White Buffalo Heart. You feel for all as the buffalo provided for all. You have important work ahead.' His index finger came close but did not graze my chest.

Aloud, he continued. "I came to see for myself what the spirits and my friend, the raven, have told me. It was my honor to fight with the Lakota. The Blackfoot and the Lakota have been enemies too long. No more. We missed an important chance to join together for our common good. We will not miss the opportunity again."

He strolled toward Grandfather, and those two walked away together, engaged in silent communication.

"How extraordinary," I murmured. I felt the others pondering his meaning- sure my dad and Rick were absolutely clueless. My questions were certainly forming.

Everyone watched the mysterious Blackfoot shaman until he and Grandfather were out of sight. Although born Lakota, Grandfather looked foreign in his jeans and flannel shirt next to his Blackfoot guest.

'He knows more than he said, Wife. Perhaps, Grandfather and Wolf Walker are comparing notes on their respective visions concerning you.'

Riordan's gaze also followed the Blackfoot, speculating, not kindly. I felt his disturbance, but a sudden onslaught of weariness prevented me from questioning the shaman's speech or why my resolute husband wondered.

4

"Handsome!" I wandered over to my stallion-he'd stopped his erstwhile flirting, proudly arched his neck and regally beckoned me with tossing head, casting his heavy mane in all directions.

"You know, he refused the dragon's protection?" Riordan informed me.

'No one is leaving me home in a coma if my girl needs me,' the stallion aggressively snorted his silent communiqué rebuke.

Ruefully, Riordan tugged at his ear, "Seems I'm the one who needed you, Thunder Wind."

The black horse's nose soared into the air; he turned up his top lip, sniffed the breeze, shook his head and displaced his long mane, forelock nearly covering his eyes.

'I like this Thunder Wind,' Handsome acknowledged with a dignified whiffle.

"A Lakota name for Handsome- thank you, Riordan," I gave my husband a kiss.

"He deserves it. See his coup marks?"

Across Handsome's chest and down onto his legs were painted four lines.

'Good thing my front feet were shod with iron. I took out four of those road apples while Riordan dismounted. . .' Thunder Wind settled a humorous, condescending glance on my gold-eyed husband.

A chill ascended my arms; I looked to Riordan for an explanation.

"In pulling out those arrows, I discovered one was extra-vigorously planted in my left shoulder. In prying it loose, I tumbled, most ungracefully, off his back. Thunder Wind bought me some time."

My arms encircled my black beast's neck. Handsome lifted me off the ground gently, with august éclat. Upon touching earth again, I assiduously examined him while he stomped impatiently. Remnants of a healing wound slashed his hindquarters, but Handsome and Riordan assured me Grace had taken care of it.

'No worries, Girl as Cat. Do you think we could run now?'

"Maybe later. Go play with your own kind. Bonnie needs to rest," Riordan stroked the noble neck before leading me away.

"Lady Shaman," Shadow fell into step with me, leather draped over her arm. Riordan excused himself for a moment.

I raised inquisitive eyes to Shadow. Seems I was always doing that around the Lakota. My 5 feet made me the shortest one in the entire nation.

"Shadow, weren't you afraid against those. . .?"

Shadow's chin, the old Shadow's, rose derisively. "Enemies come to our homes! The Plains tribes will surrender no more. We fight to protect our own. If 10 Lakota and a Blackfoot can not withstand 300 southern ghosts- HA!," she smirked and I felt a thrill of pride that she'd included me.

"They had no chance- you, Lady Shaman, struck the first blow. Red Hawk told us. You put the fear of the Lakota in their phantom souls."

I almost felt like I'd gained a sister. At least we now seemed to be on a friendly footing.

"Mary sent you this. She said to tell you of her dream. 'In my dream,' Mary said, 'I woke to a heartbeat. I thought that maybe it was my time to move on to the Spirit World. But a white light settled in front of me. Near the white light, golden eyes remained vigilant on the white orb. Soon colors surrounded the light: red, yellow, black, brown and pale imitations of the white orb. The heartbeat came from the center of the orb, it pulsed.'

Mary said to tell you- your heart beats for all."

Shadow offered me the softest, whitest leather imaginable. Unfolding the garment revealed a mother-of-pearl shell, heart-shaped, on the chest. Rayed from the shell were porcupine quills dyed in the dream's colors.

My heart skipped a beat and I felt emotional tears begging to be released. I'd have to ask Riordan about the meaning of her words, but at the moment, I could only admire the softness of the skillfully prepared tunic, and feel the love that had gone into its composition.

I somehow found the words to thank Shadow and asked her to send my gratitude to Mary and tell her I would visit.

As Riordan returned with a brooding look of concern for me, Shadow added, "Mary also said to tell you, your mutual friend is doing well." She glanced at Riordan, nodded and walked off.

We'd come to the camp in late morning- a perfect, breezy cloud-studded, Wyoming sky asserted its blessing, but I was flagging. My energy level, though not completely depleted as in my previous episodes, had not entirely recovered from the ordeal of- was it just yesterday?

In admiring my new tunic, my brain took a sudden turn.

"Riordan, do you have clothing like the other Lakota?"

"Wasn't time to don typical warrior garb, if you recall. I had to change into something a bit more. . .woolly?"

I laughed and fell into his chest. His arms stole about me, momentarily spiking my body with a particular flood of energy.

"You should catnap, Wife. If you like, I'll put on my leggings for the victory feast."

He carried me to Grandfather's lodge. It seemed the hawk's eyes smiled beneficently on us as we entered. There was no time to regard the interior, for as Riordan settled me on a buffalo robe bed I fell asleep instantaneously.

I never found out who managed it, not that it mattered, but there were buffalo ribs and steaks roasted over a fire plus tamales- these obviously courtesy of Grace, and fry bread extraordinaire provided by Singing Breeze.

Confronted with this veritable feast, I felt ashamedly useless as I'd slept the afternoon away while others cooked. Riordan chided me for being silly.

I'd donned my new regalia, and emotions stung me as the soft hide settled on my body. Riordan had lovingly positioned my moccasins upon my feet- like a veritable Prince Charming in the Lakota rendition of Cinderella, and we'd joined the others.

Sitting cross-legged on strewn blankets around the fire, I tasted my first buffalo ribs. Though I usually prefer my meat well-done, it was delicious. Everyone heartily agreed, making short shrift of the banquet.

True to his word and fitting right in with his brethren, Riordan had dressed for the occasion. His simple leggings and breech clout bore no decorations. Around his neck hung a giant claw suspended on a leather thong.

'It's a saber tooth cat's fang,' he tackled my burgeoning curiosity. 'My first vision quest when I was five. This was left by my foot when I woke. The spirits called me at a very young age. You can touch it, Wife. Of all humanity, only you can touch me whenever you like.' An insouciant grin plied his lips. One of those glorious Virginian brows rose.

My fingers cradled the 6 inch long fang- smooth ivory with its deadly point still intact.

'You knew your path when you were five?' I continued our silent talk as the others finished eating. 'Most don't know where they are going at 25.'

'Grandfather helped.' Riordan basted my lips with a buffalo rib, licked off the grease, stole a kiss and returned to eating. Blushing at his intimacy which effectively stemmed any more questions, my eyes wandered.

Sitting across the fire, Dr. Gunne with rib in hand, leaned against. . .Shadow?

"The dragon is drawn to strong women. Shadow fits that description. She has matured in the past 6 months. Apparently, the feeling is mutual, for now," Riordan chortled.

Shadow presented the Doctor with half of her tamale and he accepted it from her fingers- the lady's man plying his courtly ways.

My attention flew to Cloud's position at the fireside. His upbringing served him well; I couldn't determine how he felt about what he was witnessing. Staving off my shamanic probe- anything less would be an invasion of privacy, I bit my lower lip. But I felt for him.

'She's not the one for him. Finally, he realizes this,' Riordan sighed, reading my speculations.

'Is Cloud a shaman?'

Riordan's eyes enigmatically rested on me. 'Soon,' was all the answer I received.

Stomachs gratified, Grandfather addressed us. A low, slow drumbeat stroked the air. It was coup recounting time- a way to honor participants and celebrate together as in days of old.

Grandfather nodded at my dad. Apparently, he'd been schooled on the proceedings, and of their importance.

"I, uh. . .I'll pass," my dad flushed. His discomfort could not hide in the firelight, and protesting murmurs erupted.

Grandfather shook his head as if at a recalcitrant child.

"All right, then. There wasn't much left to do from my position at the head of the canyon."

Had my dad realized he'd been positioned there for his safety? I hoped not; I didn't want him to be embarrassed, to feel as if he were dodging. . . 'Stop worrying, Wife,' Riordan chided me.

"The Lakota and Wolf Walker had already dispatched nearly all the creeps. I know of four that my arrows took down, or out. Never shot a ghost before." My dad shook his head, not believing where he'd come from or what he'd been part of or what he was saying.

"Girl as Cat's father is too modest. He should add 3 more marks to his count," Running Antelope cut in, in English.

My dad's eyebrows rose at me as he mouthed, 'Girl as Cat?'

Uh oh, I thought. Riordan playfully grabbed my ear in his teeth. 'You'll think of something, Lioness.'

"HEY YA!" A chorus of approval resounded, temporarily drowning the drum beat- I wondered who was drumming as I didn't see. . . Riordan gigged me to attend the overt activity in front of us- each warrior-participant joyously celebrating the victories of another.

My dad elbowed Rick, who stuttered- as bashfully reluctant and dumbfounded as my dad had been.

"I…uh. . . I…I gotta tell you, I was more afraid th…than I've ever been in my life. T…to experience the occult like that, wow! I've never shot at a l…living thing."

"Still haven't, Rick," Riordan assured our stymied friend.

Encouraging, expectant silence reigned.

Rick swallowed, shrugged his slumping shoulders, "Three," he belted out.

In turn, each warrior had his say and was roundly HEY YA'ed. Fourteen-year old Black Bull counted 15, BJ- 10, Running Antelope- 12, Standing Rock- 20, Shadow- 16, Blue- 8.

Grandfather, the commandant of the skies, had initially sent 20 wraiths back to hell. Cloud had remained near my dad and Rick to ensure their safety, but he had the furthest reaching bow and strongest arm- 35.

Wolf Walker tied him with 35- his placement at the canyon's mouth.

Riordan refused his chance to boast, but instead spoke of me, to my complete embarrassment.

"My Wife, Girl as Cat, used her wind skills and brought thunder and hail upon our enemies. No telling how many she returned to the beyond. HEY YA!" Riordan's shouts were echoed for what seemed an interminable time, and there was no place for me to hide. Grinning, boyishly, he winked at me.

"I wish to speak for Man Who Walks as a Cat, my teacher," Cloud rose. All eyes followed him, eager for his words. Except for Riordan, who ducked the attentive focus- I sensed his wish to run, but knew he would not.

"Once the battle was over, I walked the route taken by Man Who Walks as a Cat. I stood where he stood when our enemies first encroached on our people. You know each man's arrows are his own and bear his mark. I retrieved 107 arrows bearing the Cat claw. Each of these bore a sluice of gore- spirit world blood. HEY YA! Man Who Walks as a Cat!"

The shouting roared and roared, attendees on their feet, fists punching to the skies. In the old days, the most proficient warrior was accorded great respect. The counting coup ritual only added to the legends surrounding my husband.

The Lakota were extremely proud to have Riordan associated with them- even if his blood was half white. And now, I, too, had a place among them. My dad and Rick were also accepted as brothers. Historically, Native Americans were more accepting of those who respected them, white blood or no. Unlike white men, who had generally placed the People on a lower scale- even considered them less than animals at times, conveniently forgetting horror breeds horror.

Repeated shouts rent the night. The drumming picked up in intensity and the fire soared higher into the sky. Wolf Walker pitched a powder into the fire. I thought I was the only one who saw him do this, for the others had begun to dance to the drum beat.

He winked at me through an opening of firelight. His shamanic eyes probed me with respect and curiosity and something else.

5

"Come, Wife, I've prepared a resting place for us," Riordan lifted me as he rose.

"You're not dancing?" I glanced at the panoply of Native Americans and guests in action, enjoying drum and fire.

"Not tonight- my passion is for you, not the dance."

I felt Bonnie's thrilling, anticipatory shivers as I carried her to a secluded spot with conifers for walls and the drama of stars for a canopy. While she'd napped, I'd arranged our bed with privacy in mind.

Bonnie's mind tried to get a grasp on. . . Here it comes, I mused.

"107! Riordan, how could, how could anyone be so fast and accurate with a bow? 107, wow! That must be some kind of a record! But, I guess. . .I guess nobody's ever called the Guinness Book Of World Records for shooting ghosts, huh?"

"I'd just as soon discuss another of my skills tonight, Wife." I gave her a quick sample as we entered our evening's quarters.

Too soon to set her down- her knees weakened with my ardent sample and I gladly picked her up again.

"I so enjoy carrying you," I felt the heat of her blush.

"Riordan, will Cloud be. . ." My all-too-caring, curious Wife.

"Cloud will be fine. As for the dragon, Shadow will give him a hard row to hoe, but then, the dragon fancies himself a lover, more so than a fighter. Now, me," my cat's eyes caressed her upturned face, "I can handle both venues."

I placed her on our buffalo robe. The contrast of Bonnie's creamy skin and Lakota tunic upon the dark hide was magnified as a star shot across the heavens.

From behind a downed limb, I pulled a leather parcel. Out came another of my surprises.

"A flute," Bonnie gasped; wide eyes intently admired the pair of carved mountain lions wrapped about each other gracing the top of the flute.

"This is a love flute. Native Americans were/are not above indulging in romantic gestures, or in fun, contrary to what many whites believe. A few overly zealous heartsick souls even sought love charms from their shamans, or medicine men."

Bonnie looked doubtful so I surrendered and expounded on the theme.

"One enterprising fellow used a root charm which he fastened to a small stone. Creeping up to the object of his affections, he threw the charm at her. He claimed multiple successes with this. . ."

"Sounds like he was just after. . ."

I laughed, "probably all too true, but it's told a Shoshone man visited the perspicacious medicine man, offering to buy such a charm. The next spring, the Shoshone presented his Wife." I shrugged my shoulders, and grinning rather like the Cheshire Cat I sat cross-legged, prepared to serenade her.

"Hmmm," she ruminated, "I bet you never needed a love charm- the way women look at you."

"Ah, but my eyes suffered chastity in love before you, Wife." I savored her squirm with pleasure, and released the haunting notes from the flute I'd carved earlier. In our alcove, the tune wafted about us, physically plying our bodies with invisible feather notes of rapture.

Bonnie hugged her knees, eyes zestfully alight. I continued my love song until the sight of my Wife lured me to hasten the music's denouement.

Upon finishing my serenade, I speculatively reminisced, "Maybe instead of a woodpecker, I should have used this." I was promptly bowled over as she flung herself into my arms.

Lying beside her, our fingers entwined, our attention was drawn to fireworks above.

"Our friends are out." We savored the Pink Lady's show along with her cohorts, Mr. Green, Yellow and Blue- who employed their best maneuvers to keep pace with her. Fat chance, she was spectacular with her unique, divine arabesques.

"Riordan?" Bonnie's perplexed voice questioned.

"I see, Bonnie. She's. . . What I'd hoped to show you on top of Mato Tipila, but the clouds interrupted. The Pink Lady is tracing the Milky Way." My fingers followed the star's movements.

"Wanagita Canku- the road of the spirits. The Lakota teach that Wakan Tanka, the Great Spirit, created the Heart Of Everything That Is- the Black Hills, to make us know we have a special connection with the earth, our mother, and this includes responsibilities.

The Great Spirit's breaths are the stars-she's showing us. They are set in the sky as mirror images of what is on earth. What is in the heavens is on the earth and what is on earth is in the heavens.

Our ceremonies and prayers come from the 'bible' of the heavens.

Indeed, the buffalo represent the power of the sun on earth- the people followed the sun, from the spring equinox to the summer solstice. The sun moves through 4 Lakota constellations-three of these are connected to specific Black Hills' sites.

By timing their travels to arrive at each of the three sites in synchronicity with the sun's movements into the corresponding star groups, the people followed the path of the sun on earth as mirrored in the sky.

Mato Tipila, the whites' Devil's Tower, was an historical site of the Sun Dance. We know it as Bear Claw Mountain, remember the story? It is a sacred place to the Lakota. The greed of white men took it from us and consigned it to a park. Can you imagine Pearl Harbor being given to the Japanese?

My friend, Osiris, cringes every time he visits the Nile. I digress. There are injustices all over the world. This particular injustice happens to be part of my heritage. My red blood feels it."

Bonnie stroked my bloody shoulder patch, empathetically. "Go on, Riordan. This is all very interesting."

"Other Lakota doings were time specific. There were no calendars. There were and are the stars. Civilization misses so much. By living in high rises, the stars are blocked to human vision, and so are the inhabitants' minds blocked from what is most important.

Stars were used as teaching symbols. Follow the 'religion of the stars', follow the path of the sun upon earth, follow the buffalo- it was all part of living in harmony and balance with the sacred powers of the universe."

"Beautiful, Riordan. Beautiful, but. . ."

I could feel the scholar in my Wife forming a question. Though she was privy to the answer by virtue of our closeness, she voiced aloud her queries- hey, I didn't mind.

"Riordan, th...the Mato Tipila is geographically outside the Black Hills."

I rolled over to face her, "OK, Smarty Pants, but the constellation that correlates with Mato Tipila is located within the track of the stars. So there." I kissed away a further flurry of inquiries.

"For thousands of years, Native peoples studied the stars and we know. . . There she goes! See her new outline? Remember the race story. The red clay valley surrounds the Black Hills. She is tracing that race track in the sky set inside the Milky Way.

The race's, the story's origins, were not told out of boredom, but because two-leggeds were getting a little above themselves and needed to be taught a lesson.

Inside the border are landmark stars," I pointed out the Pink Lady's movements again.

"These stars and constellations represent landmarks in the Black Hills. Each Lakota sought his own relationship with the Spirit World. We had nothing called 'religion'. One followed the Road of the Spirits daily to arrive at the place of Wanagi Yata- a place of never ending happiness and respect for all.

The Road of the Spirits provides hope for all- for life after death. In fact, there is no 'death' but simply a passing to another world. Lakota of old attempted to mirror the ideal of a good life every day.

There are many who have visited Wanagi Yata in near death experiences and visions. These people were told it was not their time to die. These visions are known among our people- visits with departed loved ones. They await us in the place of Spirits.

Just as the ancient Egyptians knew their paths through the study of the skies, so do we, the Lakota, and other Native peoples. Those locked in cities could not conceive of the miracle of the stars. And don't get me started on blind religious club/cults and intolerance and. . ."

My senses momentarily rankled, settled and stirred anew, not altogether from Bonnie's continual stroking of my arm. The art noveau Pink Lady began forming a new design.

Near, but outside the legendary race track in the sky, she settled sedately and took on the shape of a heart. Not the pointed Valentine's Day heart, but the shape of a living heart.

Bonnie went still beside me. Reflective.

With her position now static in the sky, the Pink Lady gleamed mother-of-pearl colors. Arrayed about her, Mr. Green, Yellow and Blue stars and another pale star placed themselves- rays emanating from and in return embracing the Pink Lady.

Rarely in my life, until Bonnie, did I receive such a tremendous jolt.

"Riordan," Bonnie whispered.

"I know, Wife."

And as if this wasn't enough of a miracle, a single ray of light softly glided down to us- a starry spotlight.

As if to ensure our realization of this extraordinary event, the star spirits held their positions in Wanagita Canku for a considerable time and then slowly faded.

As the colors dispersed, a new star held sway where the Pink Lady had donned a heart mask, and this star remained.

'Great Spirit?' I intoned.

In answer to my unspoken request, the star was joined by another- a wedding of sorts. They were separate, yet one.

"What does it mean, Riordan?" Bonnie's tone reflected her awe and confusion.

"I think we should discuss this with Grandfather," I bowed out, not caring to commit my idea aloud- the idea that we were being sent a most powerful message.

"Riordan, I think I'll find the little girl's room, uh, behind some bushes." I stood, swiped my tunic and sauntered off looking for suitable privacy.

"You could always travel home and use a real bathroom," Riordan politely reminded me.

"I don't mind, I am a cat." I felt Riordan's ardent gaze on my sashaying fringe as I left.

Finishing up, my mind intent on the Pink Lady's spectacle, I began my trek back to my husband when my wild senses warned that I was not alone. I hesitated, searching.

'Do not be startled, Girl as Cat.' A silent plea.

From the deep shadows of the evergreens, padded an enormous wolf with his tail held high as if it were a flag of surrender. The enigmatic eyes of Wolf Walker held me in place.

His muzzle and collar were black, but the rest of his body was reddish-gray. Only the very tip of his tail exhibited an incongruous white.

'I'd hoped we could speak. . .alone.'

"You must realize I'm never alone," I replied aloud, with confidence. My senses cautioned he was not altogether benign.

'I assumed as much in studying the two of you together. I would give everything in my power to have a mate such as you.'

"Surely there must be someone for you." Wolf Walker was extremely attractive- ooh, I hope Riordan didn't misconstrue that.

The wolf lowered his head, his paw scratched an ear.

'It would seem not. The spirits have not revealed. . .unless, you?'

The power of his forceful eyes attempted to fascinate me and I was fascinated, but not as he hoped.

All of my life I'd been a loner except with animals. Lately, I had admirers stepping out of the woods, so to speak. A brazen raven, a Casanova dragon, this mysterious wolf, even Handsome expressed. . .

As I mused on this phenomenon and Wolf Walker's attempt to mesmerize me, I felt my mate step to my side.

Lovingly, I placed my hand on his tawny, black outlined ears, fondled his forehead and tickled his whiskers.

'Man Who Walks as a Cat,' the wolf conceded.

'The spirits have designed us for each other. I do not hold her with spells. She is free to do whatever she wishes,' Riordan advised Wolf Walker.

'Care to see how a dog lives, Girl as Cat?' Wolf Walker's low voice flirted with a suggestion.

"No, shaman. My heart belongs with Riordan."

'Your heart belongs to all. You will see.' He once more offered this mysterious portent.

A flash of inspiration begged release from my core.

Wolf Walker nodded his lupine muzzle at my husband and turned to go.

"Shaman, your mate exists, but not where you might think. Find her. Ask your guide for help."

He paused, studied the two of us together.

'My ears are always open if you need my aid. I will study on your words, Girl as Cat. I hope you are right. Thank you.' And he vanished.

From a long way off a goose bump-raising, yearning howl reverberated- a lone wolf calling. Seeking.

Hank Winch's latest episode of seeing a hairy elephant in the high desert brush of Cody, Wyoming brought him to a long overdue decision.

His pickled brain had a difficult time as new sober brain cells attempted to reproduce with the dissipation of alcohol. He faced the seated, expectant group. They patiently waited his story, his admission, the first steps to a new life.

They had heard and seen it all before.

He coughed to clear his throat and steady his voice.

"My name is Hank Winch, and I'm an alcoholic."

The group, consisting of males and females of all ages chimed back at him, "Hi, Hank."

6

I could tell by Bonnie's breathing that she was near to waking. The fireworks in the sky, the potentially auspicious import arrayed, had kept me from sleep. In my mind, I outlined the design Mary had worked on the white leather tunic.

"What exists in the heavens also exists on earth and what is on earth is in the heavens," Bonnie murmured, eyes fluttering.

"The Pink Lady couldn't use black or brown in the night sky, as Mary did here," I mused with my finger tapping Bonnie's chest, "so she employed other colors."

The implication had staggering significance- exactly what, I did not yet know. But how often do the heavens directly speak to humans via such blatant star language?

Coupled with Wolf Walker's strange monition. My Wife apparently had an eminent role to play at some point in the future. Of supereminence, it would seem.

Hopefully, Grandfather could help decipher this puzzle, or perhaps the spirits were just giving us a heads up as they held the full tenor close to their proverbial 'chests'- until their idea of the appropriate time was at hand.

Bonnie had slept til almost noon. The elemental powers she indulged still tired her, though not as much as in their initial onset.

"Will it always be so?" She read me as she stretched gracefully, endearingly catlike.

"I honestly don't know, Wife. The spirits will reveal as they see fit. I do think you're growing stronger with the use of your powers- you didn't faint this time."

My stomach interrupted our discussion, protesting the lack of breakfast- Bonnie's enthusiastically chorused a reply.

"They're gone!" Disappointment registered in her every cell as she stopped dead.

We'd returned to the prairie meadow only to find trampled circles indicating where lodges had stood.

"They've been here some time, Bonnie." Still their absence struck a discordant note.

"Why didn't anyone tell me, Riordan?" She accused, rounding on me. "I would have loved to learn how they put up the tipi and to study the artist's designs on them and. . ."

"It would seem Grandfather knew you'd say that," I inclined my head at an orderly pile of poles and a parcel of hides.

"More importantly, I smell buffalo stew." I pulled her toward a Dutch oven hanging over a lingering fire by means of an iron tripod.

We breakfasted heartily on the succulent, well-basted stew with a stack of fry bread for dipping.

"I see they left you a t-shirt and jeans, but conveniently absconded with my jeans," I said, sifting through the hides. "Don't laugh, Wife," I anticipated her response.

"You could travel home and. . ." she giggled.

"I just might do that," I quipped.

"But don't, Riordan. Your leggings and breech clout are extremely attractive."

"How attractive?" I sauntered to her, cat eyes glittering.

My Wife fought for air as I closed on her.

"Um. . . Shouldn't we," she fumbled, "set up a lodge?"

"You do realize this is women's work," Riordan grumbled, his bare chest glistened with sweat.

He'd shed his leggings and stood Tarzan-like in a breech clout alone. The light bronze of his tanned chest continued down the long powerful muscles of his legs. His bloody shoulder prominently displayed as if he carried a perpetual shield.

The statue of David had nothing on my cougar dream. Focus, Bonnie, focus. I could wax poetic on Riordan's ultra good looks, but. . .

It was an incredibly hot day for early June in Cody, Wyoming. Off again in musing, I speculated that ice cream sounded good, but couldn't compete with the glory of Riordan Catskill.

"Ice cream, now there's a cool idea."

"I don't think they'll let you in the ice cream parlor in downtown Cody- not dressed like that," I blushed.

Riordan grinned, "Might earn the shop more customers. Did I tell you this is women's work?"

"Only about ten times. This is hot work."

Sun beating on us, we'd spent what seemed hours trying to erect a tipi.

If battling phantom armies doesn't put a strain on a recent marriage, putting up a tipi might fill the ticket. No wonder it was considered women's work- only women would have the patience.

Yes, fledgling married couples could rise or fall by raising a lodge, I presumed.

"Couples in the old days did not raise tipis. Women did- helped each other out- no divorce that way," Riordan chuckled as once more I didn't hold up my end of the deal, er, pole.

I'd never even erected a tent, so I was completely at a loss.

Loudly remonstrating, a red tailed hawk sailed above us.

'Pitiful,' Grandfather sent us his amused comment on our inept undertaking.

"Bonnie," Riordan took a pre-historic hammer from my hands before I could further inconvenience my thumb. Self-healing or no, a blow was still a blow and needed at least a minute to heal.

"That's it! I, myself, have never raised a lodge. What would a cat need a tent for?"

We ended up imitating knights of old, and jousted, using lodge pole pines, until we could no longer hold the poles for our sweaty palms, not to mention laughing.

"Enough, Wife." Both of our chests were heaving.

I'd parried as many blows as Riordan had delivered and got in a few of my own. I knew he graciously extended marital courtesy and kept our conflict simple yet exuberant- what a workout!

"On one hand I could recount the times I slept in a tipi. But, if you're adamant about knowing the process, I'll tell you a story," his eyes glittered with innuendo. I waited for the qualifier.

"I'll instruct you by means of dirt drawings on the basics of tipi construction if. . ."

"If?"

"If we can break for a cooling swim," Riordan beguilingly raised a brow.

"Not swimming?" My spirits sank, knowing my body would follow suit when in water. "How?" I briefly considered traveling home to an ice-cold lemonade, cookies, anything to distract him from my personal bane.

"Wait a minute. There's a great skinny dipping spot right over there and it's not over 4 feet deep. You can handle that."

Skinny dipping! He wanted me to take off my clothes, here?

"Who's going to see? For crying out loud! C'mon." Not waiting for an answer he hoisted me over his shoulder and proceeded to. . .

He dropped me and his breech clout and jumped into the small shaded pond in the midst of the flowing stream- thoroughly dousing me in the process. I looked about furtively.

"Sheesh, Bonnie, swim in your underwear, c'mon, it feels great."

Riordan upended like a duck, reveling in the keen, spring-fed water, sluicing his sticky, sweaty body.

I turned around and divested myself of t-shirt and jeans. The water did feel refreshing- my innate climate control kept me from chilling. An ordinary human might suffer frostbite, but not Riordan or me.

After dunking a few times, I stood up- the water leveled at my chest. I twisted my wet hair behind me and caught sight of Riordan's eyes and how they fastened on me.

"Underwear was a great idea, Wife," his voice was sultrily hoarse. "Better than lingerie."

While savoring the last of the buffalo stew, and while we still had light, Riordan picked up a drawing stick and in an area devoid of vegetation, he started class.

"Remember, what is in the heavens is on earth and vice versa," my grinning professor tousled my hair.

"The cottonwood has always held a place of importance in Lakota lore. Of course, everything is important, but if you study a cottonwood leaf," he placed one in my hand.

"What do you see? Think along. . ."

"It has the basic form of a tipi," I whispered, fascinated.

"You're beautiful," Riordan winked. I heard him silently chide himself to 'focus'. I could empathize.

"Building a tipi replicated the world. The first step, once you've gathered straight poles, is to triangulate 3 poles-creating a star.

The foundation of the lodge, this star, represents light- star light- power. This strong tipi foundation centers the world- the lodge.

Next step is to mirror the seven directions in our home. Seven poles represent east, north, south, west, heaven, earth and center. These symbolize order.

Now there are 10 poles- the laws of nature. This shows the Lakota's respect for law and order.

Two more poles- the ears, are outside the lodge controlling the flow of air in the tipi- air, the carrier of spirit.

The tipi, once the hides are in place- the world, is now formed. Spirit can breathe in and out. Communication with spirits is open- there is no separation."

I studied Riordan's sketch, mused on his words. "Kind of like how a religion uses a church."

"Pretty much so, I guess. Though, the Lakota do not need the tipi to speak with the Great Spirit. We now have 12 poles- 12 months- the cycle of life.

As the stars are similar to a calendar ordering our days, showing us the proper time for activities in the old ways, so our home reflects this.

Once a year the people gather for Sun Dance. The tipi is also reflective of this important ceremony. With their dancing, sacrifice and prayers, the dancers make a symbolic tipi around the sacred tree.

The Sun Dance renews life on our earth and in our tribe with our gratitude. The Dance creates energy- powerful energy. Look." Riordan drew two pyramids, one upended upon a lower one, point to point.

"The sun above is light- energy shining down. The dancers on the ground create a tipi of gratitude and prayers rising up- a recreation of the world. Renewing the relationship with the Great Spirit and so much more.

Sacred above, sacred below. There is no separation, only a oneness with the Great Spirit- the One- Wakan Tanka. There is so much beauty in how the Lakota see their world, their lives, the spirits, the stars."

Riordan's voice betrayed his emotion and likewise I felt my own heart responding.

"A little more for you to ponder. Living inside a tipi is compared to living inside the sun. The smoked buffalo hides loved light and let it shine through. As the buffalo represented the power of the sun in the animal world, the people lived inside the skin of the sun, inside a star."

I nuzzled Bonnie's lips, teased first the top one and then the lower one. I felt her goose bumps rise and an inordinate gasp.

"Bonnie?"

"Riordan, look!"

The star show of the previous night was not happenstance. Bonnie's star and I guess, mine joined to hers, were present above us. As in the heavens, so below. Our stars in their relationship to the Black Hills' constellations and storied race track placed us exactly where we lived in Wyoming. We were home in more ways than one.

What did it all mean?

7

"I see you were unsuccessful- had to sleep out of tipi, so to speak," constituted Grandfather's tongue-in-cheek greeting as we visited him on the way home.

"Unlike some birds, we prefer to sleep outside," Riordan mock-huffed a rejoinder.

"Excuses, excuses," Grandfather muttered as Riordan tossed the parcel bearing Grandfather's tipi hides into a corner.

My husband pulled out a chair, spun it around and sat with arms folded across the chair's back.   I excused myself to Grace's new convenience- a real bathroom.   Riordan would fill Grandfather in on our recent stars' appearance.

"Grandfather, where is Grace?" I asked upon returning.   I sensed her absence involved more than a trip to the grocery store.

"In Sedona with friends," his expressionless answer.

A horrible thought crept from the woodwork of my brain. "She's coming back, isn't she?"

A perceptible twitch lurked at the corner of Grandfather's mouth.   Did I really detect the beginnings of humor? In Grandfather?

I had to admit he had loosened up some with Grace's reappearance in his life.   In fact, she was good for all of us, a natural mediator and an elegant, quiet-spoken friend, not to mention her special talents.

"Don't worry, Granddaughter, Grace will return. It seemed an appropriate time to visit her healing center. Now that Chac has been disposed of." And more quietly, "She's been away from her creation for a long time."

I sighed with relief, until his last remark hit home and left me wary. I was sure Grandfather felt as I did- I hoped Grace would always be near. I loved having another female shaman to talk with- surely she'd come back- this was now her home, wasn't it? Riordan leaned into me to stop my ruminating.

"Have you seen Dr. Gunne? I never had time to thank him properly." My mate issued an unintelligible spate of borborology on this particular change of subject.

And decided to interpret. "I expect he's too busy being fawned over or should I say 'shadowed'?"

Grandfather eyed my husband in reprimand, "Grandson!"

"Riordan, aren't you the least bit grateful? He did take. . ."

"Yeah, yeah, I'm thankful, but I'll never be his top fan." 'You are my territory and any male that sniffs around you. . .' silently he finished. My husband- the quintessence of male.

"Speak of the devil," Riordan rolled his eyes.

A light tap at the open door and Dr. Gunne stepped in.

"Someone call for a savior?" The dragon grinned- sort of a cat-that-helped-himself-to-the-cream smile.

Riordan tossed a silent 'blasphemy' my way, and threw an inimitable eye to the incongruously appareled dragon.

Dr. Gunne's immaculate sense of style- LL Bean button down shirt in pink, (how many men would confidently wear pink?), double pleated Dockers and boat shoes were foreign to the simplicity of the homey, western cabin- as always.

"Riordan?" Gunne offered his hand.

'Riordan,' I silently warned. His hand shot out and an accord of some sort ensued- for how long was another question.

"I'm on my way to visit the res, invited by my new friend, Shadow," Gunne launched into the mix.

Briefly recalling my own visit as the only white girl/shaman, I wondered what Gunne's reception might be like.

'Don't forget, Wife, our Lakota warriors know that the dragon is also a shaman. He'll be given all due respect. Shadow will be sure he is comfortable,' Riordan's silent smirking answer to my wondering.

'No bullets?' I telepathed.

'My fault, Wife. You know how sorry I am about that.' I did.

Gunne and Grandfather stood idly while we communicated silently. Riordan pulled me onto his lap after rearranging the chair again and softly tugged at my cat's eye pendant present.

"Remarkable conversation. Too bad I didn't understand a word of it," Gunne brushed imaginary dirt from his spotless khaki trousers, ruefully eyeing us.

"Don't let that hinder your departure," my husband rudely retorted.

"You two, honestly!" I pinched or rather tried to gather enough flesh to pinch my husband's bicep.

"Don't hurt yourself, Wife," he caught my ear with his teeth and I startled him with a snarl.

Grandfather shook his head at our antics. "You'll have an interesting trip, Dr. Gunne, but before you go. . ."

He brought the dragon up to speed on the joining of 'our' stars and what he assumed was the significance.

"I believe the stars represent you, Grandson, and my granddaughter. Their placement in the heavens relates to your home here. You are where you are supposed to be. I'm sure there is a reason for this, and the spirits will make it known in their own good time." Echoes of Riordan's insight.

"Hmmm. . .," Dr. Gunne with his finger tapping his lips thought out loud. "I've never really spent time watching the sky- gives me some ideas for nightly recreation at the res- no ambient light to spoil the view."

Riordan almost said something inappropriate, but I ran interference with a well-placed boot.

"I suggest you ask Cloud to fill you in on Lakota star knowledge. May come in handy for the future. I assume you are making your home here?" Riordan rubbed his ankle.

"Haven't the spirits made that plain?" The dragon smiled fondly on me. What was I going to do with them?

Grandfather's eyes lighted on me- my cue.

"I…I haven't thanked you for…for saving me and my home. I'm most grateful, and happy you are well."

The dragon gazed at me softly, "Anytime, Bonnie, anytime. You all know how to reach me."

He nodded his goodbye as I felt Riordan's upheaval at the dragon's response to me. Wild animals, indeed.

"I'll be off then." The sound of his expensive sports car clearly dictated his mode of transportation.

"What is the significance of the stars mirroring my, our home?"

"Historically, Granddaughter, shamans were culturally and therefore, site specific. They travelled with their own tribe, keeping somewhat separate, but always available for whatever was needed by the people. As their time to go to the spirits drew near, they designated a likely successor and diligently educated their replacement. And so on through time."

"But, Riordan and. . .us?"

"We are different, in our life spans and talents. Riordan is an anomaly- half white, half Lakota. His path seemed split. The Lakota always welcomed him, the whites reviled him. But, as he could pass for either, depending on his mood and how he wore his hair. . ."

Riordan's eyes glittered, amused.

"Grandfather, you've grown color blind- the blonde threads in this hair- not at all like yours," my husband raised his long hair to better show off the light strands.

"I decided to travel to any location that drew my interest- wherever the spirits called me to go. One of those callings put me in the right place at the right time to acquire your ring. No coincidence. Simply being tuned in and listening to the spirits," my husband continued his story.

"And now, do the spirits. . .?" I cringed. My husband was done traveling the world, wasn't he?

"Wife, the spirits put us together. I go nowhere without you. At least, I can conceive of no reason to leave you behind, now. Some things were kept from you leading up to Chac's arrival. I wanted his focus on you, and you not dwelling on certain things. All the better to ambush his evil intentions. I expect, whatever our future holds, we are meant to be here. That is how I see the stars' placement."

"Bonnie, you look well rested. Glad you're home. These kittens have been driving me crazy. Do you know there isn't a single place in this cabin that they can't get into or onto? I find my razor under the kitchen table, toilet paper strewn throughout the house, pieces of cat food, well, suffice it to say, our home has become a soccer field with cat kibble and all the teams are ready to play all the time. Especially at 3a.m. Beats me why 3a.m. is the kitten witching hour."

Even as my dad described it, 6 black and white kittens and 1 golden one were each battling around tiny bits of kitten chow. Once in a while, a squabble erupted as one kitten decided another had over-stepped his bounds and stolen an erstwhile claimed soccer piece.

Riordan and I fell into each other chuckling at their antics. My dad joined in and as for Amore, she perched on the kitchen table, regally playing referee.

Over a fried chicken dinner with mashed potatoes, gravy, salad, and of all things, cookies, my dad came up with a first class question.

I pretended to check on another batch of cookies as my dad swatted kittens away from his plate and addressed Riordan.

'Good luck, Husband.'

'Hurry with the cookies, Wife. Maybe we can distract him.'

'If 7 kittens can't distract him, uh, make that 8,' Amore lay in my dad's lap cadging bits of white meat. 'Don't hold out much hope for these cookies.'

"Riordan, son, can you do that illusion trick whenever or does it require a lot of practice beforehand?"

Dad was hinting around about the wooly mammoth. He gave Riordan one of those 'you're not fooling me' looks. To his credit, my cougar didn't squirm, whereas I almost dropped a tray of cookies fresh from the oven, in anticipation of what kind of explanation my husband might come up with.

"Jim, I. . ."

'How about the truth?' I silently suggested. Riordan eyed me thoughtfully and dispatched a handful of cookies, gauging his response.

"You accept the means we used to rid ourselves of those wraiths?"

"I'm trying to come to terms with the results- too much like a RETURN OF THE MUMMY flick when those dust dogs attacked the Arabs on horseback. But, I'm working it out."

I was amazed at how well my dad seemed to be taking it.

Of course, he had personally seen me redirect a flash flood. But, somehow I thought he thought it was more a matter of coincidence. I'd forgotten the puddle of rain I'd encased his feet in when I turned it to ice. Maybe, he was accepting that. . .

"You weren't meant to be in on the final action, Jim, but since the Lakota all raced back on horses. . ."

"I had to see my girl was safe, and you, you know," my dad failed to cough-hide his being choked up.

'Tell him, Riordan.' I put my arms around my dad's shoulders and hugged.

"You knew we couldn't use bullets. About the only thing a jaguar might fear in the real world other than a gun-toting hunter, and that is no guarantee, is an elephant."

"So you...what, conjured up a ghost mammoth to stomp the ghost jaguar to death?"

My dad hadn't the distinct misfortune to see Chac in his shamanic pseudo-human form- only as the jaguar. So if my dad assumed the jaguar was a phantom, then. . .

"Right, Jim, magic. I think you're beginning to get the picture," Riordan chuckled, glad to be let off the hook, and clapped my dad on the back.

Not completely convinced, Dad opened his mouth to ask another question- Riordan had to see I came by this honestly.

I staved off the next query by placing a plate of cookies before them. Riordan grabbed the entire plate. My dad's brains switched to more important things, like his share.

8

"OOF!"

So this is how it feels to be punched in the nose, er, beak. In trying to rub my injured proboscis I inadvertently forgot I had wings and poked myself in the eye with a black feather and landed on my avian caboose with two raven feet sticking out in front of me.

Riordan was barrel-rolling and caw-caw laughing at my inefficient fledgling antics. 'Just jump off and catch an updraft,' he'd told me. Fat chance. And the day had begun with so much promise.

"Do you think I can change into other animals?" I'd asked, all innocent-eyed and eager.

"Haven't forgotten that blasted, feisty, feathered flirt raven, huh?" Riordan's brow shot up.

I bit my lower lip. Being teased about a flirting raven was one thing, but I had something completely different in mind.

"Maybe I should challenge him to aerial combat for your affections- kind of like a duel." I watched my husband mull over a Red Baron routine.

"Aerial combat? You've actually fought other birds in the sky?" I could tell Riordan was extremely glad I asked.

"Let me tell you about. . ."

"No, I don't think I. . ."

"C'mon, if you want me to help you become a raven. . ."

How could I resist those golden eyes alight with exhilarated remembrance? I ran a finger over the dark, shadow markings accenting his tempting mouth.

His eyes instantly flamed with another purpose. If I weren't careful, I'd be waylaid. Which wasn't an altogether unpleasant thought, but. . .

"OK," I conceded, "tell me, and then. . .?"

"And then, we'll see what kind of a raven you'll make. I'd just fished a rainbow trout out of the clearest stream- long before all those damn factories and dams destroyed the innocent, stunning clarity of a mountain stream. Delicious fish- pure, fresh and. . ."

"Raw?" I still had a problem with certain aspects of our wild nature.

"Of course. Have you ever seen a raven light a fire and cook a fish? Come to think of it, I was crossing a few bird boundaries by fishing as a raven. Oh, well, I digress. I felt a shadow above me and as fast as you please, a golden eagle swooped and stole my fish. Right out of my mouth. Without a by-your-leave.

Now, I wasn't in a sharing mood right then, so I took after her."

"As a raven against a golden eagle, wasn't that rather foo…bold?" I quickly amended.

"Ah, Bonnie, you should have seen me. The Red Baron would have been proud, and probably learned a few tricks, too." I rolled my eyes.

Riordan gently elbowed me and continued. "I shadowed her just within plucking distance, divested the bold belle of several tail feathers; I banked and spun away, ascended and nearly landed atop of her, but then, she decided I was serious."

My husband had me. He drew out a long silence, sat there reflective.

"Riordan," I urged.

"Bye, bye went the fish." His arm dropped. "And we locked together, somersaulting in the air, pecking and grasping for better talon holds.

I didn't want to kill her, just teach her a few manners. Suddenly, I managed to glimpse we were headed down onto a rather nasty looking branch. I barrel-rolled away, hoping my weight would deflect her from being injured. We unlocked and. . .I let her go."

"You let her go?"

"Yeah, turns out she had a nest full of hungry youngsters and. . ." his lips twitched.

I reckoned the punch line was coming up.

"Go on," I had to hear the end.

"Just below our disengagement point was a guy fishing. He'd pulled out a nice fat trout. . ."

"Who got the fish?"

"Well, it so happens, I let the eagle steal the fish- she had more practice at theft. But, as the man went for his gun, which he never located in time, I swooped down and knocked him into the lake with a bit of fancy footwork and I, the raven, made off with his stringer, bearing two fish. What a day!"

Riordan rested back on his elbows, savoring his exploit.

"And then there was this other time. . ."

"Riordan," I brought him back to the present. "You change into other animals. I'd like to, too."

"Wife, as easily as you communicate with beasts and birds, it ought to be a piece of cake for you. If you've decided on a raven, picture and feel as if you were a raven."

I thought on our feisty raven guide- his intelligent, black eyes, his movements. I pictured other ravens I'd seen on sunny days like today, enjoying the always-prevalent Wyoming draughts.

I began to feel light and my arms and feet felt pretty strange. My cougar's feet were like home, but this. . .

A wolf whistle from Riordan heralded my success.

I extended an arm-wing and tentatively spread my fingers-feathers to survey a black that was almost blue in the rays of the sun.

"I'm certainly glad, for the flirt's sake, that he's not around to see this," Riordan marveled. "You are one beautiful bird, Wife."

With that whistled compliment, Riordan transformed into my raven mate.

A twinge of apprehension struck and I began to have second thoughts. Whereas the mountain lion felt like a second skin to me, after innumerable, trying, initial escapades, the idea of flying seemed awfully dangerous.

'Don't be silly,' Riordan scoffed. We'd resorted to telepathic communication. 'Follow me,' he ordered.

I fluffed my feathers and experimented with walking as a raven. 'This feels weird,' I hopped and stumbled with my first efforts.

'Stop complaining. C'mon, we're going up to that ledge,' he inclined his glossy raven head, winked a beady, black eye, and using talented beak and wings proceeded steadily up a rough path.

'When an updraft comes our way, we'll jump off and let the wind carry us up. Don't flap your wings like you're beating up the air. This should not be a replay of your first swim lesson,' he stopped and looked directly at me, hopped and continued up the incline, negotiating loose rock.

We reached the ledge, Riordan heartening my haphazard attempts all the way, until I finally looked down, and quailed.

'Wrong bird, Wife,' he cawed.

'It's a long way down, Riordan.' What had I got myself into?

'Sure, but Wife, we're not going down. We're headed up, remember? Get ready. Spread your wings and let the wind carry you. As the wind subsides, gently flap your wings and we'll drift slowly to earth. Here it comes. Go!'

Riordan extended his wings and jumped off the ledge. Immediately, he was aloft, gliding perfectly in tune with an avian nature.

'Bonnie, c'mon. This is great!'

I swallowed, took a deep breath- which felt very different from human and cougar actions. Briefly I thought of all the ravens I'd seen enjoying themselves, gulped, and I stepped off.

Unfortunately, the wind took that moment to cease or maybe it simply changed course- leaving me without a parachute, dropping like a rock, flapping faster than. . .

'Bonnie! Don't flap so hard!'

OOF! Just drop and let your wings catch the draught, he says. . .

I plowed, beak first, into the ground. And where was my loving husband? Snickering-cawing his head off, somersaulting above me- the great show-off.

Effortlessly, I sailed to a nearby limb and promptly rolled off, laughing at the spectacle of my Wife, the raven, sitting on her tail feathers.

It was the old swim class chaos all over again, except this time it was the battle of the flailing wings-v-the flailing limbs, beating air-v-beating water.

I gained some idea of what mother birds went through when their babies left the nest or tried to, for the first time. My fledgling Wife, spirits help me.

Feeling her discouraged embarrassment- she wasn't hurt, I curtailed my amusement and hopped closer to offer further advice.

After three more botched attempts, I suggested we retire from raven-hood and take it up another day.

"What's wrong with me?" Bonnie transformed back to human form and muttered, disconsolate. My Bonnie, the over-achiever.

"Absolutely nothing, Wife. You almost had it that last effort. Study birds more, especially ravens' flight. Perhaps you have more of land animal tendencies rather than flight or swimming."

As she grew more irritated, I added, "Maybe, we should have tried a road runner, first."

9

"I want to try again," I badgered Riordan for the next two days. For my pestering, I received everything from a chuckle to 'not today' to 'you need to study ravens more'.

Finally, I put my foot down. "OK, Riordan, if you won't help me I'll. . ."

He pulled me into his chest, his arms straitjacketed me and sparkling gold eyes diverted my attention. He was inordinately pleased with himself, at my knees buckling in response to the twitching at the corner of his lips preparatory to engaging mine.

As we came up for air, I pled my case again. Wasn't much effort behind it, but it had worked in the past.

"Riordan," I put a whisper-soft, sexy tone in my appeal. "Please?"

His eyes and sensory tentacles swept me. I felt his examination- more personal than any physician's. Because I was actually part of him, in ways no other human could unite with another.

"You are a most necessary part of me, Wife. If it will make you happy. . . As your continuing education instructor, I'm proposing a change in the curriculum."

A frown creased my brows. I was confident this changeup would invoke my dispute. Amusement bubbled in Riordan's chest.

"Today, we'll work on a land-based critter. My pick. Be a good student and listen."

He kissed away my erupting 'but'.

"I allowed you to get too ambitious the other day with choosing a raven. Human to mountain lion- human to raven- worlds apart. I don't want you losing self-confidence or beating yourself up, so today we'll become. . ."

He let the suspense build until I was ready to explode.

"Horses," Riordan gave in with a glorious smile.

"Horses!" I liked the sound of that.

"I knew you would. A few caveats. Humans and mountain lions are predators. Horses are prey animals. A horse prefers to flee rather than fight, unless he's cornered. Horse eyes are set on to be of greatest use- to give the wary animal time to potentially effect escape. Use all of your senses to remain constantly vigilant. And I suggest we repair to a more congenial spot. Don't want Handsome to see you as a potential mate. That's all I need, to duel with him after we've reached an amicable plateau."

"Where?" I asked.

"Hold your horses, Bonnie. I'll take you."

There are still stretches of Wyoming considered wilderness. Just have to find them. I'd picked out a section of high desert country with rounded hills and sage galore- enough room to run.

Maybe I'd even take her up to the ancient medicine wheel. First things first, CatSkill.

"I'll change before you; then, if you have any difficulties, which I don't believe you will, you can look through my eyes to help you adjust."

"You're beautiful," Bonnie's face flushed with surprise at my transformation. "Your color. . ."

'What did you expect of a half-breed?' I snorted, literally.

My four-legged form involved burnished light bronze body, black mane and tail shot with streaks of gold and auburn and a bloody patch ran down my right shoulder.

"Riordan, that color. . . If you were prepotent for that color, wow!" Her hand thrilled my supra-natural coat.

'I'll show you prepotent.'

She giggled and in a flash my mate was a mare. A cream colored one with mixed shades of gold in her mane and tail. Huge dark eyes in a refined head that tossed with pleasure.

'Catch me if you can,' she taunted, and kicked up dust and tiny bits of rock into my chest as she bolted.

Glad of her successful venture, I allowed her a head start and admired her haunches tucking under and propelling her glorious little body forward.

She nearly flattened parallel to the ground as she put on more speed- racing the wind as it bantered with her tail and lashed her mane back and forth over her neck.

Better not let her get too far ahead, CatSkill, I advised myself.

We raced for miles, kicking up dry Wyoming dirt, jumping tumble weeds and eroded rivulets, flattening sage brush, running down into and thundering up ravines.

Being without shoes, I guided Bonnie's path from the worst of rock, and when she deviated to spite me- not seriously, I nipped at her sleek, sweet hindquarters. Isn't that what a stud does with the mare in his care? Could also earn the stud a swift kick from a lead mare. . .

For my attentions, I received the flick of her tail on my muzzle; her tiny heels kicked up and a 'Better watch it, CatSkill' squeal stopped my errant speculation.

Until the clamor of uninvited hooves disrupted our fun.

I pulled up with a scant caution to my mare. We stood together and read the intentions of two riders headed in our direction.

They slid to a stop on a rise looking our way and the four of us gauged each other- pair to pair.

One checked his lasso.

'Got any speed left, Bonnie?' The terrain was wide open- no place to hide. The nearest cover was five miles away.

'If we can make it to a tree line we can hide, transform and travel home.'

'Then let's go,' Bonnie sat back on her haunches, pirouetted and raced off toward the goal line.

The miles we'd previously playfully covered had us at a disadvantage over the shod geldings in hot pursuit. Hard ground and rocks wouldn't have made a difference to our feet during our joyride, but now we were running, well, not for our lives- more like for convenience' sake- no time to regroup or consider the terrain. Changing in front of them was not an option I wished to consider.

Dust blew off in clouds behind us. Too bad it wasn't enough to hide our supra-natural activities from the cowboys.

I guarded Bonnie's flanks, keeping ahead of the roping talents of the riders.

We'd have made it easy, until the proverbial wrench, in this case a hole, interrupted us on our escape.

'Bonnie!' I screamed as she crashed down- her hoof caught fast.

I heard the snap. The momentum of our pace propelled me forward even as my stride was cut dead. The surprise of my fall delayed my vocal cries.

Hurriedly, I took stock of my injuries. The worst was I couldn't rise. Riordan bucked, reared and screamed around me- baring teeth and warning the riders not to approach.

But the range riders came on. What cowboy could resist the challenge of roping a wild horse?

'Bonnie, I'm going to throw out a frequency, make them sorry they ever thought of roping a wild horse.'

'Riordan, wait!' Breathing was a bit difficult as I lay on my broken right shoulder, not to mention my leg. 'Let me talk to the geldings.'

'Better hurry, Wife.' Riordan challenged the riders' horses. The cowboys reined their horses to a standstill to plan their next move.

From their vantage point I knew they believed my situation was hopeless. This was confirmed as the chestnut's rider pulled at his rifle scabbard.

I addressed his horse, 'Chestnut?'

The rangy gelding's ears twisted back and then perked forward- honing in on my telepathic voice as if they were tiny satellites. His gray buddy listened in, too.

'Can you help me by taking your rider away? Give me a chance to recover? I'd really appreciate your help. I'd owe you a favor.'

Bribery usually worked with horses if applied in the correct manner. The chestnut nickered and tossed his head.

'I'll give you all the time you need, pretty girl. Too bad you already have a mate.' And with that promise, the red gelding bucked, fish-tailed and bolted.

His rider scrambled for a hand hold on the saddle horn which caused him to drop his rifle. A shocked look of surprise stretched his features at the impromptu upset.

The rifle lay inert, a useless tool without a hand to guide it, and the chestnut raced away with his off-balance rider tenaciously trying to regain control and keep from falling.

His gray buddy decided the best idea was to follow suit, regardless of what his rider believed. Suddenly rearing, the gray gelding's bony poll hit his rider's cowboy-hatted head; he rolled back and roared after his equine buddy- leaving his stunned rider swaying and grabbing for the saddle horn.

With the change back to my human form and the loss of the adrenalin factor, my injuries began to throb and worse, my foot was still stuck fast in the hole.

My husband knelt, chuckling all the while, shaking his head.

"I suppose you thought that was fun?" I gritted my teeth.

"Yeah, pretty much so. That, and watching you. You know you were in no danger, right?"

"Between the rifle, the lasso and the cowboys attached, I thought there might be just a suspicion of jeopardy." Guys could be awfully blasé in a perilous situation- at least, Riordan could.

Riordan kissed the tip of my nose. "I'll not let any harm come to you."

I struggled to get my foot loose as I continued to heal myself. Torn tendons, knee, ligaments, sprained ankle, broken shoulder. . .

"I feel so useless," I mumbled, watching my husband, gaining some idea of how Riordan had manipulated his claws to cut my jeans the night I was shot- this, I got to see firsthand.

The fingers of his right hand extended, curved slightly into the expert claws of a cougar. He grinned at me as he deftly employed his claws to dig out my foot.

"How in the world?"

"Just a little trick I picked up. There. All better."

My foot was free and his claws disappeared as his fingers encircled my ankle. With his powers added to mine, I felt good as new in seconds.

Physically, that is. I rested my head on my knees. Hid my face from him.

"Oh no you don't," he tapped my head.

"Riordan, am I the most pathetic shaman you've ever seen?"

"No shaman is pathetic. The spirits think I should spank you for saying such a ridiculous thing. Just because you've crossed over into becoming a shaman doesn't mean everything will come easy to you, Miss Overachiever. This isn't a typical school. It's much more catholic than any class."

Riordan brushed back his sweaty, long hair, sat back in the sage-speckled dirt.

"How many wild horses or domestic ones, for that matter, do you think step in holes?"

I started to object and he hushed me with a serious, raised brow. His words began to sink in.

"You're right, Riordan." Wasn't he always? His grin returned as he read my silent question.

"No shaman is omnipotent. Perhaps the hole was placed there in order for you to learn something." My husband, my teacher.

"I'll think about it," I promised him and rose to test out my legs. Like I thought- good as new. The sense of his teaching was rooting inside of me, and I gratefully sent a prayer to the spirits.

"Shall we go home, Riordan?"

"Good idea! I'm starving." What else was new?

He jumped up and suddenly stopped, his eyes swept the terrain.

"Riordan?"

Grimacing, he said, "I was just thinking. Not many wild places left for a wild creature to just be. . .wild."

10

"Kids? Bonnie, Riordan?" We'd popped back into our bedroom in time to hear my dad's call.

Eight quartets of paws abandoned us and raced to the sound of my dad's voice- they'd conquered his heart just the way they wanted.

"Anybody. . .here? Wait a minute!"

Riordan and I laughed at my dad's admonitions to the feline entourage barraging his person. A sudden thought flashed through me.

"Oh, no! It's Friday!"

"So?" Riordan's mouth twitched.

"I was supposed to have dinner ready. The fights are tonight." Hastily, I brushed at my clothes.

Riordan raised his head, "Grandfather's here."

"Oh, boy. Do I look all right?"

"Perfect," he winked.

He followed me into the hall with his hands grazing my behind.

"What?" I whispered.

"A patch of dust," he grinned.

"There you are. Help me with these kids," my dad begged.

Three kittens were climbing up my dad's jeans. Three others were perched on a shelf preparatory to jumping on his shoulders. The golden one sat before him, meowing fit to deafen a person- begging to be picked up.

That's Amore, on the kitchen table, cleaned her paws, watching the three-ring circus out of the corner of her eyes.

Grandfather, arms crossed, stood back, appreciating the show. A glint of humor lurked in his eyes, but his face was impassive.

"What's for dinner? I don't smell. . . You didn't forget?" Was my dad actually whining?

I was too busy detaching the Velcro kittens from my dad's clothes. Unfortunately, I couldn't hold all of them at one time. Those I couldn't hold reattached and climbed back into my dad's patient arms.

"Pineapple upside down cake," Riordan broke in.

My dad turned puzzled eyes his way, "For dinner?"

"I thought you asked about dessert," Riordan said, nodding to Grandfather.

"Dessert, now that is a great idea. Get down, Cali, Fragi, doggonit!"

"More like cattonit, eh?" Riordan and Grandfather laughed. "But, pineapple upside down cake sounds good to me, too."

Three pairs of male eyes turned in anxious anticipation to me. "I guess that seals that. Riordan, you'd better dig up some pineapple," I conceded.

That satisfied the human male contingent. Oops, I spoke too soon.

"What about dinner?" Dad repeated his original question. "And what have you two been up to, rolling around in the dirt?" He mock-scowled as he suffered the continued kitten onslaught.

I stopped and actually looked down at myself, at Riordan. Silently, I gave him a hefty dose of what-for.

And silently, he retorted, 'We're married, sheesh! You think your father doesn't know we. . .'

'Riordan!' I silently screamed. He laughed aloud and pulled me into his arms.

Flushing, I detached myself and hurriedly ran through what occupied the freezer. "How about the last of Riordan's fish?"

"Great! Come on, Red Hawk." A strident squeal hit the air waves as my dad inadvertently stepped on a kitten tail.

"Sorry, sorry," the offended kitten was hoisted up by my dad and kisses rained upon its little head. I swear the whole squeal was a ruse to get his attention, by the look of the satisfied grin on the kitten's face.

"First things first. Super, Cali, Fragi, Listic, Expe, Ali, Docious, That's Amore, let's eat."

Seven pairs of kitten eyes harkened my way and with That's Amore playing the Pied Piper of Hamlin, a rough formation of a line followed me back to Riordan's and my bedroom, where I placed 8 dinners on a serving tray and set it down for the kids and Amore. She gave me a particular look to make sure I'd not classed her with the kids.

"What's with these fights your father is so keen on?" Riordan had returned with 6 cans of pineapple.

"Just how much dessert do you think I'm going to make?"

"Enough, I hope," he tilted my chin and offered inspiration.

"Riordan, son, come watch the fights with us."

I walked into the living room where Grandfather and Jim were comfortably ensconced, waiting dinner and checking on the evening's line-up of mixed martial arts combatants.

I shook my head as Jim indicated a seat. "Not my thing, Jim. Grandfather will keep you company, though. I'll help Bonnie with dinner."

"No fights, no sports. Isn't there anything you like to watch on TV, son?"

I gave it a second's thought. "Any reruns of The Virginian? I'd like to get a look at his eyebrows."

That would give him a Rubik's Cube for thought.

"Grandfather, I'm sorry I've not had you to dinner sooner, with Grace away. When will she be home?" Bonnie asked, setting out a bowl of biscuits.

Grandfather took his time buttering a biscuit and adding jam. "By and by," he answered in a mysterious tone that left no room for further inquiries.

I was aware of Grace's quandary concerning the future of her center in Sedona and her future here with my grandfather. It was their business, and I simply hoped for the best.

Back to studying over her perceived failures, Bonnie remained much too quiet over dinner. I guessed there'd be question and answer time later. No way around it. But, at least I had a whole pineapple upside down cake to myself-girding up for what she had in store for me.

I scooped my Wife into my arms.

"Riordan, the dishes?"

"They're not going anywhere, Kitten."

"But?"

"Let's do something different tonight," I kissed her and hurried to the inevitable.

"Spit it out, Kitten." Her cute little antics to act as if she didn't know what I was thinking about tickled me. I almost succumbed and to the devil with her questions.

When she began to chew on her lower lip, I gave in, restrained my baser male inclinations.

With my hands behind my head, resting against the brass head board, which wasn't very comfortable, I reiterated, "Spit it out. I'm waiting."

"All right," her eyes glistened with unshed tears of frustration.

I knew she felt as if she'd failed some kind of self-imposed test and I knew Bonnie had never had the experience of flunking at anything before, not counting swimming. Not that she'd failed at anything now, but knowing how her mind worked. . .

"It was so easy to become a mare today. Why is it so difficult to be a flying raven?"

"How much time have you spent studying horses?" I'd use a bit of coyote learning. Question instead of outright answer- make her come to the solution in a roundabout fashion.

She frowned at my not answering straight out. I lifted a brow as in 'where's your response?'

Rolling her shoulders, she said, "Years. My dad started me very young, teaching all he knew, helping me see and I never stopped and when I found I could talk to. . ."

"And not counting our flirtatious guide in Banff, how many ravens have you studied and conversed with?"

Her delectable lips twisted, nose scrunched. Resist, CatSkill, resist.

"None."

"Need I say more?"

Bonnie went quiet for close to a whole minute. I saw it forming- yes, the next question would be a doozy. In for a penny, in for a pound- I'd heard that expression somewhere.

"Did you have d…difficulties? When you crossed into other forms?"

Temporarily, I blocked my brain's ramblings. No, I'd not disclose the time I attempted to switch genders- what a fiasco! But, there was. . .

"I want you to realize that I've had 150-plus years to gain the experience I've acquired. I also grew up in the wild. No home or the spiritual death-knell of civilization such as you've grown up with to hinder me. It's only natural that many animal forms and spirits are open to me. My spirit guide, the mountain lion, was as easy a metamorphosis for me as breathing. Our shared guide was relatively easy for you to become, right?"

For a loaded moment, she reminisced on her initial transformations.

"Granted, your first shift was a trial by fire."

"Yeess," she tentatively agreed.

"So what's the problem?"

"You're not disappointed with how fast I'm not learning?"

A great belt of laughter burst from me and kept on coming until I was nearly in tears. Her face reddened, agitation brewed.

"Bonnie, you've been a shaman for less than a year. You're perfect. I love watching you learn. I can't wait for you to learn more about your special powers- we're all agog wondering about them. I love discovering you. Remember, simply crossing over into shamanism and having complete control of your body does not imply complete control of other bodies. It takes time, practice, lessons. For instance, today, you took to being a race horse like a duck to water- say, there's an idea!"

My lovely Wife rolled her eyes.

"Stop being so self-conscious about your development. I'll let you know if I perceive a problem and we'll deal with it together. Now, once more, your homework is to study birds, especially ravens in flight. Talk to them. Study hard for say, at least a couple months and we'll try again."

"Months?" she wailed.

"Yes," I fervently replied and leaned in for a kiss.

"Will you tell me about some of your early misadventures? Were there any?"

Here it goes. Give it up, CatSkill. Prove to her you're only. . .half human?

I leaned back into the headboard. "OK. I was trekking in the rainforest, enjoying colorful birds, tree frogs, etc. I got this crazy idea, and I use the term with all its connotations, to try transmuting into a snake.

A lovely specimen was hanging out in a tree above me. I spent, oh, an hour or so studying the reptile. He/she seemed intrigued with me. It was easy to become the boa."

"A boa constrictor, you picked a boa constrictor for your first reptile transformation?"

"First snake," I clarified.

Bonnie's eyes widened and I realized I'd opened a whole other can of worms. Digging yourself in CatSkill, digging in, I mused.

"Anyway, there I lay in all my boa glory, strung out on the detritus of a rainforest floor, when hanged if I didn't remember I'd not studied the boa moving. . ."

Bonnie stifled a laugh. A hand on her sweet mouth, where my mouth should be. Focus, CatSkill, focus.

"Basically, you constrict certain muscles and this pulls you along, right? Huh! Could have fooled me. I was pretty well stuck in limbo. As I weighed my options- reclaiming my human form or continuing to figure out snake propulsion, I learned the sex of the boa in that tree I'd left behind me.

Female. Hot. Sexy. . . Well, you get the picture. Before I could get my act together, she had begun to entwine about me."

Bonnie was getting the biggest kick out of this and truth to tell, it was pretty funny in hind sight.

"Before she could further embrace me, I rolled and wrapped about a small tree. Unfortunately, the tree barely hinged on a river bank. In dislodging the lady serpent, I up-anchored the tree and down I went, tree and all, into the river.

Luckily, I had the presence of mind to change into a fish- catfish, of course, and as I hit the water. . . To this day, I don't know how or if boas can swim, but I managed well as a fish.

Relieved to be out of her grasp, I was shocked when BAM! My tail was punctured by a fisherman's spear point. I erupted from the water as myself- my cougar self- scared that youngster into a faint."

By this time, Bonnie was spellbound, but no more laughter. I thought it was pretty funny, myself.

"I went back and laid a memory fog on him. Why did you stop laughing, Wife?"

A small, feminine hand graced the side of my face, stopped intimately at the corner of my mouth and then strolled down my chest.

A catch in my breath, in my heart rate.

"The very idea of anyone, snake or whatever, infringing on my territory and you are my territory. . ."

Great Spirit, help me. Bonnie crooned my own words to me. I groaned. Bonnie, my Wife, my never ending source of surprise and pleasure.

11

"That should be illegal," I wolf whistled as my Wife entered the living room.

There is a soft black leather that emphasizes a woman's curves. It was this leather that molded to Bonnie's tiny feet, ankles, calves- up to her knees.

I'd surprised her with a pair of custom- made-for-her-riding boots. Only the best for my Wife. Knowing an Italian shoe maker who owed me a favor helped.

Continuing up those glorious thighs and highlighting the perfect curves of her hips were butter-cream riding breeches. Only my hands had the right to caress her that way.

A thin, long sleeve, cotton shirt, open at the throat and framing her cougar pendant, completed the picture. Her hair was ponytailed and her face blushing.

"Honey, you gonna wear that in public?"

"Dad, Riordan," she frowned at me, "this is English riding attire."

"Huh, looks mighty. . .uh, never mind," an equally blushing Jim looked away.

'He was about to say mighty sexy, Wife.' No brag, just fact. Bonnie moaned silently in reply.

"You ready, honey? Better get that beast in the trailer. We want to be there early for your lesson."

"You coming, Riordan?" She looked at me hopefully.

"You kidding, I'm not letting you out of my sight."

At the head of the Bueller's drive a black tinted window SUV blocked us. A black-suited individual with an all-too-serious mien stepped up to Jim's side of the truck.

"State your business."

"What is this? My daughter has a scheduled riding lesson this morning."

"That's too bad." Before the suit could continue, a barrelling Bob Bueller slammed on the brakes of his pickup, spewing dust and bits of rock on the suit. With fire in his eyes, he exited and pushed his bulk to Jim's side.

"Can you believe this, Jim? Some so and so tore up my hay field last night and now the place is crawling with Feds and guys dressed in camos taking over my fields, worse than trespassers! I've got stock to tend to. Sorry, Bonnie, I had no idea. Couldn't reach you in time. Got a hold of Mr. Peters, he'll reschedule."

Jim got out of the truck. My wild senses dictated the same. I lifted Bonnie down. The suit didn't like that. I could sense his position. Like, maybe he wasn't getting the proper respect. Huh, fancy that. Guy takes over somebody's property and the owners don't appreciate it.

The implacable suit warned us to leave.

"Tell us about what you found in your field, Mr. Bueller," I asked, ignoring the suit. Something important was in the air. More so than any Feds could conceive of.

"Near as I can tell, Riordan, it's kind of like those crop circles you hear about on the TV. Never did pay them any never minds except, now. . ." The rancher scowled at the agent.

"You need to leave," the suit advised again, more forcefully.

"Look here Mister, this is my property. You have no rights here. This ain't California. This is Cody, Wyoming."

'Bonnie,' I silently instructed her, 'I'm going to fly over, look through my eyes.'

I pretended to check a trailer tire, turned the corner and shifted into a more covert operative- a raven would do. I put in a call for Grandfather to join me in the air.

"Where'd he go?"

My dad and Mr. Bueller were engaged in mutually supportive conversation. No one we'd ever heard of around Cody had been treated to a property take-over before. At least not in the 21st century. Unbelievable.

"Who?" I played innocent.

"The long hair," an imperious retort from the black-suited agent had me ready to snarl.

"I don't know anyone by that name."

Westerners did not appreciate government interference with their ranch operations or being treated as second-class citizens anywhere.

A frown threatened down on me. He thought he could scare an ordinary girl- too bad for him that was not me.

The suit scurried about, trying to locate Riordan and keep calm over losing- what? A suspect? He hesitated with his hand hovering over his walkie-talkie.

I envied my husband's mastery of the skies- his dance with the winds. Below him, I saw several camouflaged men and other dark-suited individuals checking out a. . .

From Riordan's and then, I saw the red tail hawk gliding, vantage point high above I saw a picture. Not exactly painted in the field, more like sculpted with natural colors in an unnatural way.

A central blackness radiated out- blackness, again. I shivered. Was I to be plagued by another black horror?

The blackness seemed to be blocked, walled in by four different colored impediments. The colors encircled the ugly dearth of color, contained it.

A premonitory kick made me clutch at my stomach.

Grandfather, the red tail hawk, swooped lower. Riordan had perched, perfectly hidden, on an evergreen limb.

I saw the flash before a sharp retort sounded. The wings of the hawk faltered. Blood poured from the speckled chest and the swoop faltered into a hapless dive.

'Grandfather!' I nearly screamed aloud. And then I had the shamanistic foresight to scream over the telepathic hot line for Grace.

Silently, I beseeched Grace, but received no reply.

Hurriedly, I stepped into the horse trailer, pretending to check on Handsome and traveled into the lower evergreens where I'd last seen Riordan- my heart at a standstill.

I arrived next to my kneeling husband in his human form. He had one hand on the seeping bloody breast. I placed my hand on his shoulder, offering further healing energies.

In the past when I'd sent out healing frequencies, I could feel them being absorbed by my intended patient. But, here? Now? Nothing!

Spirits help us! What did this mean?

Throughout my system a shock of blackness. . .nothingness. . .   Was Grandfather. . .?   No, it couldn't be! NO!

Riordan's body turned rigid. He became part of the blackness- not with death, but a deadly calm of retribution. A truly angry Riordan was more implacable, more formidable than any weapon.

'Bonnie, go back to Handsome.'

'Riordan? Is Grandfather?'

'Is gone. Go. I have something to attend to.'

'No, I. . .' His ruthless stare fixed on me, ordering obedience.

I refused to concede. Yes, retribution was in order, but I'd not leave Riordan to it, alone.

He started away from me. From the distance, I heard the agents.

"Stokes, what the hell are you doing shooting at birds? Our orders were no weapons to be discharged."

"I think that hawk had something on its leg."

"You moron, biologists tag birds to study them."

"Nah, this was more than. . ."

"You better hope you're right." Footsteps.

"Riordan," I whispered. I grabbed his arm. He snarled at me and threw it off. Undeterred, I reached for him again.

"Riordan, I won't let you go alone," I whispered, adamant.

This time, he rounded on me, loosed my grip, began to stalk away when. . .

"Riordan, look, look!"

A tiny bird hovered over Grandfather's defiled hawk body. Blue-black wings, forked tail, russet breast- the swallow. She remained like a humming bird in place, hovering right above Grandfather.

"Riordan, look," I beseeched.

Now we could hear it. Riordan's eyes squinted. From pain to surprise and. . .hope?

The tiny bird slowly, gently settled upon the hawk's breast. I heard a frequency that I'd not heard before.

'I've not, either, Wife.' His arms went about my waist and he rested his chin on my head.

The wings of the hawk imperceptibly- did they move? The swallow was still. Silence reigned, portentous.

Grace had heard my call. The tiny bird rose and in an instant, Grace was standing next to Grandfather. A repaired, resurrected, standing, human Grandfather.

"Still making decisions that aren't yours to make, Red Hawk? I thought we'd moved beyond such. Seeing as how many. . .so many years. . .?"

Grace addressed Grandfather with tears rolling down her face. She didn't try to hide them or wipe them away.

Grandfather almost looked. . .sheepish?

"Riordan?" I was puzzled.

"Never mind, Wife. Not right now. Grandfather, Grace- bless you, I suggest you continue this discussion elsewhere."

Stumbling noisily in our direction was the cause- an irresponsible. . . I couldn't find words vile enough.

Riordan released me and winked. Grandfather gathered Grace into his arms and disappeared.

"Care to help, Wife?"

I nearly laughed aloud at Bonnie. "I said coyote."

She whined at me. Her coyote resembled Stalker more than the dog's wild cousin.

The murderer, not used to negotiating western terrain in dress shoes and a suit, was about to get his comeuppance.

In a great noisy commotion, he burst into our area, sweating and cursing.

Bonnie growled, dripped foamy saliva and in general, attempted to appear menacing as she advanced on our 'culprit'.

From above on a suitable limb, I waited until she brought him to the mark. The nervous agent stumbled, felt for his pistol, and Bonnie sprang. She knew what that wandering hand portended.

This backed the suit right where I. . .

My cougar-self landed, knocking the malefactor to the ground, face first.

'Bonnie, go ahead, Wife.'

Bonnie hit a frequency that released the downed suit's guts and bladder. I'd once experienced a portion of her talent in that regard. And so had Gunne.

The contemptible jerk trembled. We were about to give him a daydream he'd never forget. I shifted back to human form, but kept the cougar claws.

"How many animals have you hurt in your lifetime? 10 or less?" No response.

"Less than 100?"

"Uh, wh…who are y…you?" The miscreant stuttered.

My claws settled on the back of his neck-tips ready to pierce. No way he could mistake my meaning.

"P...p...m...may....maybe...m...more," he sighed and began to sob- the usual response of a bully who's been apprehended by the king of beasts.

Bonnie growled and her chops drooled on his head.

"I'll tell you how the rest of your life plays out. You will become the greatest animal rights advocate on this planet- got it?"

I leaned in, let my face take on bear and sniffed loudly at his neck.

He moaned, his senses almost giving in to his terror. I didn't want him to black out- not yet. The festivities had just begun.

"I've got your scent now. There's no place in the world you can possibly hide from me. Do you understand the conditions of your release?"

"Y...y...yes. I...p...p...promise. I s...wear."

Bonnie growled, dissatisfied, and made a silent suggestion.

"Have at it, Wife." A pungent stream saturated the agent right before he passed out.

12

"What is so funny?"

We'd just returned home from gathering specimens at the Bueller's hay field. A great adventure, covert ops- a mountain lion's favorite activity- pursuing an agenda while remaining under the radar, so to speak. And the radar/suits/armed personnel were out in full force. Except for Grandfather's assailant- nowhere to be seen.

Grace had insisted on the necessity of studying the origins of the unnatural colorings of the grasses. What we'd brought home would keep her scientific-bent mind busy.

As for me and Grandfather, although we'd not had a chance to discuss the phenomenon yet, I believed there was tremendous augury extant in that field art.

The message wasn't for the military though. My senses told me the extraordinary telegram in the field was meant for us. The interpretation. . .

Bonnie had not stopped laughing. Every time she looked at me she released anew further gales of hilarity. They dared not try and subside.

"Riordan," she hiccupped, "you surprised me. I didn't realize you had a comic side."

"I'll show you comic," I picked her up and dumped her on the bed. The rebounding mattress displaced a few cuddled kittens. My bounding next to her sent the remaining die-hards off in cat huffs.

"I wish you could have seen yourself." Bonnie held her stomach's convulsions.

"Hey, I think I did a better job then you did becoming a coyote- now that was a howl." I nuzzled her neck, blew strands of hair away from her delightfully scented jugular vein.

Maybe vampires had the right idea. Bonnie's blood was certainly perfume to my nose. Kissing along the length of her exposed neck seemed to check her frivolity.

Good thing, 'cuz I had something in mind.

"Riordan, you were the most splendid, attractive, manly. . ."

I'd hit the right spot. Glancing up our eyes locked- green to gold.

"How'd you like those eyebrows?" I gave her my best Virginian look. Brought on the giggles all over again.

"Riordan?"

"Hmmm," I'd almost dropped off.

"What did Grace mean about Grandfather making decisions alone again?"

"It's not my story to tell, Wife. You'll have to ask Grace." I curled her into my embrace. "Sleep, Kitten," I murmured.

"Son?"

Uh oh, I thought. Bonnie's father had been perusing flyers lately and practicing his bow skills in all of his free time.

"What's up, Jim?"

"There's an archery competition coming up. I hoped to talk you into signing on. Uh, I'll spring for the entry fee if. . ." He broke off as my expression registered disinterest.

"That's kind of you, sir, but no thanks." I really, really didn't want to.

Jim frowned, couldn't figure me out, and now felt as if he'd put me on the spot.

"If you like, sir, I'd be happy to coach you," I offered.

"But you aren't interested in participating, not at all?"

"No. Competitions are not my thing. Hope you understand." Knowing he didn't.

"Darned if I can figure, son. You're talented beyond belief. No fear anywhere in you. Complete self-confidence." Jim tapped at his jeans, fiddled with his ball cap.

"I heard about your escapade with the football team, so I know people, with all their misguided ideas, don't make you nervous. No sports, no competitions. . ."

Men, as Mr. Lance saw it, shared beers, watched sports, engaged in 'manly activities'. Many of them also needed to prove something. Not me.

"Sorry if you're disappointed, sir. My hobbies, other than Bonnie, are solitary pursuits."

He nodded, thoughtfully. Not comprehending-and why should he understand a mountain lion's preferences? I realized he wanted quality male time with his son-in-law. Activities beyond who could snatch the most cookies. Even chopping wood was a solitary endeavor.

"How about fishing, sir?"

Jim's eyes brightened, "There's an idea-fresh fish for supper. Bonnie does a helluva fish fry. I'll dig out the poles. Maybe Red Hawk will join us. Sure you won't enter the competition?"

"I'm sure, sir." Positive.

"Well," he rubbed the back of his neck, put up his bow. "I guess I'll take you up on the coaching. Hope you'll come and watch me?"

"Dad's got something up his sleeve." I cornered Riordan while mucking stalls.

"He wants me to go with him and compete at an archery tournament."

"Oh," I considered his disclosure, hung up the manure fork, but Riordan wasn't forthcoming with further details. "So, are you?"

"No."

"Why, Riordan?" I felt my husband's unease.

"Simple, I'm not into competing."

"It's not exactly like other contact sports." My husband had a perfect talent and I'd love to see him win.

He leaned against a stall wall, deciding on how to continue in whatever veins he wished to conceal or keep private. "You know, the target might have a difference of opinion."

I rolled my eyes. "I guess Dad would like to hang out with you more. Like fathers and sons do."

My husband hitched his fingers under his flannel shirt and into his jeans' pockets. "I suggested fishing."

"That's good." I hesitated, sensing he'd prefer to speak of anything else. I knew he knew I knew, yet I persisted. "Can you tell me why, Riordan?"

A wry smile studied me. "Does it matter, Bonnie?"

"I…I'd like to understand. You're so talented. What would it hurt to enter?"

"You're worse than your father, Miss Persistent." Grimly, he shook his head. "You won't like what I have to tell you."

"It's not a matter of liking or disliking, I simply want to understand. Will you tell me?"

His jaw clenched momentarily, relaxed. I sensed when his indecision turned to decision.

"Before you, Bonnie," he looked at me intently. "Before you, I kept mainly to myself. In my traveling, yes I'd be among people here and there, but for the most part, I preferred the solitary route, or inconspicuously on the outskirts of humanity. Camouflaged, like a good mountain lion." A genuine smile curled his lips.

"Behind an obstacle, observing. Occasionally, I'd enter into a situation to help someone or to acquire some knowledge. You know of some of those doings." I nodded.

"With my looks and heritage, I especially make it a point not to enter areas where groups of males in situations inherent with high levels of testosterone are in play. Bars would be an example. Sports activities, licensed or impromptu, are other examples."

I started to protest, but he waved me off.

"Listen, Wife. Invariably, if I walk onto certain stages, some loud mouth, bully, bigot etc., will try to start something. I know I can take care of myself. But I'm not into protecting trouble makers- it's much more fun to teach them a lesson.

However, in general, I gave that up a long time ago.

I guard my people on the res, of course, but I prefer quiet, solitude- except for you, or peaceful people-watching on occasion. I still tend to my shamanic duties- it would be remiss of me to deny when I'm needed, but I'd much rather observe wildlife in unpeopled wilderness than join a crowd."

"I understand that, Riordan. I always kept to myself. My favorite things to do- painting, working with animals, the horses, were singular activities. I never cared for organized sports, even when I was talked into them. Didn't care to compete. Running by myself, until you came, was enough. I didn't need to convince anyone else of anything." Emotions were swirling inside, stirred up by memories pre-Riordan.

"You were destined for me, Lioness. Our shared spirit guide, the mountain lion, chose us for each other. And I'm sure Irusan had his paws in the mix, too. In this whole world, there is only you."

The fervor of his feeling for me not only surrounded me, but filled me with reciprocal joy. And then his lips were on mine and all else was obliterated. For a time.

"Do you dislike people for the most part?" I thought of the friends we'd made. I believed Riordan liked Rick and even Matt, now.

A semi-relieved smile replaced Riordan's concerned look. "No, Wife. I just don't care for groups, on the whole, especially ones outranked by men trying to outdo other males. May be necessary to wander in at times, I accept that, but I'm not going looking for trouble. Don't borrow trouble, seems someone once told me. "

"What about school?"   Why had he entered high school?

"Grandfather's idea.   He's a cunning bird. Can't complain- that's where I met you, as he well knew."

With eyes plunging into my soul, he came toward me.

"You are the joy of my life.   In fact, you are my life and all I need."

"What if we just go to watch?"

"I'm glad you're not a pit bull, Wife."

"You would be uncomfortable. . .watching?"

"I'd not be uncomfortable, Wife."

"Oh," Bonnie replied, confused all over again.   I felt the twitch at the corner of my mouth.   Bonnie didn't fully fathom my earlier explanation.

And why should she?   Her youth and inexperience. . . Block yourself, CatSkill.

"If you want, we'll go."   As one who could read the signals, I'd be prepared.

"I don't want you to do something against your better judgment.   I thought it would be nice to support my dad at the competition.   Do something as a family.   I mean besides fight monsters."

I sighed.   "It's all settled.   We'll go." I'd not be the one to start trouble, but knowing. . .

13

I stepped out of our old jeep. Jim excused himself to register. Competition today would involve luck- the Wyoming winds had come to wreak havoc.

I scanned the grounds, turned and lifted Bonnie down, shut the door and nodded to my right.

"See the guy with the crew-cut, the one in the jersey?"

"Yes," she frowned in the direction indicated.

"He'll be the first to make a snide remark," my scenario reading skills were at work.

"How do you know that?" She knew I knew, but didn't comprehend my unique talent.

"Wanta bet?" She tried to make sense with her wild senses what I inherently knew.

"No, Riordan, I trust your judgment. We should go." She grabbed at my arm, tried to open the jeep door.

"No, Wife, we'll let it play out."

"But. . ." I kissed the tip of her upturned nose and stifled her protest.

"Will you look at that? Two long haired girls walking hand-in-hand. Don't see that every day," my suspect jeered loud enough for everyone around him to hear. A typical loudmouth.

I swept my long hair from my eyes and tilted Bonnie's chin up, gave her a mischievous wink and a warning.

"Don't interfere, Kitten- no matter what. Understand?"

"I hear you." I was afraid of that. Comprehension and agreement did not necessarily follow hearing. I well knew my Bonnie.

"Shut it, Stokes. I know that young man and he's more of a man than you'll ever be." A beaming policeman strolled to us with hand extended for my husband to shake. From my Riordan's eyes, I recognized him, too.

"Mr. CatSkill, if I remember?"

Riordan reciprocated the greeting, "Officer. Bonnie, this is the police Captain who interviewed me at the hospital." He explained for the officer's benefit.

"I'd heard everything worked out for you, and you, too Miss."

"My Wife, Bonnie," Riordan introduced me.

"Hello," I offered my hand, glad of a mediating force. The policeman offered congratulations with a pleasant look of surprise, before cautioning Riordan.

"Don't mind Stokes, son. He's always a first-class a… Well, never mind, you know."

"I do," Riordan solemnly averred.

"Are you competing?"

"No, sir. Came to cheer on Bonnie's father."

"Give my best to Jim, wish him luck." The man turned, stopped. "You know we never found that cat's body- only part we have is its ear. Hope you're careful out there. If it's alive, he could be even more dangerous."

"We'll watch it, sir, thanks."

Riordan and I giggled into each other's bodies as we pictured the end of Chac at the bottom of dancing mammoth feet, and we went to join my dad.

"Hey, CatSkill!" A grinning Rick, bow in hand, pushed through several conversing groups of contenders and their fans.

"Hey, Rick, didn't know you were going to be here."

"Hi, Bonnie," Rick's genuine, friendly smile graced both of us.

"Where's Lil?" I asked.

"Uh, she's not into this sort of thing." Rick and Riordan shook hands while I construed the meaning behind Rick's words.

Not interested? How could your girlfriend not be interested in watching you strut your skills? Riordan, reading me, gave me a silent warning.

"I'd like you to meet my father," Rick presented a graying model of a man, expensively clad and matching his son's height of 6'8".

Mr. Winslow eyed Riordan with certain misgivings before extending his hand. To Rick's annoyance.

"Dad, lighten up. Riordan was not only an A student and world traveler, he can beat me in a game of HORSE and he's probably the best archer on the planet."

"Mr. Winslow," Riordan allowed Rick's father to gauge him better with a firm handshake, and steady eyes assessed each other in turn.

"Bonnie, Riordan, I'm up next. Hey, Rick, you my competition?"

About that time, the rude loudmouth hustled by us, saw my dad and stopped dead.

"Should've known you'd have a pansy for a son-in-law, Lance. Always sticking up for the odd balls, eh?"

His remark kindled my inner nature into fire-mode, even as I felt Riordan completely calm and cool at my side.

'Don't mind him, Kitten. He hasn't got a clue.' Riordan silently reminded me.

I burst out laughing while directly eyeing the bulk of the bully. His face reddened, not so sure of himself.

"Hey, Lance, once I kick your butt and all these other wannabees. . ." he blustered.

To my dad's credit, he remained steadfast while the bully continued psyching out his competition. At least, that's how Riordan described Stokes' behavior to me.

I wondered what that comment about my dad sticking up for odd balls meant- certainly a topic for conversation on the way home.

"Good luck, Stokes," my dad, the sportsman, said as he went to join the contenders lined up facing the first targets.

"Only one going to need luck is you, Lance," Stokes practically spit back.

The wind played havoc with the first arrows fired. Only Stokes seemed to find an acceptable score in the colorfully ringed targets, some 60 yards out.

"No, Wife." Riordan settled his hands on my hips and whispered in my ear. I'd considered asking the breeze for a favor as my dad notched his last arrow.

Stokes won the round. My dad came in fourth, which I thought was pretty respectable for a man who'd only unretired his bow within the past weeks and that was to stave off ghosts.

I was positive Stokes lived with and breathed his bow.

"Probably sleeps with it, too. Can you imagine a woman being attracted to that?" Riordan's quip brought a smile to my face, mirrored by his own.

My dad didn't seem put out, certainly not ready to quit; he'd entered the 90 yard round. "Make a nice practice, if nothing else," he shrugged with a wry grin.

Rick, surprisingly, did not finish at all well. Between Stokes verbal boasts and insults and the winds playfulness, he had trouble aplenty, and disappointment reigned on his face.

"Hey, Lance, got you a baby score, huh? Tough luck." Stokes baited my dad again as he corralled the other winning scores.

"It's just a game, Stokes. Lay off."

"Ha ha! That's the typical response of the loser."

Faces in the crowd frowned or smiled depending on who they supported. Most were used to Stokes and his consistent wins and irksome boasts.

Rudely, he knocked into Rick as he strutted by. Rick's bow loosed from his grasp and fell.

Mr. Winslow stepped in front of Stokes. "I suggest you pick up that young man's bow and apologize."

Stokes looked around, moved closer into Mr. Winslow's personal space. "And if I don't? You going to do something about it?"

The bully's eyes raked up and down at the expensively dressed gentleman. "You going to. . .sue me?"

"Here, Rick." Hoping to check trouble, my dad picked up Rick's bow- the one with all the bells and whistles.

"Got your boy a good bow- better get him some lessons. Hey, Long Hair, you do anything besides paw that little girl?" Stokes dared to give my husband a condescending look.

"Listen, Wade," the Captain broached the crowd to intervene, "we don't want any trouble here. Why don't you go celebrate? Your friends are waiting."

"They can wait. Am I getting to you, girly?" The bully overstepped without a clue as to what he was stepping into.

I felt Riordan's lethal, calculating calm next to me. Through his eyes, I saw his gaze never wavered from the muscular, crew-cut roisterer.

I knew if Stokes blundered one inch into Riordan's or my space, there would be a fight. No doubt who would win. An understanding of Riordan's words from the previous day dawned clearly.

My arm slid along Riordan's forearm. The braggart didn't miss a chance to chide my husband again.

"Your little Missy keep you safe, boy?"

"Stokes, that's enough," my dad, without hesitation, stepped between Riordan and Stokes.

By now, Rick's large frame had straightened with grim, tight-lipped resolve. He wasn't above wading into the fray. Mr. Winslow's element was more of a courtroom than a free-for-all- he looked entirely discomfited amidst ungentlemanly sorts.

A few of Stokes' supporters threw out suggestions varying from 'let's get a beer' to 'let's run the long hair out of here'.

The officer took his cue and acted his official role again.

"Break it up, here," his voice commanded.

"Nothing to break up, just having a little fun with this. . .this. . ." Stokes made a rude gesture at Riordan.

It must have had a greater significance than I knew of because I heard intakes of breath, a few muttered curses, and my dad's and Rick's fists clenched.

Riordan, however, smiled in a saintly fashion, obviously nothing he'd not encountered before was transpiring.

"All right, big mouth. You want to have a little fun? I'll oblige." Riordan's imperturbable tone seemed to feed the fire.

A circle widened around us. Apparently, the men took this as a challenge to fight.

"Riordan, son. . ." my dad broke in, but Riordan, nonchalantly, held up his hand.

"Do I understand that you are the winner of this tournament? That you consider this your sport? Your house?" Riordan's smile widened.

His earlier explanation of men, sports and heightened testosterone made all too much sense, now. Belatedly, I knew I'd been wrong to ask him to come. He winked at me, as if to say it's OK.

As a reader of situations, I knew today would play out just this way. As Jim Lance had hoped, I was going to compete- only not quite the way he'd expected.

"Might I suggest a little contest? Call it an archery duel, between the two of us."

"You going to challenge me, boy?"

Stokes thought this extremely funny. As did certain numbers of his coterie- the ones most like him.

"Are you afraid?" My voice, serpent smooth, slipped into the overflowing machismo.

Wade Stokes' jaw dropped in surprise, and I swear a fly landed inside, must be all that trash talk creating a fetid odor that fascinated the run-of-the-mill critter.

Granted, Stokes had talent with a bow, but his best ally was his single-minded focus, and he was assiduous in psyching out his competition. So, even competitors who might have given him food for thought generally dissembled before stepping up to the mark.

As the number of his conquests grew over the years, this, coupled with his braggadocio, kept him in ascending ego mode- completely unchecked.

Ah, but he'd never met a contender like me.

"Put your bow up, boy."

"Terms, first. I suggest three separate rounds or tests. You pick one, I pick one and a neutral bystander picks the third test."

"Boy, you don't know what you're getting into."

I chuckled. I knew exactly what I was getting into. On the other hand, he was truly clueless.

"What's your pleasure, boy?"

Right now was not the time to say just how gratified I would be to knock the word 'boy' down his throat, but soon.

"After you," I offered.

"All right then, girly. One arrow each- flight competition. Let's see how far those girly arms of yours can send an arrow," Stokes had the nerve to hoist a sizeable bicep.

"Riordan," Rick interrupted, sure I didn't know- he motioned at Stokes' compound bow with its stabilizers, magnifying front sites, special arrow rests- a bow built especially for Stokes to compete and win with.

I shrugged off Rick's offer to use his custom bow.

My choice of contest was along more natural lines- field archery: 10-30 fake, target animals arrayed on a course, a timed event, a shot for the kill- one arrow for each target.

Stokes hesitated a fraction of a second before agreeing. Perhaps he was finally gaining a sense. . .

As there was not a single disinterested bystander standing by, Captain Frey decided the third test, a standard Olympic target at 70 yards.

"I assume you brought my bow, Jim?" Bonnie's father glanced away, abashed.

"Riordan, you can't compete in all three tests with your long bow. Please, take mine," Rick pushed his custom bow at me.

"Now what fun would that be? Cheer up, Kitten," I stroked the side of Bonnie's face. Although she believed in me, the stricken look in her eyes was full of self-recrimination.

A brief respite in the wind allowed Stokes a more than respectable distance in the first test. Unfortunately, it then kicked up as if laughing at me.

I slipped off my moccasins, stepped to the mark. This was not a timed shot, but I'd not be allowed unlimited time.

Stokes mouth was busy in the background when a sudden, endearing bolt out of the blue was tossed into the equation.

"$500 says my husband wins this tournament."

I grinned- Bonnie, Bonnie, Bonnie, my never ending sweet surprise. At least she seemed comfortable with her new financial status.

"Let's see your money, Baby Cakes," Stokes belted out.

Baby Cakes? I'd see he ate those words, too.

"Here's 500 to back her. Stokes, where's your money?" Mr. Winslow had bankrolled my girl's support.

Stokes' friends were pulling at their pockets.

The wind almost stilled. Bonnie looked at me, imploringly.

'No cheating, Wife.'

And in a movement that would seem impossible to the onlookers, I turned, nocked an arrow and let fly. Murmurs from behind admired the flight path.

Oblivious to the result, I strolled back to my Wife and to her embarrassment kissed her soundly until the distances were recorded.

It was all in the hands of the spirits, anyway. Might as well do something pleasurable.

"Robin Hood and the Road Runner," some witty onlooker cat-called.

"Riordan, I'm so sorry." He laughed at my apology.

"Whatever for, Wife?"

"For asking you to go. I didn't know it would be the football team scene all over again." I felt terrible.

"I did try to explain. . ."

"I know you did. Please don't ever compromise your principles for me again, please."

"Bonnie, you're being silly," he pulled me onto his knee. "I went to support your father. He wanted me there- to meet Stokes."

"You think my dad wanted you to fight?" My eyes flashed in disbelief.

"No, Kitten. Not fight, but he hoped I'd take Stokes down a peg or two or three."

He was calm, collected, no regret in him. I sensed all through his body, which tickled him no end. His mouth settled on my neck.

"I told you I'd not be uncomfortable. I've had years to study bullies, unlike you, my young, young Wife."

"Oh, Riordan!" My whole body melted and erupted at the same time.

"Yes, Jim?"

Horrified, I looked up to see my dad, hesitant, hovering in the doorway. I hid my blushing face in Riordan's neck.

"Son, I should apologize."

"No need, sir."

"Honey, Riordan's right. Secretly, I hoped he'd enter the competition. I…I didn't want. . ."

"It's all right, Jim."

"Son, no man alive is a better man than you are and I'm damned proud to have you as part of my family. Why don't we go out for supper, my treat?"

"No, thanks, Dad, I'd rather stay home," I popped up from Riordan's fragrant neck. "Fry up some fish. And bake something."

My dad lifted and replaced his ball cap, smiled, and turned toward the kitchen.

"Jim, great punch, by the way," Riordan congratulated.

"A most satisfying moment, shoving that last 'boy' down his throat," I couldn't believe I heard my dad right.

"I think a few teeth went with it," Riordan chuckled. Men!

"Couldn't let you have all the fun, Riordan," my dad laughed along with my husband.

"You won't be disappointed in me for showing Handsome, will you, Riordan?"

"Now whatever would give you the idea I could possibly ever be disappointed in you?"

"I mean it would benefit the ranch, promoting him by showing how perfect he is. . ." my voice trailed off.

"Perfect?" One of his beautiful brows rose.

"Not as perfect as you," I soothed his teasing countenance.

"Competition is great for the right reasons. I'm all for it," Riordan's hands rested behind his head. His tangled multi-colored locks lay strewn about his gorgeous head, like a lion's mane.

He rose up on an elbow, reading my thoughts.

"Is the reason you don't compete, I mean other than. . . I mean is it because you'd always win?"

Win!! He'd smoked Stokes something fierce. Tales of Riordan's expertise would be discussed, expounded on for years. No one would believe the truth. It would all be considered tall tales, except for those who'd thought they'd actually seen my husband defy the Wyoming winds for perfect shots- except for the cell phone cameras catching it all. Every single one. I had no hand in it. As natural as if he were part of the wind- I was in awe of my dream.

"Competing, winning- it's all a matter of focus. I know how to help Rick, now. Get him up to Olympic caliber."

Riordan's lips were feathering my brows, my cheeks.

"You know," I pushed at him, half-heartedly, "dressage shows won't be anything like today- it's mostly girls showing, at least, until the higher levels. Oh, Riordan. . ." His lips never ceased.

"And you'll be performing at the highest levels in no time. And who watches these girls showing horses in tight breeches and black boots? Husbands, boyfriends, brothers. I'll be there protecting my territory."

What more could I say?

14

"Robin Hood and the Road Runner? Give me a break! For someone who likes to live on the quiet side, you've become a local hero- the talk of Cody- even made USA today for the love of the spirits! Must have been some hotshot reporter at that shindig, the way he wrote you up. 'Not since Robin Hood'. . .blah, blah, blah. . ."

Riordan smirked, "Jealous?"

But Gunne was on a roll and rolled right over my husband's suggestion, which seemed to bear some merit.

"They'll have you running for president, next."

"Gunne, how nice to have you back," Riordan sarcastically snickered. "Did you happen to learn anything from the Lakota, like personal reserve, impassivity, how to contain yourself?"

Dr. Gunne, with his flair for GQ apparel in full hurrah, stood with hands on expensive, immaculate-clad hips. I'd almost expected his nose to seek airtime as he snorted, neck extending from his white silk shirt collar.

"If you two are done with your bantering, there are important matters for us to address," Grace played mediator as Grandfather sat, eyes twinkling, watching my husband and the dragon who were, as usual, at odds with each other.

'We're not at odds, Kitten. This is simply the nature of our relationship,' Riordan silently corrected me and pulled me onto his lap.

There were extra chairs now, but I preferred his lap and he apparently preferred my preferment and was happy to comply.

Sunday school was in session and today's lesson featured Grace as the professor.

Briefly she filled Dr. Gunne in on the strange doings in Bueller's hay field and of our own adventure in obtaining samples from different areas of the crop circle art work.

"And how did you manage to sneak past all the security? I assume it was locked up pretty tight and invisibility is not one of our attributes," the dragon asked.

"I went as a kitten," I spoke up. "One of the soldiers actually tried to pick me up."

"Did you take off his ear?" Dr. Gunne smiled sweetly and winked at me, to Riordan's disgust.

I blushed before answering, "No, I hissed, spit and clawed his hand and peed on him."

"Great diversionary tactic, Wife."

"Thanks, Riordan," I nibbled his ear. "Grace shifted to our director rabbit and. . ."

"Riordan was extremely useful as an opossum," Grace finished.

We deleted Grandfather's being shot- a little too private (and I still was in the dark as to what that all was about) and too close to emotions to rehash.

"Come again," Dr. Gunne hoarsely asked after choking on his chili and spattering red spots on his camel dress pants and white, custom-fitted silk shirt.

"A 'possum, Dr. Gunne. His pouch came in handy for carrying the grass samples," I explained, stifling giggles as I pictured the comic sight.

The doctor had rushed to the sink to apply cold water to his spots.

"An opossum?" he managed, while diligently attempting to save his apparel. I don't believe he believed me.

"You know, a rat-tailed creature, marsupial pouch," Riordan joked.

"I'd give anything to have seen that. Good chili, Grace, though I'd prefer it off my shirt. I should don an impervious shroud before meeting with the CatSkills," he ruefully eyed his sacrificed shirt.

Grandfather's hand hid a grin.

"Anything?" Riordan's lips twitched enticingly, baiting the dragon as always.

'Riordan,' I fastened my teeth on his ear lobe. 'Be good.'

'I'm always good, Bonnie,' his Virginian eye brows rose and I pictured his 'possum form with those brows and burst out laughing.

"I think we should get down to serious matters here," Grandfather remarked. His return to concerned mien should have put me on alert.

It took great effort, but I curtailed my giggling fit and focused as Grace explained her findings.

"The central blackness is completely charred- burnt even into the top layers of the soil. The force of heat to accomplish this without drawing any attention in the process. . ." Grace's tone belied her professorial emotion at encountering something she couldn't fathom.

Our wild senses sensed each other. Curious.

"Today's science doesn't cover any part of my findings. The very center of the black had exploded out towards the colored ring which seemed to contain the spread of the inferno.

I was right to insist on gaining these specimens on that night. As you will learn in a moment, the entire site was meant for a short period of time- less than 24 hours. So we believe," Grace nodded at Grandfather and Riordan, "that this message was for us, and perhaps especially for Bonnie."

"Me?" I squeaked. To me, black was Chac, coma, nothingness. . . "Chac is dead, Riordan? What more could that monster throw at us? From beyond the grave?" I shivered.

Riordan held me closer, "No worries, Kitten. I assure you Chac is history."

"I'd have to go along with that. Nothing could withstand the 'Mammoth Stomp'," Dr. Gunne averred.

"Granddaughter, I've not seen anything yet, but there definitely is. . . The stars, I believe, are warning us by providing the crop circle, near at hand. Whatever is coming involves us and is probably site specific. Remember the new stars in the sky? Grace, please tell about the colors."

Uncharacteristically, Grandfather laid his hand over Grace's and kept it there. The dragon was quick to chide Riordan and me, most likely because of our age, but not one word did he kid Grandfather with.

"Red, brown, white, yellow. It's a fascinating miracle how the stars managed to color the grasses- there is no question of this circle being a fake, by the way. Not a matter of paint. Each color held great significance- a veritable treasure, in fact.

The red hue consisted of copper and ruby dust- enough scattered over the grasses to imitate, and this is my conjecture, the red of native peoples. The brown- dark amber dust crusted with iron. The yellow was gold dust and the white- silver."

She gave us a moment for this to sink in. Valuable gems and minerals dispersed on a field as a picture. No wonder the officials were all over it. To my knowledge, no crop circle had ever involved precious materials.

"There is no separation of the colors, no borders between where the colors come together. They mesh. Remember the melding of certain materials lends strength. Red Hawk?"

"I flew over the site. More carefully, this time," he pointedly eyed Riordan. "With the sunrise of the next day, the hayfield, other than the charred inner section, had returned to its normal use. As if nothing had transpired."

"I'd have loved to see the suits' faces."

"And the military," Dr. Gunne added and he and Riordan chuckled together.

"Gotta love it when the Great Spirit wishes to defy humanity's attempts to keep Him under wraps," Riordan quipped.

They all sighed in a moment's respite of relief. My instructors. But not me. Once again, something black was. . .coming for me?

"I've never told anyone my genealogy before, but I think it may be pertinent. My mother was a Quadroon Queen- my father met her in New Orleans. My blood contains Native American, black and white and Oriental," Grace said.

"The swallow- no wonder you can resurrect," Bonnie murmured.

Grace had a combination of many powers- of all the races- fantastic, I thought.

"What's that?" Gunne asked.

"Later, please, Dr. Gunne," Grace begged to continue. "Riordan, you are Native American and white. Red Hawk, although hundreds of years ago. . ."

"Yes, Grace. Norse blood is far, far in my past," Grandfather admitted.

"And I'm Oriental and of African blood," the dragon added.

All eyes turned to my Wife.

"Bonnie, you are the only one of us without mixed heritage. The ring of colors around the black has the colors meshed- possibly to represent us. I don't feel that you are of the circle."

I felt my Wife begin to tremble. Sweat broke out on her temples.

"Bonnie," I soothed her.

"Am I. . .to…to be blown up? Is that what you. . .th…think? I'm. . .d…de…destroyed by wh…what…ever is. . .go…going to…to explode?"

"Sssh, Wife. Of course not."

Seriously concerned looks were exchanged and refocused on Bonnie. My wild senses studied Grandfather, Grace, Gunne. They didn't know. Neither did I, but. . .

"Look, that is not possible. Remember the stars. . ." I broke off and blocked my thoughts.

Stars. . . Spirit, help me. Stars were believed to be souls gone on. If Bonnie passed. . . Then so would I.

With grim resolve, I stated, "It's not going to happen that way."

"Grandson and my Granddaughter, calm your selves. We don't know what is coming. We must wait for the Spirit to enlighten us," Grandfather held my eyes.

"Nothing will take Bonnie from me. The ancient art. . ." I bristled.

"Dealt with events prior to this, perhaps," Grandfather stated.

"I don't believe the cave's artwork has an end to it," and I wasn't saying that just to bolster everyone's courage. I really felt it. We were protectors of Bonnie, for always.

The dragon had remained unnaturally quiet, for him.

One inappropriate word. . . No, even he would not add to Bonnie's distress, and she was in the throes. Bearing up in front of the others, but inside, disquieted. The phrase 'basket case' came to mind.

I needed to sweep her away. Coddle her. Make her know I would always be with her. I'd not mention it, but that included even unto death.

"Let's look at this from another direction," the dragon began. "I think Grace is right in that the four of us are represented on the circle. But, maybe it means more than just us, and I don't believe Bonnie's destiny is that of charred grass.

When I was at the reservation, Cloud spoke with me on Lakota star knowledge. He pointed out to me a new star formation, relevant to this part of our earth. Two stars joined, creating the symbol of infinity.

Riordan, I believe you would know if your death and therefore, Bonnie's, is in the near future. The stars were set in the sky prior to the crop circle warning. I think it's a type of 'support'?

I believe the infinity symbol is Riordan and Bonnie's union. I believe the stars were set there not to indicate your demise, but to reassure you- of what, I don't know. I'm simply stating my conjectures."

Never had I felt so kindly toward the dragon. And he'd given me food for thought.

"B…but, it, it could m…mean that. . .I'm to, to join. . .th…the sp…spirits?" Bonnie quavered.

I pulled her firmly into my embrace. I would know, wouldn't I? If I were about to lose my life force?

My end was supposed to be up to me. Spirits willing, I still believed this. In which case, my life and Bonnie's were tied together.

But, what if the Spirits had something else in mind? What if that charred remains devoid of life was stopped only by my Wife and me and the others? How was Bonnie part of it, if not indicated by the silver? Was she. . .above the colors?

The stars had a purpose- what was it?

15

'Irusan sends you a message.'

Surprised out of my semi-depressed reverie, I stopped washing dishes and glanced up at Amore perched on the kitchen counter. Usually quite self-indulgent in her grooming, for the moment she was perfectly still, staring at me.

'He couldn't come?' I continued our silent conversation, not that my dad would give a second look at me talking with my cat- more like the subject matter might cause consternation.

'You didn't ask for him to come, did you?'

'No,' I sighed. Couldn't argue with logic.

'You're not his only concern, you know,' she chided me.

I nodded. Did I really think, even in the fantasy moments of my new life, that I was the pre-eminent regard of the King of the Celtic Cats?

'Don't get maudlin,' Amore swatted at me.

'You can read my thoughts?'

'Isn't that kind of what we're doing right now?'

I dried my hands. 'OK, what's my message?'

'He wishes you to know he's disappointed in your attitude. He expected a greater rise to your new challenge.' Amore's nose sniffed the air. 'Best check the oven.'

Ooh, the pie! I rushed to retrieve the apple pie, got it in time. Riordan and my dad would be grateful.

'Even if it's the end of me,' I continued.

'Maudlin, maudlin,' Amore hissed.

Getting a grip on myself, 'You're right. I've been so inordinately blessed for a 17-year old. I should simply be grateful. Riordan promised I'd not be alone, but I don't want to be the end of him. On the other hand, what's so bad about crossing completely over into the world of the Great Spirit?'

I heard myself, rattling away. What indeed? Except I absolutely enjoyed my heightened existence and being part of so much after my lonely growing up years. How could it all end this soon?

'Snap out of it and focus! You're bringing Riordan down with this sort of thinking and that's nearly an impossibility. No daughter of mine goes down in defeat- is Irusan's message. Think about it. Whatever catastrophe, no pun intended, comes your way, rise to meet it instead of dissolving at the mere thought. Live in the moment as your spirit guide extols you to. I'm done with the sermon. I would like a piece of fish now.'

That brought a smile to my face. I mean, you hear of cats all the time telling their people when to feed them, but mine were particularly succinct in their druthers. Seven additional little pusses' faces turned up to me in expectation as I opened the refrigerator.

"Twinkle, twinkle little star. . ." It had been awhile since I'd serenaded my Wife- lying on the cabin roof, sky watching, provided the perfect opportunity.

I segued into WHEN YOU WISH UPON A STAR, threw in a few special effects with my eyebrows until her giggling had her rolling into my side.

"Now this is my Bonnie- not that puny, pale imitation of the past few days. Your father even asked if you were pregnant."

"Oh no!" interrupted the giggles.

I quickly delved into locating her ticklish spots. After all, laughter is the best medicine.

"There's our star, if I'm not being too presumptuous," I pointed after a brief tussle, and banking of the resultant fire. Bonnie's head rested on my outstretched left arm, which I curled about her, and our breathing stilled.

At the word 'presumptuous', the Pink Lady burst into frantic action. A plethora of colors surrounded our mirror image in the sky.

"I wonder if she's trying to tell us something?" Bonnie mused.

"Wouldn't surprise me, Wife. Wouldn't surprise me. We'll just have to wait for the interpretation. So, you OK now?"

"Yes, Riordan. I'm sorry I lost sight of us together."

I leaned in and kissed her breathless under our sparkling canopy. "No apologies, remember? I've an idea. You up for an adventure?"

"Yes," she bubbled.

"I'm going to do a sweat lodge ceremony for Rick. He's dealing with a few bumps in the road of life. It might help him clarify his path."

"Did he and Lil break up?"

"I can't say. Maybe, just a small separation."

"You are the best friend a body could have. No gossip, not even a hint," Bonnie tried to tickle my close-to-the-chest side in mock frustration.

"I didn't think you were into gossip, Kitten."

"I'm not. Not at all. I happen to think I could help someone if. . ."

"Hence, the sweat lodge. Care to join us?"

"Do you feel I might learn something?"

"The spirits pick and choose as they will. The worst thing you could do is expect them to. . ."

"I don't expect, Riordan." She was silent for a moment. "Maybe it will be a good centering adventure."

"That's my girl!"

In a clearing we'd used for the purpose many times, Grandfather and I had constructed a willow branch sauna of sorts.

Gunne had agreed to help Grandfather with the heating of the rocks we would use to 'sweat' the participants- Bonnie and Rick.

The inside of our lodge had a pit in the middle into which the heated rocks would be laid. A bucket of water near my position, fireside, would be ladled at intervals upon the hot rocks, creating a dark cave of extreme heat and humidity.

An entry flap of hide would be opened to decrease the heat, if necessary. In exchange for Gunne's help, we'd agreed to conduct a sweat for his own experience.

"Anyone bring matches?" Gunne studied the pile of rocks, the pit and the chopped wood outside the willow tent.

Grandfather had a speculative look on his face. He patted his pockets.

"Grandson?"

I shrugged my shoulders. "I'll round up the makings for a bow drill."

"What's a bow drill, Riordan?" Bonnie asked.

"A simple, primitive device using the friction between a spinning wooden spindle against a chunk of wood. Voila! Fire. I'll show you."

"Wait, Grandson, let my Granddaughter try."

"OK, but I've got to gather. . . Interesting. Yes," I intuited Grandfather's designs.

"Granddaughter, you have made friends with wind and water. Another element is fire. I believe you sent it against Chac's spear. Care to start this fire for us?"

Bonnie looked at each of us. Rick hadn't arrived yet.

She seemed unsure of what to do, "I don't remember how it happened."

I felt her curiosity as if it were my own, only I hadn't her power to address elements.

'Ask, Kitten, that's all,' I silently urged.

She raised her ring hand and as clear as day, I heard a retort rankle in her brain- 'Testing me, are you?'

At the same instant as the voice remonstrated with my Wife, the pyre of wood in the pit burst into flames.

Gunne jumped back, startled. "Warn a guy, will you?" He brushed at his chest, checking for burn marks, on an old shirt, for once.

Grandfather and I fed the furnace its due.

"Excellent, Granddaughter."

"I don't think the spirits were happy I asked," Bonnie conjectured doubtfully.

"Thank them profusely and hopefully they'll be appeased," Grandfather and I reminded her.

Rick trotted to us from a path through the woods and he and Bonnie shed their outer clothing. If it had been just us guys, we would have shucked down to our birthday suits, but in deference to my Wife, and my sense of territory, swim suits would suffice.

I'd drug out my breech clout. With Bonnie's admiring eyes and flushed face, I considered wearing it more often. I winked at her as she read me.

I distracted Gunne and Rick as Bonnie's pink clad rear crawled inside. Briefly, I described to Rick the dark and heated interior, no outside impediments. Earth and heat- that's all.

The dearth of distractions helped focus minds and could help some commune with the Great Spirit- maybe receive a special, pertinent message or a thought-provoking lesson.

"Some liken the experience to birth. The lodge is the warm womb and if one is very lucky a blessing from the spirits is bestowed before exiting or being born."

Rick mulled this information over before getting into crawling mode and entering the lodge. With Rick's height, he had to sit closer to the heat source as it was a small lodge with sloping, rounded walls.

I warned him to indicate if the heat got to be too much. Some couldn't take it- the stifling, claustrophobic feeling. Once in a while during Grandfather's sweat lodge sessions with his lesson groups, a man or woman had to bow out.

Sweating to the point of passing out. . . It wasn't an easy experience, but for many, it led to an unimaginable experience.

I opened the sweat with a prayer of gratitude, stressing our openness to the spirits.

With each addition of fired rocks and intermittent ladle of water thrown upon them, I addressed the spirits of all directions: east, south, north, west, the sky, earth and heart.

I kept my wild senses open to any distress on Rick's part, knowing I would feel Bonnie inside my own body.

To my deep gratification, Rick quickly gained a meditative state as his body poured sweat. He neared faint mode, but I sensed his inner strength and determination to carry on.

And then suddenly, a shock, as if a lightning bolt striking, slashed through me, "Bonnie!"

Her little body toppled over without a sound.

16

Involuntarily, I shivered as I took my place inside the close confines of the small willow lodge. With Riordan's and Rick's entrance, the space seemed to shrink further.

Not only was there no room for personal space, we each had to sit cross-legged, knees practically knocking knees, about the fire pit. With the flap closed, the intensity of the darkness acutely troubled me.

'Bonnie,' Riordan silently instructed me. I desperately tried to remain calm and 'hear' his words. 'Your wild nature embraces dark. Open your lioness eyes, Wife.'

That did help, my allowing the cat's eyes to have superiority over my human ones. Cats are comfortable in the night. Thankfully, I found it wasn't nearly as 'dark' as I'd initially thought.

'Do not regulate your body's temperature-let that part of you remain human. Allow the experience, Kitten. I love you and I'm here for you and with you.' His words soothed me as did his intonations to the Great Spirit.

And then the heat intensified. With each hiss of water Riordan poured on the fired rocks, my body responded. I quelled the wildness in me that sought to keep my temperature neutral.

In no time my swim suit was saturated with sweat. My skin's flood gates poured. Was I being reborn or oozing all vital fluids? Was one dependent on the other?

'Hush. Quiet, Wife.'

My clammy hands rested on my thighs supportively and still the temperature climbed.

"Rick, are you all right?" I heard as if from a remote distance. And also, Rick's grim affirmation.

I stumbled over my own 'OK' and felt Riordan's solicitude. I concentrated on the glowing rocks before the sweep of fog-steam enveloped us in added ghost-like moisture.

And still the temperature climbed. I wasn't sure if I could stand it- perhaps I should travel out and not disturb Rick?

'Focus,' a voice rang into my reverie. I didn't know who was speaking to me, but I bucked-up in an effort to persevere. If there was a message for me, I could, I would see this through.

I glued my cat's eyes to a single point on a stacked fossil bound rock.

My shamanic-wild nature attempted to come to my aid, but I forced the wildness to stay under wraps.

Slowly, I began to feel as if I were alone in a dream state with no lifeline to shamanic power- no tie to earth- no tie to. . .

I swallowed or tried to. My mouth, contrary to the rest of me, was completely dry. The aloneness I felt was a pre-Riordan feeling- as if. . .

I shuddered and the voice from out of nowhere demanded of my brain, 'FOCUS'.

A dark veil closed in on me from all sides. A singular path opened. A path with red coals at the end. Suddenly, that sole light turned black- blacker than black. It grew inexorably and I was held prisoner in the heightened darkness.

The black wave-wall kept growing in front of me, until in my trance it outgrew the willow lodge and it towered over me and advanced malevolently.

I opened my mouth but I couldn't cry for Riordan. There was no sound. Why hadn't he felt what was happening to me? Had I done something wrong? I was strait-jacketed by. . .

The black wall descended on me. Powerless, I. . .

The voice broke in, but I'd already approached an insane state of fear and immobility and. . .near deafness.

It was the dream again, the one that had relentlessly kept me from sleeping not so long ago- the one of black, and curiously, this time also, I felt my body upended in the descent of the black wall. Somersaulting and sucked under, claimed by. . .

A voice barely permeated the volume and violence of the blackness. 'The light. Ask the. . .'

The fog in my brain refused to clarify the message. Ask? I couldn't form the words. I was inundated, no more myself.

Light? What was the rest? What light?

I never heard the last. For some reason I had. . .had I allowed myself to be walled off? From Riordan? Why? I no longer had the means to sense anything. Even to fight to spare Riordan. I thought I heard a desolate moan before I succumbed- like a dead leaf caught in a black maelstrom.

My attention momentarily focused on Rick, I almost missed Bonnie's tiny body toppling headfirst into the pit. I called for Grandfather to attend to Rick as I grabbed Bonnie and traveled with her in my arms outside the lodge.

Gently, I placed her by the outside fire where Gunne rushed to her side and reached for her wrist. My wild, territorial nature snarled to rebuke him.

"Get a grip, CatSkill. I'm a physician."

"So am I. She doesn't need a doctor," I seethed.

"Right. I see you're tending admirably to her needs. Was she well hydrated before entering the sweat lodge?"

I felt my teeth aching to attach to his neck. With great restraint, I checked Bonnie's body with every sense I possessed. It seemed as if a great block was between us. Even touching her I couldn't get a reading. A tremendous, disturbing shock raced through me.

"Her pulse is elevated. I thought perhaps this was simply a fainting spell, but. . ." Sensory alarms rang in my system.

Gunne studied Bonnie's systems and his voice showed his distress. "Her inner powers should have already alleviated any harmful attacks on her body."

A frightening shock hit me. What had happened in there? And why wasn't I apprised before anything out of sorts occurred to Bonnie? Or as it occurred? It was almost as if I didn't exist. . .

"Wake, little one," Gunne addressed my comatose Wife. "This is not a faint," he puzzled. "Maybe we should call Grace?"

I leaned over her soaked body. My hands grasped her waist and with the full force of frequencies I could draw up, I commanded her, "Bonnie, wake. NOW!"

I felt the shock of recognition roil through her as the block between us dissolved in an instant. She was once more open to me.

Her eyelids fluttered, opened, fastened on mine. I felt a convulsion building in her and I held her as she turned and threw up.

"Great bedside manner, CatSkill. Hmm. . .almost like an hypnotic trance. Self-induced?"

I growled at him for even thinking of such.

"What or who could do that to her?" His question echoed mine.

As her trembling subsided, I picked her up.

"R…R…Riordan? What happened?" I could feel her trying to get her bearings.

"I'm taking her to Grace," I nodded at Gunne. "The sweat's nearly over. Please come as soon as Grandfather can get away."

"Are you chilled, Wife?"

She seemed to take stock, frowned that I asked. "No. Should I be?"

"Here, Riordan. Get her out of that wet suit. I'll make some tea. Give her a few minutes without questions," Grace told me.

Grace's healing energies were in force along with my own. Bonnie seemed oblivious, as if someone just waking from a coma- all too clearly did I recall those horrific days. She was still shaking and not from cold, as I helped divest her of her single piece, pink swim suit.

Keeping one arm about her, I towel-dried her. She didn't protest. Was too complaisant for my liking. My wild alarms were on stand-by. I pulled a sweat shirt over her head and helped her don sweat pants.

"Dear, sip this tea, slowly. Stay quiet for now. Allow yourself time to catch up with your experience. When Red Hawk and Dr. Gunne return, if you feel able, we'll listen to what you remember."

The three of us sat in silence. My fingers kept contact with my Wife's hand. She had returned to me, but of her revelation in the lodge, I was strangely ignorant. And profoundly frustrated.

"Granddaughter, how do you feel?"

"Better," Bonnie tentatively smiled, ducked her head in embarrassment at being the center of so much anxious scrutiny. "Thank you, Grace."

'Thank you, Riordan,' she telepathed to me.

"Granddaughter, if you can recount to us what you saw, heard, felt, anything at all, perhaps we can help you to understand. Take your time. It is important that you tell us everything- even if you think it inconsequential."

Each of us studied our youngest member as she hesitantly spoke. After she finished her halting story, Grace replenished empty tea cups.

"Dear, can you tell if the blackness was the result of fire?"

Recalling the unusual warning articulated in Bueller's hay field- that the black center was the result of tremendous heat- mutually set up in our minds. Was Bonnie's experience related to the crop circle? Was it about to happen so soon?

And why had she blocked me? What kind of message was this? A single lesson for her or. . .?

"I had no feelings, no sense of touch. It was as if all my senses shut down," Bonnie related, distraught, confused.

Normally, the chewing of that lower lip would have ignited a certain feeling inside of me, but the import of this night's revelation stymied my desire.

"And the only words you heard were 'ask' and 'light'?"

Bonnie nodded, trying with all her might to conjure up the rest- a futile attempt.

"I…I know there was m…more. I. . ."

"Don't push yourself, Bonnie. I suggest you go home and rest. For now, it should be enough of a reassurance to know that the spirits have not abandoned you. They were speaking. Perhaps you did not receive all the message? But we won't dwell on that for now. I'm sure they will repeat the words when it's necessary. May I check your pulse? Even though I can read it from a distance, I may glean clearer information. CatSkill?"

I gritted my teeth. My fingers grazed my Wife's wrist.

"Her pulse is normal," I told him and rising I picked up my Wife and took her home.

Watching her sleep, peacefully curled into my side, I telepathed to Grandfather. Instantaneously, he responded.

'Grandfather, I do not like how Bonnie was separate from me. That has never happened. Not since the coma. This is highly irregular.'

'I understand your frustration, Grandson. Her experience is prophetic on an unheard of scale. I'm not sure, but maybe more than one message is inherent in her trance state. It concerns all of us that she had no cognizance of you while she was in the throes of this new nightmare. As Gunne said, we must keep in mind that the Great Spirit is watching her. We can only wait.'

'Grandfather, I don't believe this is related to the portent in the field. In this instance, she felt herself alone.'

We commiserated in our unease. The sole fear of my life was the period when Bonnie was apart from me, trapped in her coma- completely out of my reach.

How could I fight what seemed not to exist for me, what excluded me?

Briefly, I remembered Bonnie's showing me she was well while I was away, so I'd not return to her immediately, leaving off my res work. When I had returned, she was physically and mentally exhausted. This had an eerie resemblance to that.

Bonnie was designed for me. Who or what would dare to take her from me? Other than the now defunct Chac?

'Grandson, this may be a learning experience solely meant for my granddaughter. She is young. The spirits may feel they have lessons to impart that were not addressed in her education. We must trust in the spirits, as always.'

I had to take a measure of comfort from Grandfather's words, especially recalling some of my own spiritual lessons which hadn't the extreme trials Bonnie seemed to be tried with.

But, I was not at ease. Great Spirit, I prayed, don't take her from me.

17

"Riordan, you can't eat. . ."

"Ouch!" I smacked his hand with the spatula.

". . .all the cookies."

"I beg to differ, Wife, I most certainly can." His lips twitched beguilingly.

I studied him. We were completely open to each other. The events of the sweat lodge rested on a shelf, for the time being.

My husband, who never brooded, assured me that the spirits might have a lesson in store for me which Grandfather and he were not privy to, but that he would not let me out of his sight. Whatever the lesson was, it was important but not fatal.

Only. . .how did he know? And he hadn't experienced the blackness, again.

"No worries," Riordan tried to calm me. I felt his advice related to both of us.

"Trust in the Great Spirit. He made us for each other- to be one," he murmured and his lips left off the cookies and descended on my pulse points.

"Hmmm. . .better than any cookies." I shivered in response, my only thoughts directed at my husband's expertise in regaling every one of my cells.

A palpable change in the air about us broke off Riordan's concentration on my neck. Reluctantly, he drew his lips away and raised his head, senses alert.

The rolling frequencies in the air physically surfed us.

"What is it?" Whatever was transpiring was beyond my experience.

Eyes alight with knowledge he had but I did not, he grinned as he related a surprise. "We're about to have illustrious guests, Wife. If you accept?"

"Who?"

"Accept and see," Riordan chuckled.

"Friends of yours? You never speak of friends. . ."

That quirky smile and tilted brows, he wasn't going to tell me. And all information remained blocked from my sensory tentacles.

"Acquaintances, and friends," he allowed to my frustration.

"Well. . .," I hastily looked around the cabin. Guest worthy? I guess it would have to do. "We'll serve cookies," I stated. One had to offer guests something.

A greedy glint appeared in Riordan's eyes. "These aren't normal guests. They probably don't like cookies."

"You can always hope," I plated some anyway and began putting unnecessary stuff in drawers, cabinets.

"Not here. We'll see them. . ." he closed his eyes as if sending an invite. "By the creek."

Riordan carried the basket of refreshments, directing me to a most unusual group waiting patiently near a grassy, sunny creek-side meadow.

Five individuals.

The more arresting figure of the bunch faced us. Tall, swarthy, regal, black eyes, hint of a smile framed by a trimmed mustache and goatee, shoulder length black hair. The ends of his hair curled up in a way out of character with the masculine countenance attached.

He nodded at Riordan, smiled warmly at me. Awkwardly, I stumbled forward- he was that handsome.

Riordan steadied me. 'Careful, Wife. I'd just as soon not challenge my old friend, Osiris.'

Osiris? I gulped. An Egyptian god's name?

Turning at our approach. . . I'd been wrong. The most arresting figure was not the tall, casually clad, darkly tanned man, but the stunning white-blonde woman at his side.

She easily fit under his arm. Was my age or close to it. Osiris was older and acted as attentive to and possessive of her as Riordan was of me.

The beauty was glued to his side. These two were as one as Riordan and I were. I intuited it, felt it in my gut.

Above her sky-blue eyes, nearly turquoise, were black raven-wing brows, perfect skin. . . Incongruously dressed similar to my own attire of flannel shirt and jeans.

Riordan's hand at my waist propelled me on. I couldn't take my eyes off the beautiful couple and so missed the other visitors until we stopped- me half stumbling, totally unlike a cat, and Riordan introduced our guests.

"Wife, Osiris and. . ." Osiris nodded. Visibly pleased, Riordan continued, "and his wife, Isis. Congratulations!"

"Felicitations to you also," Osiris' deep timbered voice caressed the air.

"My Wife, Bonnie," Riordan kissed my temple.

I was star-struck and tongue-tied, but a movement to our side had my wild senses taking control. Vigilance is paramount to a wild creature, in all instances.

Twins. Small, dark haired boys with intent, eager eyes- young teenagers in jeans and t-shirts stepped forward as one.

"Romulus and Remus, and Zander, the Greek," Riordan calmly stated as if illustrious visitors came to call every day. The last name belonged to an older teenage male sporting loose cotton clothing, a shaved head and an indifferent attitude.

Unlike ordinary greetings among friends, there were no hands proffered. 'They know I'm not into contact, Wife, and except for Osiris, and by dint of relation, Isis, we're not really friends- more like acquaintances.'

The black eyes of the young male visitors examined me closely. Too closely for Riordan's comfort. With a subdued hiss/snarl, he guided me from their intrusive scrutiny, set the basket down. Isis seemed bemused by his actions.

'Riordan,' I silently asked, 'who are these people? Are they shamans?' My wild senses had already detected that these five individuals were beyond normal human range.

Riordan's silent, amused, 'Not exactly' stoked my curiosity. Until really knowing my husband, I'd only counted animals as friends, and Grandfather, of course. Somehow, I assumed, perhaps, it was the same for Riordan- although he was totally comfortable in company of any kind, unlike me.

He'd never mentioned anyone from his past, other than the elderly man from India, and some mental images of folks he'd helped in the past, but never any names. And yet, here. . .

I smiled tentatively at our guests, only to be met by piratical blank stares from the youths- they had accurately gleaned Riordan's warning. Ignoring his fellow visitors, Osiris' attention settled on Riordan. Only Isis' smile openly mirrored my own. Here, I knew, was a kindred spirit- one who'd understand my past. Perhaps, I could make a new friend. Osiris bestowed a warm gaze on me- almost as if he'd read my thoughts.

"Why don't we sit down and you can tell us why we are blessed with your presence," Riordan cut into my silence.

Isis and Osiris sat close together on a downed trunk. Romulus and Remus, in a pas de deux move, sank to the ground, cross-legged and expressionless. Zander failed in attempting to inconspicuously stare in my direction as he leaned against a cottonwood.

I took a seat on a low boulder peeking from long, prairie grasses, opposite to Isis and Osiris.

"Uh, Bonnie, why don't you sit over here," Riordan looked at me skeptically.

"This is fine, Riordan. There's room for you, too."

He winced as I patted a place next to me, "But not room for the three of us."

I frowned at his words. The three younger men ignored our repartee, but Isis and Osiris smiled congenially and lovingly tilted heads together. Had her eyes turned green in the shade of the trees? Or was I seeing things?

'What?' I silently asked the edgy Riordan. I followed his eyes to a crawling denizen with prior rights to the rock.

"Oh, a daddy-long-legs!" I grinned and picked up the tiny body perched on long, spindly legs.

Riordan was immediately dumbstruck. "Wife?"

I placed the spider on a safe spot away from our feet. The others watched our interplay. The twins looked bored; Zander disagreeably gazed into the cottonwood canopy. Only Isis and Osiris seemed to be enjoying themselves.

I shrugged, "I don't mind daddy-long-legs, Riordan- only those other spiders."

"The ones in the bathtub?"

"Exactly," I affirmed. Isis giggled gleefully, a delightful sound.

And while Riordan regained his tongue from the proverbial cat, I played hostess.

"Would you like some cookies?" I opened the basket and spread the contents on a cloth.

Riordan belted a laugh, shook his head and recovered his aplomb in time to warn our guests they'd not care for the cookies. "Too sweet," he told them.

'Riordan,' I shot him a telepathic reprimand, 'where are your manners?'

Osiris' brow rose; his eyes swiveled between my husband and me.

"If I know you, CatSkill. . ." He picked up several cookies and extended his hand first to Isis. She accepted, but the others made no move to join in.

"Just as I thought, delicious!" Osiris dared to wink at me as he complimented my handiwork. Isis eyes sparkled with her commendation.

"We've heard of your wife, shaman, and of her unusual talents," one of the twins, I couldn't tell if it were Romulus or Remus, spoke with decisive skepticism.

'Riordan, who? How?' I sensed he was not happy with this opening gambit.

"Wife, do you recall the legend of the founding of Rome?"

I filed through my catalog of facts about ancient Rome. "The twins suckled by a wolf?" What did this have to do with. . .?

Riordan's grin was tight.

"Romulus and Remus?" I whispered, thinking. I stared at the twins, as alike as two peas in a pod.

'Do all legends live?' I silently asked.

'That depends on who you ask,' Riordan silently smirked.

My Wife was having difficulty comprehending a living legend 2000+ years old. Who could blame her? My 150 plus years had put her in a faint. Wait until we got around to Osiris and Isis- I was sure she hadn't caught on, yet, and I wasn't going to let the cat out.

"Many legends have factual basis, Wife." The rest might as well hear.

"B...b...but. . ." I pulled Bonnie into an embrace, my eyes, intent on my Wife. Defiantly, I snarled anew at the blatant examination the youths accorded Bonnie. I was quite willing to play Miss Manners with a malicious twist for their edification.

The twins dropped their gazes, apologetic. "Shaman, we mean no disrespect. As we said, we've heard your woman has a rapport with the elements. We've," Romulus glanced at the others. "We've come specifically to implore her aid."

I knew I wasn't going to like this. "Osiris?" What had my friend brought to me? To us?

I'd met Osiris, of all places, in the northeast woods- once the home of the Iroquois- who Osiris told me had befriended him long ago. He still kept in touch with certain descendants of his original Iroquois friends. Especially, an interesting ageless elder.

"The Oracle," he stated. I rolled my eyes at the mention of an old nemesis. "The Oracle has seen a cataclysm in the Mediterranean- a catastrophic eruption and flood waters destroying the ancient civ. . ."

"These things happen around the world, Osiris. You know this. So now it's the Mediterranean's turn. Unfortunate- warn people to leave." The fate of the world was not my Wife's to fix- she was not a god or goddess. Good grief!

"There's no time. No one would believe, anyway, as there are no visible signs."

"Then that's it," I rolled my shoulder.

"Venice would suffer, too. Perhaps irrevocably wiped out this time."

The hint regarding my palazzo disconcerted me somewhat, but grimacing, I held fast with, "Unfortunate."

"The Oracle believes your wife can help." Osiris, the spokesperson for the legendary contingent, wasn't blithely taking no for an answer.

"No," I stated unequivocally.

'Riordan?' My puzzled Bonnie asked.

"As a shaman in her own right, she has the right to decide."

"No!" I stood. If necessary, I would challenge Osiris- friend or no. "This jolly get-together is finished. Come, Wife." But, of course, she didn't.

"You said, Oracle?" My curious cat-Wife would not let it go.

"The Oracle at Delphi," the irritatingly soft voice of Zander finally made an entry.

Bonnie began to chew her lower lip. "The Oracle at Delphi? Riordan?"

"Bonnie?" I felt my jaw clench, brow rise in aggravation. How dare they bring this here and lay it on our doorstep!

"Riordan?" Bonnie hung on. I think I actually muttered a curse.

"Might as well sit back down," I griped. "History may claim that the Delphi Oracle was destroyed or died out, but the Oracle has always been. It simply went deeper, into total seclusion."

"Legends? Oracles?" Bonnie tried to come to terms with the newfound, startling information.

"Zander is a servant of the Oracle," I added.

"Servant, as in, paid employee?" Bonnie struggled.

"No, more like slavish acolyte," I stated, and immediately blocked my next thought- glad she'd not assimilated Osiris and Isis, yet.

"The Oracle wishes to meet you. There is more information for your ears alone. Will you come?" Zander softly appealed.

Inwardly, I did curse, blocking more of my thoughts. Not a good idea to take Bonnie. . .

"You, you all think I…I could stop th…the flood of the Mediterranean?" I felt Bonnie's heart hammer. "I…I'm new. . .to these. . .powers. I…I can't. . . I'm not sure if…if they are at hand at any given time. Just because of. . . How did you know of. . .?"

"The Oracle," Zander replied.

"I've also dreamed, er. . ." Osiris began.

A rumbling of protest, of territorial protest, erupted in my gut.

'Riordan,' Bonnie placed her hand on my chest.

"Let me amend that, the spirits have led me to you," Osiris tried to placate my burgeoning disgust by casting responsibility on the spirits' doorstep. Didn't help.

Bonnie stepped in front of me to stem my advance on Osiris.

"You're not easing my mind, Osiris," I warned.

"Please, CatSkill. If she would only consent to hear what the Oracle has to say."

"Why not call on your god friends?" Oops, I'd let it out. "This is more of a threat to their temples, etc."

"They are bowing out. Ra, as always, refuses to meddle in humanity's problems. He's grown tired of the overt intransigence," Osiris jaw tightened. I knew what Ra was ticked off about; too bad most of the rest of the world was oblivious to their mess-making. "But he will welcome the worthy among the deceased."

Osiris' eyes remained steadfast on Bonnie and me, with a semblance of regret lurking in their black depths.

Isis silently importuned her husband and he silently replied. This did not go unnoticed by my Wife.

'Riordan?'

'Yes, they can commune as we do.' Fascinated, she leaned into me and observed Osiris and Isis with our shamanic abilities. Mentally, she was already compiling questions for later. No surprise.

"When is all this supposed to happen?" My heart constricted at Bonnie's question.

"Soon. Perhaps ten days," Zander answered.

'No, Bonnie.'

'But Riordan, what if I'm supposed to do this?'

"Will you at least consider talking to the Oracle? You can always leave, pop back here to safety," Romulus ended on a sneering note.

"Watch your manners, twin," I spit back challengingly.

"CatSkill's right. We really have no business asking this of you," Osiris stated, head bowed in surrender.

"If I can't. . .help?"

"Bonnie," I tightened my grip on her.

"Then Rome, Venice, Egypt. . . All the ancient civilizations within miles of the Mediterranean will fall," Zander's soft voice announced.

Indecision and turmoil vied within Bonnie.

18

'We'll discuss this later with Grandfather,' I placed my finger on Bonnie's about-to-protest lips.

"I will wait for you at the base of the granite rock beginning two days from now. I will wait all night, and hope," Zander bowed slightly to my Wife and walked out of sight. Literally dismantled his form as he stepped into oblivion.

Romulus and Remus, as one, focused full attention on Bonnie as if they could actually compel her. This rudeness I would not tolerate-legends may die, I mused on a frequency sure to reach their ears.

"Apologies, shaman," they offered without remorse, and they also faded from sight. I considered a nightly mission to Rome, but Bonnie forestalled my intention. For now.

"On a lighter note, CatSkill, how about a race?" Osiris tipped his chin in friendly rivalry.

"Cat-v-dog, Osiris?" Like myself, Osiris was quick to lay aside things beyond our control as well as tedious, serious talk, and seek a little pleasure.

"Seeing as how you are so versatile, CatSkill, I suggest two bouts. Lion-v-wolf, and wolf-v-wolf?"

"You're going to race?" Bonnie questioned in disbelief as if the men were purposely skirting the weighty issue at hand.

I kissed the crown of her tawny head. "My Wife is also a formidable athlete," I proudly admitted.

"The Road Runner," Osiris acknowledged, and before Bonnie voiced another protest or worse, an inquiry, "I've studied you prior to agreeing to this visit."

Bonnie's mouth snapped shut- amazing.

"The boys want some male bonding time," Isis' singsong voice graced the odd situation.

"Kitten?"

Bonnie donned a wide smile, and excited eyes fed into mine, "You go race, Riordan. I can run with you any time. It's not often I can spend an afternoon with a. . .Goddess?"

'You're incredible, Lioness,' I silently applauded her.

'You weren't going to tell me, were you?'

'Eventually,' I felt my lips twitching around that admission.

'Have fun. I expect victory,' Bonnie winked provocatively at me.

Osiris and I threw back our heads and roared. Apparently, we'd both been instructed along similar lines. We left our young wives avidly embarking on a new lifelong friendship.

"Your wife is enchanting, CatSkill. I would like to hear how it came about."

"Osiris, in order to prolong our friendship, you will refrain from discussing my Wife."

"Touchy, touchy. I see wedded bliss has only added to your territoriality."

"It's my lion nature- reciprocated in Bonnie."

"She transforms?" Osiris was openly awed- a difficult visage for him to pull off.

I suppose I could concede that point. "Admirably. On land. Still learning aerial ventures. I assume Isis. . .doesn't?"

My friend shook his head. "No, but she is an incomparable healer. And it doesn't matter to me. At last, we're finally together and that is what is most important."

I changed course, recognizing my friend's heightened emotion- the legend of Osiris and his love, Isis, and the tragedy they'd suffered was well known. "Tell me what you've seen of this impending Mediterranean catastrophe."

"I cannot pledge what I've seen relates to the Mediterranean. My vision is of a shrouded Ra."

"As in an eclipse?"

"Not. . .an eclipse. More like a shadowing of all light. The darkness is not from a body moving upon Ra, more like an eruption of night from a source I can't pin down."

"And your father is of no help?"

"The ancient Sun God does not claim responsibility for humans' plight, especially after their rampant despoiling of this earth."

"And yet he sends you to us?"

"No, I came on my own. My cause IS this earth."

Osiris, the God of green, resurrection of the land- yes, he would feel remorse if his beloved Nile was buried under the sea, as well as any part of earth and its natural creatures compromised through no fault of their own.

"I thought you had a fondness for Venice."

"A fondness is nothing compared to the feelings I hold for my Wife. You can't say for sure that your vision involves the Mediterranean. Bonnie's place is here. She is much too young and inexperienced to be drawn into worldly disasters, especially those forecast by the Oracle," I felt my jaw tighten.

"The Oracle may clarify if you allow her to," he gave me a sidelong look. "But enough, let's race, CatSkill."

We morphed into different forms for our first race. Wild wolf-v-mountain lion. With my inherent love of running at any distance, Osiris didn't stand a chance.

"You are a. . .Goddess?" I hoped I wasn't being impolite.

Isis looked up at the sun, eyes enraptured, reverent, and curiously wide open. "Bonnie, we are what we were born to become. That doesn't mean we had to become what we are, but we are."

My brain cells tangled up trying to decipher this enigmatic statement. Luckily, she got me off the hook- at least before I could design another question.

"You can shape shift?" Isis accepted another cookie and a glass of lemonade.

There was no desire within me to speak of myself- there never had been. I was much too eager to learn of this one who seemed my age, only more, but how did I ask how did you get to be a Goddess? Was her development similar to mine?

I had no girlfriends growing up. Riordan's entrance into my life fulfilled all friendship roles, but how to politely answer her- I was in a quandary; I couldn't conceive of actually talking, exchanging intimacies, with an ancient Egyptian Goddess. It was impossible to fathom the idea of Isis or her true age- thousands of years?- .while she sat opposite me in her beautiful, teenage body. Focus, Bonnie.

"Yes," I finally managed. "The spirit of the mountain lion drew us together. I've dreamed of Riordan in his wild form for as long as I can remember." Unbelievably, I was admitting secrets I thought I could never tell another girl.

"I…I sensed in you mutually shared bits and pieces," the mysterious Isis took her time. "Loneliness, issues of childhood and…and now we have the most desirable, attractive husbands in the world. Bless you, Ra."

Sub-consciously, my lion side began to snarl. I flushed, part of me- the insular part- embarrassed, part. . .

"You are like him naturally, a territorial lion. Please believe me I've no designs on Riordan CatSkill. For thousands of years I've been kept apart from Osiris by ancient circumstances. We are newly rejoined and I'm not. . .ready to…to speak of my trials and long-yearning existence."

She attempted to covertly gather her emotions. Her eyes misted- chameleons- sky-blue/turquoise in the sunlight changed to forest-green in the shade. Marvelous!

I sent her soft frequencies of comfort. Her eyes widened as she acknowledged and received my empathic efforts.

She slowly smiled her thanks, and continued, "My soul is tied to my husband the way yours is tied to Riordan CatSkill."

I gulped, she knew and understood! My eyes mirrored her unshed tears.

"You can't phase into. . .?"

"No, I don't have that particular skill," she offered without the slightest regret. "Osiris as the God of the underworld is associated with the star Sirius- the dog star, and the God Anubis. He enjoys the form of wolf. Once, I saw him as a huge moose- fighting to protect an orphan in my care. But, wait, he did mention a. . .bigfoot?"

We both surrendered to fits of giggles. Wow, did I have questions for Riordan!

"A friendship of sorts with your lion mate and Bastet and Kemet are his only cat tendencies or leniencies, as a dog would probably put it."

Looking at it from Sticker and Stalker's viewpoint, I guess that was an accurate description; they variously ignored or attempted to babysit the kittens, usually with great dismay as when the tiny tots avidly climbed out of the dogs' reach. I'd catch them slinking away if the kittens taunted them from a high point, and I was quick to tell Sticker and Stalker how absolutely wonderful they were to put up with such childish behavior.

"I…I can see through the eyes of ravens," Isis revealed to my great surprise.

"Ravens?" My bane.

"My, I mean our home, is in Maine. I'm responsible for a huge tract of land. Many ravens live there. Their eyes keep me informed of everything that goes on. I share their sight. They helped bring Osiris and me back together. It's a long story. Perhaps, one day. . ." Isis broke off, turned her face to the sun whose rays seemed to encompass her fondly.

"Why do you not live in . . .?"

"Egypt?" Isis shuddered.

"I'm sorry. I didn't mean to bring up bad memories. Riordan always chides me for my unlimited questions. It's just, you…you don't look Egyptian, yet I thought you originated along the Nile, and were revered everywhere." I should have kicked myself.

Sadness of remembrance singed the glee in her eyes, now alternating colors as if to display inner turmoil.

"My mother was a slave from the far north. My father- court physician to Pharaoh. He bought and freed my mother and married her. They were a great love match. My silver-blonde hair harkens to her," Isis stroked a lock hanging over her shoulder.

Way to go, Bonnie, make your guest feel miserable.

"You mentioned caring for land in Maine?" I hoped this was a better topic. I didn't mean to be nosy, but how else were friendships to begin without questions?

Isis laughed softly. "I rehabilitate injured, wild animals and care for orphans. Hence, the baby moose Osiris helped me with. My role is that of a healer," she shrugged, uncomfortable extolling her own virtues. I could certainly empathize with that.

"Tell me something of you," Isis insisted. The soft blues of her shirt seemed to shift to hues that matched and enhanced her entrancing, black fringed eyes.

"I live on this ranch- my dad's ranch. He's away right now; he's a blacksmith, farrier- uh, horse shoer. I know he'd love to meet you." Had I overstepped?

"I would like to meet your father some time. I would also like you to visit us in Maine- near Camden. We could go sailing."

I fruitlessly attempted to drown my apprehension; sailing- that involved water, deep water, didn't it? Ravens, try to concentrate on ravens- maybe I would learn to be a better flyer. Perhaps I should take up salmon-shifting. After all, they were the source of knowledge, according to my Celtic forebears.

I tacked- no pun intended, "Would you like to see our animals?"

Isis eagerly helped me pack up. Sticker and Stalker greeted us as we approached the home-site. Immediately, they were enamored of Isis, who promptly dropped to her knees and delivered the requisite hugs and kisses and hip massages.

Hector and his harem scurried to cluck about her, too. A pleased, blissful smile graced her perfect face. That's Amore and Super, Cali, Fragi, Listic, Expe, Ali, Docious lined up for their share of affection. Isis acquiesced, but she was shy with Hoss and Lil Joe and warily retreated from their nosy intentions.

"You've not been around horses?"

"Once, long, long ago. In a healing capacity. I've never socialized with them. These seem very big to me."

I gave her some peppermints and showed her how to give snacks to inquiring muzzles. Silently, I warned the boys to be extremely careful. Isis didn't miss the subtle change in their demeanor.

"You talk with them?" Her eyes glittered in surprise.

"It's something I've always been able to do," I shyly admitted, not wanting to seem boastful.

"How wonderful! In my healing, I can sense where distress lies, but to be able to really communicate. . . How wonderful! If I have a difficult case, I know who to come to."

"I'd love to help. Let me introduce you to Handsome." The stallion was jauntily prancing to garner his due. He passaged to the fence rail, reared and pirouetted.

'Easy,' I telepathed to him. 'She's a bit leery of horses.'

'Only healthy ones,' my prideful beast replied. He tilted his head, eyeing Isis. 'She's different than you, but also a little like you,' Handsome reported.

"What is he saying?" Isis watched our silent interaction.

I repeated his impression and Isis sighed, delighted.

"He's magnificent!" She applauded his regal equine dance as he broke into full show-off mode.

"Yes, and he knows it. Would you like a ride?"

Isis shook her head, "He's beautiful, but I would be rather intimidated."

"Problem solved. I'll saddle Lil Joe."

Isis hesitantly received her first riding lesson. Once I helped her overcome her initial timidity and resultant tension, she bubbled with joy over being at one with a horse, at least at a walk. Trot could wait for another time. I hoped there would be another time.

Afterwards, we took a hike over some of my old running trails. Isis was game to run with me, but I kept a moderate pace so we might continue talking as we jogged. Amazingly, I sensed she had a love of running similar to mine.

In circling the ranch, we met our men coming in from the west. Sweat beaded both of their faces. Long, wet, tangled hair.

I caught a whiff of Riordan's enhanced scent and my mouth watered. Instantly, his eyes were on me and I raced into his arms.

'You smell too good,' I silently sniffed. His answering chuckle and light kiss with promise of 'later' thrilled me.

"Any of those cookies left?" Osiris, with an arm about Isis, began to dig into the picnic basket.

"Bonnie, will you please give me your recipe?"

This is how fantastic my life had become. An ancient Egyptian God and Goddess were visiting my shamanic husband and me to appeal for my help with a potential Mediterranean flood and ended up asking me for a cookie recipe. I was living a fantasy novel.

"Now what was that earlier about my scent?" I stroked the side of Bonnie's neck, felt the jump in her pulse which echoed my own. The scientists who'd discovered pheromones- well, I only hoped they'd gained some first-hand knowledge for all their efforts.

19

"Riordan, where were you?"

"Blowing off a little steam." In preparation for what was to come, I silently thought, careful to block Bonnie on that last meandering.

"I don't understand; why didn't we just race, together?"

How to explain? She eyed me expectant, rightly deserving to know what I'd been engaged in. Oh, well- "There are those who think it's 'manly' fun to take a pack of hounds, tree a mountain lion for the hell of it and then, shoot the sitting-duck cat," I flat out said. Nothing draws my ire more than the dolorous cry of a helpless creature, especially a cat. Not even a sporting chance to fight for its life- damn!

"Seriously? My heavens! And you...you went to help, alone? Without me? Didn't it occur to you I'd want to be there? What is the matter with people?"

Of course, she was right, but, "It's not a pretty sight. . . "

"I don't care; if a cougar needs you, I WILL help! The nerve of people, for the love of. . .!

"Easy, Kitten," I cradled her trembling body. "The next time I'm cued in to hell on earth, I will take you- might give dogs and idiots extra food for thought. I promise," I vowed to her upturned eyes, and proceeded to regale her with my rescue.

"Should have seen that scaredy-cat pack of dogs racing for home, tails tucked, with their jerk of an owner, rifle wrapped around his neck, slipping in hot pursuit. Shoot, you could have peed on him! That scent would have stayed with him. The cougar, a female with kittens I might add, went safely on her way, knowing I'd be within earshot. The wild needs all the help it can get and I assured her I'd be ready."

Now back to the reason for my wishing to blow off steam. . .

"Bonnie, Wife, just because someone asks you to do the impossible doesn't mean you have to try. I see all through you. There is nothing importuning you to go. Don't go developing a guilt complex of sorts."

"But, Riordan. . ."

"Granddaughter, do you listen to your spirit guide?"

I paused; was I completely wrong? Had I been allowed a certain power which was to be used. . .when? Why would legends and gods and- what was Zander?- come to me if I was not destined to try to help?

"Granddaughter?"

"I…I'm sorry, Grandfather, you're right. Nothing in my heart compels me to go. Is it coincidence I'm feeling? Making something out of my sweat experience that isn't?" I was flustered, more like a teenage girl, like a simple human and not the soulmate of Riordan CatSkill?

Riordan's hand swept the hair from my downcast eyes, tilted my chin up. If I asked him?

"No, Wife." That answered that.

"Granddaughter, the circle was represented in the crop circle reading. Your purpose lies here, I'm sure of it. We will unite in whatever is coming. Here." Grandfather's concern for me was potent in his dark, probing eyes.

I swallowed, gathering my courage. I was on my own, sort of. What could it hurt to at least hear what the Oracle had to say?

"I don't like this Grandson," Grandfather stated. No kidding- my feelings exactly.

Grace sat silently contemplative. I sensed her misgivings and she knew it.

Gunne, with his arms crossed, was furious with me. "Can't you control your wife, CatSkill?"

"I suppose you think you could do better?"

"Damn straight! Lock her up. . .wait a minute, that won't work, either." His mouth twisted irritably, recalling the airline fiasco.

"I will take her to hear the Oracle. Not much choice in that regard. I do have the power to bring her with me when I travel. I could always just carry her away. She will not come to harm."

"Grandson, you may be the one in harm's way. You haven't told her?" Ruefully, I shook my head- indubitably perking Gunne's interest.

"You're sure you'll be OK, Dad?"

"Honey, I took care of this place long before you were born. Though there is a bit more to it now." The feminine felines circled him with great expectations.

"I've stocked the freezer with meals and. . ."

Jim looked askance at Bonnie, scratched under his ball cap, stared into the packed freezer, noted all the filled containers on the refrigerator shelves. Eyed the stacked cans of kitty food and bravely ignored his soon-to-be-meowing fan club.

"Son, I hope you've packed food for this camping trip of yours before Bonnie froze every edible in the house."

Jim and I exchanged grins, man to man trying to fathom woman.

"How long are you gone for?"

"About five days, sir."

"Hmm. . .looks like I'll survive."

I toted our backpacks. The camping trip was our ruse to make an escape to Greece, with a couple surprise stops along the way.

"You want me to do what?" Bonnie's adorable, scrunched-up nose distracted me from the task at hand.

Of course, it was pretty secluded here. I moved in, intent on her appetizing mouth. Her groan of acceptance of my husbandly reconnaissance as my hands embraced her waist. . .

Unfortunately, a sheep-seeking shepherd emerged from a copse, drew up short and with a distinct leer sidled around us.

"Maybe we should continue this inside?" I suggested.

"You seriously want me to step into this hole?" Bonnie displayed a rather dubious attitude.

"You don't trust me?" My questioning brow rose.

In her indecision, she began to chew on her lower lip and ignite me all over again.

"I'll go first and catch you." If I didn't break this stalemate. . .

"Couldn't we just, you know. . .travel into the cave?"

In looking around there was nothing to reveal that beneath our feet lay a tremendous network of caverns previously undetected by humans, at least for some 20,000-35,000 years.

In the distant past, I'd stumbled down the rabbit hole, so to speak, and found a treasure I wished to share with my now wavering Wife. Granted, the sole physical access I presented her with consisted of a hole in the ground some two feet wide, but, beneath lay. . .

"Now, what fun would that be?"

"I bet you like all those amusement park rides," Bonnie sniffed in disdain.

I laughed, "Who needs those with all the adventures I've had? Coming, Scaredy Cat?"

That got her back up- she actually arched.

"I'll send you a signal," I instructed.

"What will prevent that sheep herder from returning and maybe joining us?"

Don't give it away, CatSkill, I warned myself. I intended to use a particular frequency and disguise the entrance from wandering human eyes.

"You're stalling, sissy," I taunted.

"All right, bu. . ."

I stepped into a twilight zone and disappeared down. No sense in not taking in a few sights on our way to the Oracle. I maintained a block from my Wife's constant perusal of my head. Finding the right time. . .

'OK, Kitten, go!'   I silently telepathed, and followed with, 'I turned into a wooly mammoth for you, do you really think I'd shrink at catching you?'

This must be how Alice felt, plummeting down the rabbit hole in search of a large, white bunny with a timing piece, except I was hurtling through space, a black, creepy, chilly space, at my husband's insistent request.

All of my senses, wild and common, were screaming at me-'Are you crazy?'   And I had to admit that seemed pretty well the case.

No animal, wild, domestic or human, would deliberately drop off into nowhere, bar Alice's rabbit.   I would never get on an amusement park ride- my thrills lay elsewhere.   This had never been on my bucket list.

Would I land on my feet, as a cat would, weightless? How far had I to go? It was hard to believe my feet still pointed down, for the hole expanded exponentially as soon as I'd stepped in.

'Riordan Catskill, you are in big. . .'

"Gotcha! Wasn't that great?"

Still in the dark, I'd landed perfectly in Riordan's arms.

"On the greatness scale, this does not exist in my book," I shuddered.

Riordan laughed, hissed out a 'sissy', stood me on my feet, gave me a second to get my bearings- what bearings? It was pitch black.

"C'mon, Bonnie, you have to admit that was a rush," he enthused.

"Definitely was that. How fast can one fall in how many feet in the dark, within a mud tunnel?" I unenthusiastically asked.

"Sounds like a terrible geometry problem," he laughed. "Let your cat eyes take over."

I did, and in focusing, minute tendrils of light showed us what sufficed as the floor of a rocky, well-like hole with clammy walls, dry ground, and I distinctly heard water softly pattering in the dark beyond.

"Duck, Wife," Riordan took my hand and we entered a 3' high passage way. The fetid odor of a long buried something-I-didn't-care-to-dwell-on-what-exactly, hung on the heavy air. Hunched over, I held my peace as we continued for several minutes. But my mind was certainly active.

"Now this is where it really gets interesting," Riordan's voice broke into my remonstrating with myself.

It came to me immediately what step three of our journey to the center of the earth involved, as it was all displayed in Riordan's mind and therefore, all-too-late, open to mine.

"Not much further down, Wife," he grinned amicably as he pointed to an even more diminished passage way. "You'll get to experience what it feels like to be an earthworm."

What exactly had I, or Riordan rather, got us into? "Earthworm?" I choked.

My shamanic powers had regulated my body's temperature, unlike in the duress of the sweat lodge when I'd blocked them. Therefore, I was not chilled by the ambient temperature which was somewhere between 45 and 50 degrees. But the idea of crawling. . . To where? And how far?

"I'll go first worm-Wife. Hold onto my feet if you like and I'll pull you through."

"Riordan, when we get out of here. . ."

"You'll thank me, Kitten."

"Alice in Wonderland to Munchkin to earthworm," I grumbled and got down on my belly. "This is progress?"

I grabbed onto Riordan's feet and was slithered along a damp, stinky tunnel. I felt ooze coating my clothes and apprehension fogging my brain. Yuck!

There was not a glimmer of light. We slinked a right angle turn and delved further into our worm hall. I couldn't lift my head to see if there was a pinprick of light pending. My vision extended solely, no pun intended, to Riordan's moccasins' soles. When had I become a wit?

"Hanging out with me, Kitten." I had to smile, even though in looking through Riordan's eyes only an impenetrable, pea-soup murk lay ahead. The scent of earth heavy in my air passages and sludge besieged my nostrils. Couldn't wipe it away. Double yuck!

Eventually, with a distinct sucking sound, Riordan oozed an exit with me in slippery tow.

"Voila!" He helped me up.

I refrained from touching my gelatinous-covered clothing. Triple yuck!

"Wait here." In a second, Riordan located and I fired a torch.

The firelight danced shadows in the large vault we occupied and the shadows played among. . .

"Oh my!" I gasped in astonished fascination, turning slowly to marvel at the gently lit rock wall.

The room barely grazed the top of Riordan's head- was near perfectly round and about its walls. . .

"They're fantastic!"

Life-size, Mongol-type horses chased each other around the rock cavern. Reddish-brown mares and a stallion, several foals- one of which had spots on its hindquarters!

"The first Appaloosa," I whispered. Whispers seemed appropriate in this wondrous, ancient cathedral.

I studied each small horse in turn. Riordan's eyes rested on me more than the animals. A smile turned up the corners of his mouth. He was terribly pleased at my surprised pleasure.

The lively brilliance of the horses' eyes- perfection in detailing imperfections- the colors of reddish-brown to fawn-colored undersides and lighter muzzles, dark points on legs, dilated nostrils to go along with the galloping strides. . . The artist had caught it all. The most breathtaking canvas imaginable!

"Could we stay here for a while?" As one who worked as an artist, I was reluctant to leave.

"As long as you like, Kitten." Riordan crossed his legs and gracefully sunk to the ground.

After a good hour spent closely studying each animal, I allowed him to pull me onto his lap.

"How did you find this place?"

"I stumbled onto. . .into it."

I sensed there was more to it than he admitted, but. . .

"Do we leave the same way?"

"Wife, please tell me you're not afraid of bats," he murmured.

"Bats?" A rustle in the dark. "I don't have any experience with bats."

"Good, then sit still. If you become frightened, put your head under my arm."

"What. . .?"
Suddenly, our art museum erupted!

20

An incredible whirring, a living rustle whooshed right above our heads, fanning us in its movement. I could not not look. Riordan's eyes fastened in wonder on our living, moving canopy.

Bats upon bats fleeing their daytime rest, bent on a bug fest outside. Another fascinating sight! So many creatures, in tight proximity, moving without quarrels, without knocking each other out of the way, without. . .

Splat! Oh poop! Too good to be true that I should escape further-accrued icky stuff on my person.

As the last bat exited, Riordan chuckled, broke into wholehearted laughter. He hugged me to his side, knowing I'd relished the overhead show as much as he had.

My fingers went in search of. . .

"Leave it, Wife. Easier to get rid of once it dries," my husband, a never-ending source of intelligence, instructed.

"Dries? In this dampness? I hope a bubble bath is the last, or one of the last, ventures you've planned for this day."

One enigmatic brow rose, "One of the last?"

I blushed. What had I become? Shameless?

"No, half of my heart, I promise the most exciting adventure after the bubble bath."

"Will we travel from here? You never explained how you found this place. How did you know. . .?"

Riordan tilted my chin, gave me a promise of things to come. "Bats 101 or. . .?"

"Begin at the beginning," I zealously encouraged. My husband had so many thrilling adventures over the course of his life- delighted, I was about to learn of another.

"I had a mind to check out the Dracula legend. Having experimented with bats in the states, I thought I'd pop somewhere close to Transylvania. Without experience of where you're going, you might end up somewhere else- remember that.

I landed in the middle of an uprising of sorts and was immediately designated a witch or spy- no difference in those days- by the rural folk of the area."

"They saw you appear from out of nowhere?" The ramifications of this were mindboggling.

"Not exactly. More in the manner of my dress and hair and eyes- very superstitious people. Instead of seeking cover and traveling elsewhere, I decided to run for the thrill of it.

The spirits directed my path and I approached a rock strewn hillside and there it was- a hole ripe for exploring."

"You know that is very dangerous. What if. . .?"

"Bonnie, I'm a shaman. I heard the spirits' endorsement of the opening. The spirits can be playful at times, but they don't seek the demise of one of their own. So I jumped."

I couldn't believe it. Had to be a guy thing. "Into. . .?"

"Right into the spirits only knew. Wow! What a rush, that first plummet," he reminisced.

"You've done it many times since?"

"Only been here a few times. I was hoping you'd think it was fun."

I fidgeted. "You know, now that I'm here I'm having a great time," I admitted.

Riordan donned a cocky smile and continued, "I followed my senses to this unpeopled art museum. As an artist yourself. . ."

"I wonder about those who drew this. There are similar techniques to the cave art at home, don't you think? Where exactly are we?"

"In the foothills of the Alps- northern part of Italy. This network leads into the veritable basement of the Alps."

"Quite a distance from Transylvania," I hinted.

"Hmm, but you have to admit the spirits led me to the bats and to this," he spread his arms out.

"Did you leave the same way you came?" The exit still occupied my greatest concern.

"Now, what is the fun in that?" I rolled my eyes. "I decided to follow the bats out. There is another entrance- pretty well hidden unless you watch where the bats go.

Anyway, this particular cavern is impossible to get to from the other direction unless you are a bat."

"So these shamans. . .? Oh my!"

"Either came in the way we did or. . ."

"Traveled." This idea sent shivers down my back. Ancient shamans. . . Were they related to, or were they the same artists who'd drawn the circle of protectors in the cave at home?

"I turned into a bat and followed the pack," Riordan finished. "Care to study a bat up close?"

I giggled, leaning into him, previous thoughts forgotten. "Yes, please."

"Ah, my curious Kitten. A few words of warning. Bats are fragile. If you don't mind, let me land in your hand. OK?"

My Wife nodded, eyes eagerly anticipatory. In a second, I was winging silently, purposefully, around her.

'Hold out your hand palm up, Bonnie,' I silently counseled.

Once she extended her hand, I settled onto her palm, kept my wings out.

'You'll notice my wings have an arm-like structure similar to humans.'

Fascinated, she examined every inch of my outstretched wings.

'Notice a thumb,' I briefly wiggled my thumb.

"Four fingers," with her eyes she traced the path of my separate bat fingers. "Five toes," she giggled as with some difficulty I roused a bat foot so she could examine my toes.

'Would you like to pet my body?' Those delicious lips curled up into a spectacular smile of zealous appreciation.

'Stroke softly from my ears back to my. . .tail.' I suppose I was reaching into a more potentially, romantic interlude- a guy thing. Couldn't help it.

I folded my wings. One delicate finger gently stroked my top side. Enthralled, she ran her finger over my fur again.

"You're so soft, and oh so cute! Those tiny ears. . ."

'Great, Bonnie. What every man wants to hear- how cute he is. Surely as a western girl, you know bats devour thousands of bugs- pesky mosquitos, in a single night?'

She nodded, still entranced by my hair. I kept up a discourse, because her ministrations were firing me.

On a lighter note, 'I bet you didn't know that when a bat has to go the bathroom while he's snoozing upside down, he rights himself, relieves himself and returns to sleeping upside down.'

Bonnie started to giggle.

'Bats are anatomically correct,' I continued bat class. 'If I rolled over. . .'

Her giggles echoed about our chamber as softly as the sweetest fluttering wind chimes.

"What are you doing with your mouth- opening and closing it? I can see your teeth. It looks like you're cussing at me."

'Echo-locating. An interchange of frequencies that allow bats to fly without crashing into things or each other.'

Parts of me were getting much too warm. I put my human body back on. Bonnie rose and walked toward me.

"I, uh. . ."

"Riordan, I didn't get to see all of you."

"You little cat," I couldn't resist her enticement. As my lips met hers, a palpable change rent the air.

"Your friends' calling card?" Bonnie asked. "Here?"

"No. No one knows our whereabouts," I was on instant alert.

A hissing, a clatter, a thundering of drums. Both of our wild natures reconnoitered for the source. Undetectable, yet everywhere.

I prepared to travel with Bonnie fast in my arms when a loud swoosh encircled us. The torch flared up and died to the merest of embers.

There was a tug on our bodies, leaching our powers, caging us.

A snarl birthed inside my gut. Bonnie's echoed. We. . .

In a guttural tongue not spoken for tens of thousands of years we heard a translation formulate in our brains.

"It's her. He's with her," spoken with voices acting in concert.

A different speaker addressed us, demanding, "Why are you here?"

"Who are you, friend or foe? Show yourselves," I ordered. "I'm not without recourse," I found myself answering their guttural language all the while trying to ignore the unnerving, impotent sense of the loss of our powers.

The torch flame reared and steadied. Before us, as a mirage of heat waves dancing above a hot, steamed roadway, formless shadows emerged.

Behind these, two huge, wavering, see-through masses of energies flitted mercurially- as if on a reconnaissance mission. This is what surrounded us and kept our shamanic powers at bay. I'd never experienced anything like it. Talk about feelings of vulnerability.

'Riordan, I don't think they mean to harm us,' my Wife telepathed.

"Why are you here, cats? Did we risk our souls for naught to travel across this world and depict you where you belong? Is this how you protect your heart?"

"You are the shamans- the cave artists?" Bonnie whispered.

I felt her apprehensive awe and shivering trepidation and pulled her close. With the subsiding of our powers, our bodies now felt exposed in an indefensible, cold position- ringed by powers beyond our ken- older and much more puissant than ours. If a single entity faced us we might have managed, but the conjoined energies of these beings outmatched us by far.

"Why do you ask what you know? Questions are for unknown answers."

"I'm sorry," Bonnie apologized.

"Sorry is a worthless word and an even more worthless emotion."

"I'm still learning," my Wife, the over-achiever, shot back.

'Careful, Kitten. These are very powerful shamans.' I refused to acknowledge I wasn't sure if I could protect her from them- and subsequently I quickly blocked this from her.

"I've been asked to help the people of the Mediterranean."

"Foolish, foolish girl on a fool's errand." The lead energy mass seemed to pace, interchanging its movements with its fellow shamans. Slowly we spun to follow its gyration.

I felt the perturbation of the many shamans even as they encircled us, quiet and waiting for their spokesperson to continue.

"Think you, Man Who Walks as a Cat, that you can protect her from her own stupidity? What you do, little kitten, must be done for the right, spirit-guided reasons and ultimately, for the good of all. We will be watching. Our advice is for you to go home, but we waste our energy. Learn then, and grow. Do not disappoint us."

"Wait," Bonnie appealed as the energy-orb shamans disappeared in high-speed streaks into oblivion, leaving a great void. All was unfathomably still- eerie to the umpth degree.

Grandfather, I, Grace and Gunne, not to mention the stars, were correct. Bonnie did not belong here, in this part of the world with its own unique set of problems.

"It's time to go, Wife," I murmured into her reverie.

"But, Riordan. . ."

"Not right now," I said, a bit more forcefully than I wished, but the shamans had left me with a distinct unease.

21

"Hold tight, Kitten, I'm going to take you to my palazzo." Bonnie's squishy arms fumbled around me. It was a measure of her disconcert that not a single question pestered me.

In an instant, I traveled to another dark passageway. One equally as dank. Only now, my right hand held us suspended, legs swinging freely.

"Bonnie, reach around me to your left. Find a lever and pull down." I clasped her firmly to my chest with my left arm as she struggled to find the solution to our puppetry.

With a grating of stone against stone an opening appeared and I swung Bonnie's body into. . .

"A fireplace? A secret passageway in a fireplace?"

"Impressed? It was most convenient for quick getaways. The downside leads directly to the canal and hopefully, for those caught in indiscretions, a waiting gondola. No one wanted to swim in the canals of the good old days."

I'd swung in after her, stretched to locate the close lever and seal up the secret as I explained. Taking her hand I danced her across a terrazzo floor of various earthen hues.

I knew we had to discuss the last events of the cavern, but I hoped Bonnie's natural curiosity would take a catnap, at least long enough to get a bath, something to eat, maybe a little. . .

"Welcome to Ca'd Gato Oro, as I call it."

"House of the golden cat," Bonnie interpreted as her eyes delighted in my home away from, well, home. Through her eyes I enjoyed the ancient palazzo anew.

Floor to ceiling windows in the front faced out on the Grand Canal of Venice- as far as I was concerned, the most beautiful street man ever helped create.

Smaller side windows on each side of my-ours now, secret- passageway-hiding-fireplace, looked out upon a smaller canal and the neighboring palazzo.

The huge room hosted two 16th century wing-style chairs with a gold gilt table in-between, directly in front of the marble fireplace.

I busied myself putting together a welcoming fire as Bonnie strolled around. The warm glow of the flames reflected in the crystals, both lavender and opalescent, of the ornate, flowing lines of the chandelier high above. The palazzo's artist had centrally placed the lighted artwork amid heavenly clouds and ocean-going merchant ships typical of Venice in the 16th century.

I flicked a switch and the crystals danced a duet with the tendrils of fire. The light cast was as romantic as the candles which it originally would have held.

The room itself was a veritable gold-framed masterpiece. Kept solely for my own use- which was seldom. Heavy drapes, of a blue Venetian artists loved, were swept in abeyance from the windows, some of whose glass was original to the 15th century.

"Venetians and glass were made for each other," I broke into my too-quiet Wife's admiring perusal. "Land upon sea, with a foundation of ancient, petrified oak trunks, and sand lapped in with the sea's waves. What do you think of my, er, our bed?"

The masterpiece of the room's masterpieces was the immense, ornately carved wood bed. All the riches of the previous owners' mercantile pursuits were carved into its headboard and towering posts. The aromatic flowers of perfumes: jasmine, roses, lilies, gardenias. Spices from afar: peppercorns, cinnamon, nutmeg, cloves, sandalwood, ginger- with a special tribute to the original moneymaker- salt.

A coverlet of gold velvet with immense, elaborate, lapis tassels at each corner set off the centrally placed bed fit for a king- lion king, that is.

At last she spoke, "This is so beautiful! How?" Her voice was that of a pious, cathedral attendant.

She ran her fingers over the carvings, gently feeling the smooth patina of hundreds of years, exulting in the skill which sculpted petals, stems and peppercorn details as well as an astronomical number of other items. What a museum wouldn't give for this- maybe the only, original, ancient Venetian-carved bed left!

"Might I suggest, My Lady, a nice, hot bubble bath and dinner, over which I shall enlighten you with the history of our palazzo? If you will follow me, Wife."

Bonnie giggled, enraptured. Luckily her sense of humor had returned. Good, she wasn't brooding.

It took all my powers of endurance to evict my Wife and myself from the warm, effervescent waters in the marble tub- a concession to the 19th century.

Winding, and I do mean winding- there's not a straight street in Venice, I don't believe, or canal for that matter- on the way to the Scuola di San Marco, I pointed out various touristy things and historical wonders.

Finally, I ushered Bonnie into. . .

"I'd like you to meet Rico, owner of this fine establishment."

"A jazz club, in Venice?" Bonnie chirped, incredulous.

"CatSkill, long time, my friend," Rico held out a hand and waited for mine. This intrigued my Wife, but Rico and I had grown used to each other.

"How were the boots?" he asked.

"Rico- Bonnie, my Wife. Rico's father made your boots, Kitten."

"They're perfect, wonderfully comfortable, thank-you." Bonnie's attention was grabbed by all the colored bras and panties hanging overhead.

'Riordan?' she silently interrogated.

'I had nothing to do with any of that, Wife,' I silently harrumphed.

"Come, my friends. Have a seat. If you're hungry I can round up several pasta dishes. I'm sure you're not into the drink specials and it's much too early for dinner elsewhere. As personal friends, however, I'm more than happy to oblige."

Rico went into a back room to prepare a menu.

Small, red and white checked table cloths covered 20 close-set tables for four. Pictures of horn-sporting musicians decorated the walls, but the overwhelming, decorative aspect was undoubtedly the veritable Victoria Secret catalog hanging from clothes pins above. Rows and rows of brightly-colored lingerie.

A tiny stage waited the entertainers at the end of the long narrow barroom. A few indifferent idlers sat at the bar, conversing over drinks, otherwise, we were the only occupants.

"Bonnie, Kitten, here in Venezia folk eat dinner late, unlike our normal schedule at home," I'd heard her stomach growl. Mine was in complete sympathy. "Shall I tell you about my palazzo?"

I took one last look at the colored underwear. "You'd look cute in that polka-dot number," I couldn't resist teasing.

"Riordan," she blushed, bit her lower lip.

Ah, don't do that, my Kitten, I thought.

"Tell me," she distracted my errant chain of thought.

"You recall your dream of a young man's rescue after being dumped in the odoriferous canal of the 1800's? He happened to be the son of an exiled duke whose family had acquired the palazzo some 100-plus years earlier.

The building's original merchant-family owners had built their home on the proceeds of spices and perfumes. Unfortunately, like many other merchants, their livelihood and line died out by the 1700's. The duke's family saved the palazzo from decay/demise, and most importantly, did not destroy the magic of the historically-significant palace, which dates from around 1400. They restored, but did not re-decorate.

History repeats itself. Unfortunately, the duke's son fell in with bad companions once again and I wasn't there to intervene. The duke had no other heirs and left the property to me.

I reserve the major room for my use alone, and rent out the other rooms. You won't believe what a room on the Grand Canal brings!

I also reserve the use of the lower portego for my self- unless, sorely tempted. That's the other reception area. You've probably guessed the room we appeared into was not originally a bedroom, but a room for entertaining.

My senses led me to discover the secret in the fireplace. I don't believe the duke ever knew of it. I can come and go, unobserved. I've so much to show you, Wife," I whispered to her glowing, intrigued countenance.

Rico set four separate Italian pasta dishes and a plate of ciccheti before us. I thanked him and explained to Bonnie the different comestibles.

"Simple linguine with marinara, garlic and clams, cuttlefish. . ."

"Why is it black?"

"Ink, Wife," I pushed the plate to her. Wrinkling her nose, she pushed it back to me.

"You, first," she looked doubtful.

Starving, I attacked the pasta peeking from the black sauce. "This plate," I indicated a piled platter, "bears ciccheti- finger foods. Real buffalo mozzarella, prawns, polenta, you recognize the vegetables."

Without much coaxing, she tried a bit from every dish. And we both ended up with black lips.

"We'll be here for only two nights, but we'll come back- if you want to?"

"Very much so. Osiris mentioned you had a fondness for Venice."

"One of the few cities historically friendly to cats, and of course there is my only possession- the palazzo." Ruefully, I acknowledged our imminent meeting with Zander and allowed the tide to turn.

"Riordan, what about. . .what the shamans said? The circle and the ancient shamans agree- I should not be here. You didn't want me to come. Why did you give in?"

"I wouldn't let you go alone. Something drives you to do this. I don't like it. However, I know the spirits often have perverse learning curves. So, we'll see, Wife."

"They said I was foolish to do this- outright stupid." Her confusion stifled her appetite. Not mine. Though I'd cleaned three plates, I eyed the leftovers on four and five until she slid them to me.

"The shamans also told you to learn and grow. I'm here, Kitten, you're not alone," I tried to assuage her misgivings while blocking my own.

Riordan pointed out interesting sites, a tour de force tour guide, visibly and vocally enthused- intent on a city he enjoyed tremendously.

We wound our way through narrow streets, crossed picturesque bridges and encountered many, many winged lions associated with Saint Mark- similar to the ones gilt in gold adorning Riordan's, oops, our palazzo. There were many prayer alcoves, apparently still in use, by the look of the candles and fresh flowers.

I paused to admire a particular frieze on the side of a colorful building- long necked birds eye to eye and beak to beak were delicately portrayed inside an arched frame.

"Symbol of luck," Riordan said.

"So many decorative touches everywhere and such lovely, abundant flowers!"

"The Venetians extolled the industries that built their republic. Gloried in their existence! Surrounded themselves with beauties. La Serenissima, beloved of the sea! Their Arsenal- the original factory workshop could build a ship during a state dinner- to impress visitors.

Everyone had a place, and their position was celebrated on buildings and in paintings. Kept the old republic going for over 1000 years. A miracle. 118 linked islands, some 400 bridges, 160 canals. In the mists of time long past, Venice represented safety from marauders. From salt peddlers to the most successful trading ventures- Venice has a most remarkable history. Not all lily white. . . Tell me if I bore you."

Riordan chuckled and kissed me lightly as I urged him to continue, "I love history."

He escorted me into a square dominated by a huge church and a monumental knight on horseback.

"Behold Colleoni- a skilled and generous mercenary. Left all his goods to Venice on the condition they erect this statue of him in memoriam. He did specify the monument to be placed in St. Mark's square, but dear Venice, always leery of one person's having too much influence, put the great bronze horse and rider here- in the Scuola di San Marco. Clever cats, the Venetians."

"Lion lovers," I hugged Riordan's arm to me, staring up at the stern visage astride the gorgeous, Renaissance horse.

"St. Mark's familiar, if I'm not being blasphemous. I couldn't have inherited a more suitable abode, eh? In the morning, I'll show you our gato oros up close. How about a gelato?"

"What's gelato?"

"Wife, you are in for such a treat!"

Never doubt Riordan. The most amazing ice cream is Italian gelato- creamy beyond belief. I couldn't wait to return just to try all the taste-bud-intoxicating flavors.

We tangoed to dueling orchestras under the watchful gaze of 4 bronze horses atop a spectacular cathedral in St. Mark's square.

"Tomorrow we'll take a leisurely, touristy gondola ride and when the crowds dwindle, we'll explore inside the cathedral- a treasure trove all in itself. The floor of our palazzo is similar to the one in St. Mark's. About the same time period as an ancient addition," my tour guide whispered as we danced.

"I wish we could stay for a week or more. I'm feeling sensory overload, but I don't want it to stop." For a kid raised in the west who'd never traveled far from home, this was over-the-top.

"I know, Wife. We'll return. Remind me tomorrow to show you the best way to spend a euro. . ."

"If there's anything to return to. . ."

"None of that," Riordan chastised me as he twirled me across the square, through a Napoleonic addition and onto a street/calle, called Frezzeria.

"I wanted to show you Max's Art Shop."

"Max?   What kind of an Italian name is that?"   I checked down the dark, narrow shop-laden calle.

"Picky, picky.   This shop carries many local artists' work.   Also, fabulous costumes for Mardi Gras.   We will attend Mardi Gras next year- in areas not overly crowded."

"Where would that be?   I've heard the narrow streets are fit to burst with party people. "

A flash of menacing steel suddenly swished in front of us at a dark intersection of bridge, canal and diverging alleys.   A bare gleam of light rayed along the blade of a rapier pointed at Riordan's heart!

22

"CatSkill, as I walk in death!"

I pushed Bonnie into an empty alley, and confronted the attacker with empty hands and a decided grin of surprise.

Inclining my head, hands spread wide, I addressed him, "Signore, you have me at a disadvantage."

"That would be a first, I'm sure," a voice in florid, antique Italian retorted, greatly amused.

'Riordan?' Bonnie queried, hackles up.

'An old friend- very old, Wife.'

'Why is he threatening you?' The rapier traced tiny circular movements, closely honed in on, but not touching my heart.

"Perhaps you'd care to share that tempting morsel?"

"I'll not share my Wife, you scandalous rapscallion! Watch your step," I snarled, most unfriendly-like.

"Wife! Please don't tell me with all the sweet feminine temptations about you've anchored yourself to this."

The silver-blue coated assailant, exuberant, rich throat lace cascading down and matched by the lace at his sleeves, peered around me with horrified skepticism.

"If you lower your blade in truce, I'll introduce you." Immediately, the rapier was sent into its scabbard.

"Wife, I'd like you to meet Giacomo Casanova- a great dis-respector of the female sex, among other things."

In the misty calle on a dark, Venetian night, a man faced me- I assumed man, in that he wore a great coat of a luminescent, brocade material that fell nearly to his masculine calves. Knee breeches of a pale moon shade, silver buckled high heeled silk shoes below opaque hose-clad legs, powdered hair tied back and of course, the ornate weapon at his side further embellished the picture of someone straight out of Mardi Gras.

Leering eyes and a speculative smile in a. . .

'Riordan? I...I can see through him. Uh, what is he, another shaman?'

My husband laughed, shook his head and continued to laugh. I only added to his amusement with my next question.

'Legend, god. . .?'

'Don't let him hear you say that! Legend comes close. Casanova already believes himself to be god's gift to females. He's a ghost, Wife.'

Ghost, I thought, would wonders never cease? My husband was friend, or foe, with a ghost? Why should I be surprised?

"Remember, Kitten, Venice is a land claimed from and surrounded by the sea. The sea runs through her canals as life blood runs through our veins. You could not find a more magical city than this liminal place- lots of ghosts hanging around if you know where to look."

I felt eyes that weren't quite eyes lingering over particular areas of my body. Embarrassing me- of all the nerve!

"Interesting mode of dress, CatSkill- leaves much to the imagination," Casanova chuckled derisively over my long sleeve flannel shirt and jeans.

"Hmm. . . Possibilities. . ." The ghost wondered aloud, casting his head this way and then inclining it in the other direction in his singular, invasive reconnaissance of my person.

He stepped er, drifted, closer to me. With absolutely no experience of ghosts, I tried to step back and hit my head on an escaping brick.

Riordan snarled, fiercely acrimonious, and the ghost's face beamed. I actually saw a statue of the Virgin Mary resting in a prayer alcove through his head, a narrow bridge through his chest.

"Is she a magical creature such as your self, Lion?"

"Yes, she is, and I'll expect you to behave respectfully, you immoral wretch."

Casanova clapped his hands in delight. "Dei gratia! Fascinating!" His examination of me intensified, if that were possible. I felt Riordan hiss, but the ghost merely smiled. Afterall, what could Riordan do to the dead?

Casanova wasn't very tall- not 6" more than my 5'- not imposing at all with his blade sheathed, discounting his ghost-hood, quite intriguing once I got over the initial shock.

"Very well, CatSkill. I shall challenge you for this tasty morsel. It's been awhile since I've indulged. She might prove interesting," the ghost smiled congenially.

"You're speaking of my Wife, you dissolute wraith. I'll not warn you again," Riordan growled.

"Matrimonial status never flawed my pursuit, so, on guard," the ghost silently swept out his rapier and knees bent, he took up the fluid posture of one well-versed in the art of fencing.

'Riordan, you're not going to fight, are you?'

'Wife, your virtue has been impugned. Honor requires me to defend your good name.'

Honor? I'd traveled back through time in this liminal place half-way around the world from my simple home, and now I was about to witness a duel for my 'good name'. Gracious sakes!

"Have another one of those on you?" Riordan asked, not the least bit disturbed as Casanova tauntingly flourished his rapier.

Good naturedly, the ghost beamed. "If you back 20 paces and enter that small church, you'll find I've left something above the door."

Riordan kept his body between me and the libertine. Obviously, the ghost was not to be trusted. I wondered about the potential ramifications of that as I recollected the history of this particular ghost.

Casanova 'tut, tutted' as Riordan swept me into his arms, 'traveled' inside the tiny church, rescued a cobwebbed rapier from the door's lintel and exited in a more 'human' fashion.

"I see you've not bothered to polish this," Riordan cleaned the blade against his jeans, examined its rust pockets, tested its suppleness, brandished it to imitate his opponent.

"What can you expect in these damp environs? But, it is good Toledo steel, my friend. Quit dickering!"

'Riordan, you're not seriously going to fence?'

'But of course, Wife. Your honor is at stake- an affaire d'honneur.'

"To the victor, the spoils," Casanova leered at me, licking his see-through lips with his transparent tongue.

'Riordan,' I appealed, to no avail.

"On guard, you reprobate," my hero challenged, kicking off his moccasins.

"Name calling- how very unsportsmanlike. Hmm. . .," Casanova mused, flicking his rapier at my husband in a testing manner. "Lion of the New World," Casanova's blade shot out seeking a hole in Riordan's defense.

I stifled a scream- see through or not, the rapier swept with great clarity of expertise. My husband- dueling with a ghost! Was this dangerous or simply another of Riordan's playful endeavors?

Steel flashing, whistling and ringing as Casanova and Riordan exchanged advances and retreats. Blades alternated thrusts at shoulders, head and opposite shoulders. Attack, parry, riposte. Two swashbucklers at work.

'Bonnie, look through my eyes, don't be so serious,' Riordan telepathed.

This is not serious? Casanova's rapier flashed under Riordan's, headed for my husband's side. I looked for something to throw. How does one rescue another from a ghost?

Riordan tipped precariously on the edge of the walkway and with a spectacular parry, catching Casanova's blade with his rapier's hilt, he spiraled to avoid falling into the canal. The attacker was thrown off. With his glorious long legs fuelled with the nature of a lion's spring, my husband vaulted up onto the parapet of a tiny bridge. The surreal incredulity of it all boggled my mind.

Casanova threw back his head, exposing his see-through teeth, exulting with pure pleasure. "A most worthy adversary, my dear CatSkill. You've been away much too long."

The summer night decided to bestow on us a light rain, quite suitable for Venice, I thought, as Riordan gamboled agilely on the increasingly slippery bridge arches.

"Coming- lover of the occult?"

"Lover of women, please. The occult can't begin to compete with a warm. . ."

"Watch your ramblings- my Wife is here!"

"Ah, so she is," Casanova turned to me and winked, provocatively.

My husband, with our marriage, had drawn me into the mystery novel of his life and I was discovering that page by page it was the greatest book I'd ever picked up. Just like with the Lakota, I understood fluently the by-play of words between Casanova and Riordan, which added to my relishing the scene before me.

Casanova joined Riordan on the bridge. My husband sloshed on the wet stones. The ghost simply hovered above the ancient wall, watching my husband's fancy footwork.

Suddenly, Casanova's blade attacked with decided vehemence and the swords clashed again. How could a ghostly blade make noise? Was it only due to the fact of its closing on another length of steel? Come to think of it, could I see through his blade?

"His blade is real, Kitten." Oh, no! And I'd begun to think it was OK to enjoy the proceedings. . .

Riordan began to hum as he deflected a thrust from Casanova. Shades of Gene Kelly, he broke into song as he did a makeshift tap dance- "Singing in the Rain. . . I'm fencing in the rain. . ."

I couldn't help myself. All this surreal stuff in the wondrous living museum of Venice! I giggled, leaned against a stuccoed, brick wall, and succumbed to belly-wrenching laughter.

"I suppose I'll have to concede- a draw, eh? I'll not be tasting your sweet. . ."

"Casanova," Riordan warned.

"Very well. The night is still young, why don't I escort you on my escape route from the Piombi?"

"The prison cells under the roof of the Doge's. . ." Riordan interpreted.

"I remember from history. You can do that? Riordan, can we go?" This sounded like fun, not that the sight of my husband tap dancing like Gene Kelly while wielding a rapier and fencing with a ghost hadn't been a. . .well, very interesting.

"The things that excite you, Wife, never cease to amaze me," Riordan's lips twitched. "Let me replace my blade- until the next time."

"You didn't tell me you've done this before," I elbowed Riordan as we exited the church.

"Wherever did you think I learned to fence, Bonnie?"

"Meet me at the Bridge of Sighs, dear friends," Casanova invited before disappearing.

Amid hearty descriptions of constipation, flatulence, diarrhea and a resultant case of piles, Casanova, showed us the confines of his first, tiny prison cell.

Riordan was at a distinct disadvantage with his height- similar to our escapade in worm-imitating. Casanova's dusty, tiny, thick stone-walled room under the lead roof of the Doge's palace would have baked the three of us with the summer's heat, not to mention disabled Riordan's back into a chiropractor's dream- if we were normal.

Luckily, one of us was a ghost and his supple companions had control of body temperatures and it was nighttime.

"After 97 days of this, God teased me with an earthquake. Unfortunately, he did not grace me with one great enough to cleave open these walls."

"Can we do the short version, my friend?"

"Ah, CatSkill! You see, Signora, how mightily your husband would have suffered in his back- if nothing else?" I didn't have to duck, but Riordan practically doubled over. Briefly I pictured him donning a smaller form. . .and stifled a giggle.

One of Casanova's influential, wealthy friends had finagled a half hour exercise- a walk in the main attic, in which he found a piece of marble and an iron rod.

After sharpening the iron piece, he devised an escape plan. Riordan crossed his legs and settled on the stone floor, 'unable' to deprive me of the entire story.

"Below," Casanova pointed one long-nailed finger, which he unceremoniously informed us also served as an ear pick, "is the room of the Inquisitors- men with absolutely no sense of humor or interest in ethereal pursuits. As for women. . ."

"Giacomo," Riordan's admonitory tone rang through the cell.

"I managed over the course of months, nearly 9 of them, to dig a suitable hole, leaving the final break through the ceiling for August 28. The Inquisitors would be away on that date. But, fate smote me a terrible blow." Casanova lowered his head in pained remembrance. His powder white pony tail fell through his dolorous face.

"On the 25th I was moved to another cell- a better one, my jailor touted. Follow me," and he walked through the walls that held him 250 years previous.

"Riordan?" My husband rose half-bent over, grasped my waist and traveled to. . .

"This cell had windows, but no escape hatch. More's the pity. A spy was sent to inform on me after my original plan was discovered. Alas, I began anew. Made a friend in a nearby cell- Father Balbi. Used my occult leanings to rein in my cell mate spy.

My prison cell was constantly checked, so the good Father used my digging stick, hidden inside a bible and carried to him by my jailor under a plate of overflowing, buttered pasta.

On the night of October 31, Balbi broke into my ceiling. Hurry, follow," Casanova's hand beckoned.

"You're sure you want to continue?" Riordan chuckled.

"I'm enjoying this immensely. But, why are we hurrying? Will we be discovered?"

"He wants to present you with the entire sordid episode, 19 hours worth of escape in, uh, three hours," Riordan smiled wryly.

"19 hours?" My brain fumbled with this piece of information.

"If we're found out, we'll not be sent here, but will have to devise a different escape plan," Riordan's lips twitched.

We were directly under the lead tiles of the roof.

"Yes, yes, here," Casanova turned to us, jubilant. "I pried open the lead roof sheeting. My reformed cell mate had cut Balbi's and my hair and beards to better affect our disguise. Another neighbor- too fat to accompany us, provided us with scant funds. I brushed my best clothes, took ropes made of sheets, and Balbi and I. . ." Casanova disappeared.

Riordan rolled his eyes and transported us onto the roof of the. . .

"Uh, Riordan, uh, we can stop now."

Perched astride a lead gable much too high above the safety of solid ground went way beyond my interest, even though I was ensconced in Riordan's arms. His high-heel, silver-buckled shoes gliding on air, Casanova simply hastened forward, unaware of my growing height fears. Again he disappeared.

"I can't look," I hid my face in Riordan's vibrating chest.

"Scaredy cat."

"You can't guarantee I'll land on my feet, can you?" I whispered.

"Do you really have to ask me that?" What was I thinking? Riordan would take care of me. But, that didn't totally relax my height-conscious self.

Riordan picked me up and carried me to where Casanova straddled a dormer window, still recounting how he'd managed to pry off a grill from the window, lodge a ladder inside, and with the use of his rope get Balbi and himself installed within.

"Follow, hurry," he gleefully dared. I assumed the end was near. But, upon entering the room in Riordan's arms, an alarm fatefully sounded.

"They've found us. Ooh, I must amend, they've found you, ha! Quickly, Lion of the New World. Good-bye, arrivederci, Ma Donna CatSkill. Please visit again, soon." And the ghost walked into another plane.

"Time to go, Wife." The sound of approaching, security footsteps hurried in our direction.

23

"How did he get out of that room? I mean, when he was alive?" I puzzled.

Riordan finished the story as we snuggled comfortably in our palazzo bed.

"By a series of breaking down doors, dragging the flagging Balbi along, descending several staircases, until fortuitously arriving in a room near an exit. He flung open a window-luckily he was spotted by a key-wielding guard and mistaken for a wealthy, Venetian patron inadvertently locked in overnight. Casanova swept past the startled guard with Balbi mumbling 'to the church'. The legendary lover took the first gondola and fled Venice." Riordan skipped succinctly through the finale.

"But he came back as a ghost. Wow!"

"Or did Venice summon him? Venice probably has more ghosts than anywhere else in the world. Most humans just can't see them. It's that whole liminal thing," my husband threw in a bit of coyote thinking.

My hand rested on Riordan's bare chest, plying the glorious planes of muscle. I mentally rehashed the events of the day which ended in the ultimate ghost story and. . .

His fingers traced a path on my arm, leaving a wake of goose bumps. "Mmm. . .," his mouth and nose explored my neck.

"There you are, Wife," Riordan joined me as I perched on the stone bannister overlooking the Grand Canal.

"Tell me more of this palazzo," I asked. The colors moving in the primeval waters danced, creating mesmerizing, hypnotic ripples.

"This portego, or hall, was originally used for receptions, feasts, balls. The rooms on both sides were for personal use, bedrooms, etc.

The ground floor served as the warehouse-storage. The remnants of the loading dock are still below, see? Our golden lions on guard at each end of this bannister- well, legends of the Cavalli, the original owners, hint that one of the first Cavalli merchants owned the ship that transported St. Mark's body from Alexandria to Venice under the infidels' very noses.

They'd wrapped hog carcasses atop and around the saint's body- you know pork is anathema to Mohammed's followers? Hence, St. Mark's body was safely delivered from 'unbelievers', shipped to Venice for all her fortunate glory, and the palazzo has displayed lions ever since- a badge of honor, I suppose. Quite fitting for my décor, what do you think?"

I leaned further out to fully reconnoiter the lions and the neighboring palazzos, causing Riordan to grasp my waist. "I agree," my eyes swept from the lion guardians to my own lion, earning me a golden wink.

"We'll take an early gondola ride. I want you to see the colors Venetian artists were famous for recreating- truly spiritual shades unique to this masterpiece of a city."

"I'm ready." I looked once more at the gold-gilt mirrored hall, its colored stone floor and the tremendous chandelier with matching sconces between the mirrors. I couldn't ignore the ornate bed, either.

"Riordan, are you disappointed in the way I dress?"

He gave me one of those 'looks' as he searched my senses. "I like the way you dress and love the way. . ."

"Riordan," I blushed, recovered. Even though I felt his reassurance, Casanova's comment on my apparel had hit home. Focus on something else, I told myself.

"Why was Casanova in prison?" I knew the old stories about women-chasing, but I didn't think that generally landed a man in prison, at least in those days.

I followed Riordan's long strides to a rear staircase, descended into a garden courtyard with its ancient well head in the midst of lush, fragrant flowers.

"The government watch dogs- think over-industrious homeland security, were not amused by colorful characters, especially those who befriended wealthy Venetians and foreigners.

Previously, they'd turned an eye from Casanova's indiscretions," he winked at me and wriggled a black brow, causing me to crack up.

"He refused to heed their warnings and don a semblance of circumspection, so they came for him."

I hailed a gondolier for a sunrise cruise of sorts. I wanted Bonnie to savor the early morning before hordes of tourists interfered.

Clad as his fellow operators had been for hundreds of years- dark pants, striped shirt, straw hat with ribbon banding, its ends traipsing down his back- Bertolli steadied the long, black, shining, high-prowed gondola as I guided Bonnie aboard.

"Do you sing?" My Wife smiled up at the agile gondolier.

He pointed to his throat and croaked, "Scusi, Signora."

"Never mind, Wife. I'll be tour guide and entertainer in one."

Silently, we glided under a head-caressing bridge, veered left onto a small canal and then swung right onto the Grand Canal.

I pointed out a few famous palazzos along the way, heard Bonnie's gasp of surprise as the sun stroked our palazzo and caused its pink and gold marble and gold gilt lions to glisten. Istria stone balconies came alive as waters lapped fondly at its foundation.

"Riordan, it's magnificent!"

"What would you expect, Lioness?" I hugged her tiny body to me, no longer mindful of breakage potential, as we nestled inside our velvet love seat. The gondola gently rocked and glided forward as the refrain of an Italian song itched to escape.

"Volare! Nel blu. . ." Bonnie's smile encouraged me. A passing gondolier saluted us.

The interplay of colors, sunlight and shadow, the intermittent resplendent cathedrals, Rialto bridge- the hum of a singularly wondrous, antique city waking into the 21st century- better than a movie.

I felt Bonnie's sigh of pleasure and saw with her artist's eyes, beguiled as were the famous Titian, Veronese and so many others. "We'll come back, Kitten, as often as you like," I promised.

Venice overflowed with remarkable experiences and I'd share them, and discover more with her.

Arriving at St. Mark's square, I located a deserted nook and traveled with Bonnie inside the ornate cathedral. The magnificent bronze horses atop the Byzantine edifice (another 'fortunate find' for Venezia) were a big hit, and the gold of the storied mosaics and Palo D' Oro craved our attention also, as well as the relic room. I could have kept her there all day and she gladly would have complied, but there were more colors to admire and pressing business ahead. And, of course. . .

"Riordan, I'm kind of hungry." I rested my case.

The blues of the Venetian sky, the canal waters changing chameleon-like as the sun moved across Venice, the different marbles, colored stucco facades, carved column capitals, gothic arches, winged lions everywhere. . . Oh, and those glorious horses from ancient Greece or Rome— no one knew for sure of their origin, or how they'd traveled to Constantinople, but now they proudly stood in the finest display position of all- atop St. Mark's cathedral.

Thank the spirits, Paris sent them back after Napoleon 'acquired' them, and that the originals were inside, safe from chemical-laden air; those prancing atop St. Mark's were superb copies set in the grandest of sites.

Venice was a feast for the artist's eye as well as the lover of history and we'd not even visited inside a museum. No time for that. The whole of Venice was a living museum.

In an off-the-beaten-path square, Riordan greeted a deli owner who provided us with paninis of different hams and cheeses. Fruit and gelato for dessert. Delicious!

With the progress of the day, the crowds became oppressive. Riordan skirted the more popular areas and suggested a nap- as most of the Mediterranean people retired during the worst of the heat.

But I was anxious to see it all, even though it was an impossibility. As the time to meet Zander neared, all the words of warning and my innate confusion returned.

"We can always go home, Wife. The world's plights are not your responsibility."

"I guess we should at least hear what the Oracle has to say." Riordan fell strangely silent, almost resigned, when I made my pronouncement.

I almost slid into the Mediterranean upon Riordan's transporting us to a rocky ledge on the coast- a baptismal font of sorts.

"Remind me to caution you about paddock boots next time we travel, Bonnie."

"Good idea," I breathed a sigh of relief, safe in his arms, safe from my nemesis- deep water.

The surf belted noisily at the rock and spit at us as if peeved at my appearance and even more at my rescue. Night had fallen and a crescent moon played peek-a-boo with an overcrowded racetrack of fast moving clouds.

What sufficed as a path lit up momentarily, but a flickering ensued, died, and then we were suddenly plunged into darkness once again. Cat eyes certainly came in handy. My anxiety level ascended as I slipped on user-unfriendly terrain- I felt like a trespasser. What was I really doing here?

Uncharacteristically, Riordan ignored my thoughts and pulled me along, intent on finishing what he considered a fool's errand.

Beside an arch of rock reminiscent of Stonehenge pillars, the white-garbed Zander awaited us. Bowing his head in a sign of respectful acknowledgement, he thanked us for coming.

"The Oracle will be most pleased," his right hand tapped on impervious rock and without a sound an ocean-doused rock wall appeared and swung into a cave.

A sandy footpath lit by torches ensconced in the brooding rock walls drew us. Shivers of déjà vu slithered along my spine- I felt most unwelcome.

'It's not too late,' a voice inside my head advised. Riordan had not said a single word since my near tumble and I began to get an eerie feeling of. . .aloneness.

The path ended in a damp, dank 'reception' area with a single sheepskin covered bench. Guest reception was a most optimistic description.

My hands hung at my side. Adding to the strangeness, Riordan maintained a distance- not open to me. What was he thinking of?

"Wait, please, I'll announce your arrival." No expression on Zander's olive-colored skin. Deep set, brow-less eyes lowered. He turned, placed a hand on another well-disguised rock door which opened at his touch.

"Open Sesame," I whispered. No response from Riordan. Maybe he didn't get it.

"I got it," he tersely replied. He was not happy. My take-everything-in-stride lion- where was he? Why had my situation taken on such a dire aspect? Why was Riordan ignoring my unspoken questions? Maybe I should. . .

Zander rejoined us in what seemed a blink of the eye, "The Oracle will see you first." The acolyte inclined his head at Riordan. "Alone."

My husband shrugged; he seemed to expect this.

"You'll be all right," he reassured me. I gripped my lower lip as a child latches onto a pacifier, and nodded.

'Look through my eyes, Wife. Use my ears,' he silently instructed, before disappearing through the rocky portal which closed ominously behind him. At least he'd granted me that- so, I wasn't entirely on my own. . .

"May I bring you refreshment, my lady?" Zander asked without the usual solicitude of a true conscientious host- perhaps his respect was solely for Riordan.

"Some water?" I tried to appear confident- without any sense of success.

Zander handed me a heavy, gem-encrusted, gold goblet. As I lifted the antique to my lips, the stone in my ring flashed angrily. I allowed my inner guide to examine the contents. The water had been tampered with.

Zander's eyes never left mine. I pretended to drink, found the semblance of a flat-topped rock, divested my hand of the suspicious cocktail and perched warily on the edge of the bench. I'd not leave without Riordan, but escape surely seemed the appropriate course of action.

Why did the Oracle wish me drugged? Almost immediately, I found myself looking through Riordan's eyes, and I listened, intently.

"Welcome, my dear, dear CatSkill," a strikingly beautiful siren of a woman floated towards my husband.

His hiss of displeasure at her approach was an echo of my own. Nonplussed, she gracefully stopped just inches from Riordan. He didn't retreat, but his ire was palpable.

Long, flaming locks- all the colors of a pine cone fed fire, swept back from a milky-white face. Flawless perfection- no freckles on this one. Black brows and long, heavy black lashes framed amber eyes that intermittently flashed as if she were gauging something, clinched on Riordan.

"Still having difficulties with touch, my darling? I remember when that wasn't quite such an issue between us."

I felt a rumbling in my chest and queasiness in my stomach. The Oracle was not only every man's dream girl- a siren beckoning a sailor to shore, but she'd also been. . .intimate with my husband.

'Wife, calm yourself,' his voice broke into my snarls and imminent melt-down.

Zander eyed me in a new light, as I bolted to my feet and paced furiously while my wild nature begged for release.

'Wife?'

She was an unparalleled beauty, the perfect woman, a temptress, an undine. . .

'Bonnie, you are the only siren song I hear. Peace!'

The Oracle strutted model-like on the catwalk, before Riordan. Her diaphanous, turquoise toga, slashed from her hips down, revealed her perfect legs with every stride. The gauzy material outlined every feminine curve- no panty lines or other underwear for that matter. Gold bracelets wreathed her arms and gold sandals left no imprints as she walked. My hackles bristled as she paraded herself.

My senses were strangely confused- I wanted to tear her apart and yet. . .

"The drama queen roll suits you, Oracle. But, as I'm not a fan of drama, state whatever it is you have to say and have done."

"You would dismiss me so lightly," her ruby lips pouted. "Come, sit. Let's reminisce."

She could have no knowledge of mine and Riordan's simultaneous shared use of our senses. Or did she?

"Seems to me someone mentioned a timeframe. If I'm mistaken on that point, well, perhaps we'll return at another time- not," Riordan pronounced, definitively, and prepared to exit.

"Very well. For now." The Oracle swung her hair, reminding me of Shadow. How did women beguile men with such a simple, silly movement?

But Riordan didn't seem interested.   Or was he blocking that part?

The Oracle retired to a throne of giant clam shells.   Its sheepskin padded seat provided the pearl with a cushion.   Her fingers gently jostled a gold bell resting on a side table.

"You may go in now," Zander's hand offered. I skirted his personal space, he was not to be trusted, and obviously his boss was of the same ilk.

I prepared to meet, no, confront my husband's ex-lover.

24

I didn't think it would be 'correct' to go in snarling and spitting; I kept the wild in abeyance- for the moment. Using all the grace of the cougar, and fingering my cat's eye pendant, I entered the Oracle's chamber without a sound.

My hand proprietarily slid up Riordan's back. I took his hand, and felt his lips twitch. With one eye on the Oracle, he leaned into me and kissed the tip of my nose.

A flit of annoyance, (I swear), swept across her face and was immediately replaced with an imperious look. She crossed her legs, which completely bared the one, and proceeded to play stare-down while waiting us out.

"Oracle, I believe you had some information to relate," Riordan pushed.

"You may go, my dear Riordan. What I have to impart is for the girl alone."

"The girl has a name- Bonnie Lance CatSkill," my husband replied, stressing the CatSkill.

"Yes, I heard you'd married, however, I'll speak with her alone."

"No way. Come, Bonnie, we're leaving."

'Riordan?' I placed a hand on his chest.

'I'd not leave Grandfather alone with her, let alone you, maybe Gunne. . .'

"I supposed your 'wife'," a modicum of spit resided in the way she said wife, "to be a shaman in her own right. If so, did I erroneously believe she could speak for herself? Ten minutes is all I require."

The Oracle's amber eyes had turned nearly black with flashes of malevolent red, and she glared at us as a snake wishing to charm its prey to death. Our senses warned us, but we were not without our own protections, right?

I felt Riordan's indecision, and the instant he conceded. He knew I'd not go without trying to help. We should be able to handle. . .whatever. Shouldn't we?

"Five minutes, and then I'm coming for you," he vowed to me, and warned the Oracle. I felt his senses momentarily delve into mine before he disappeared.

"Now that the male influence has departed, we girls can chat." The Oracle pretended a friendliness belied by her black eyes, singularly arched brow and ultra-cool countenance.

I refused her proffered seat, recalling my drugged water, and the prescient drop in temperature.

"What of the Mediterranean waters flooding?"

She pelted me with an hypnotic frequency which I surmounted- easy enough. I'd been there before.

"Block Riordan from our conversation," she politely requested.

A sense of unease shot through me, my ring finger tingled, but I refused to drop my gaze from her. Block my husband? I wondered if I could pretend.

"No, you cannot."

If this was the only way to find out if I could help. . .

'Riordan, I'm going to block you.'

'Bonnie, no!'

My wild nature strongly objected as I shut the door between Riordan and myself. I maintained the block with extreme trepidation and difficulty. What was I doing, ignoring all the signs?

With no trace of rancor at her failure to trance me, she shot me a question, "Would you die for your imagined lover?"

Her sultry lips curled up- a veracious adept in the art of seduction. Imagined lover? What was she talking about?

Relentlessly, she pelted my psych by vocalizing all the reasons I wasn't the. . .

I swallowed, trying to keep myself from disintegrating or going up in flames. I was but a girl, and Riordan deserved a woman- the basis of her alternately reproaching me and cajoling me to step aside for what was best for the powerful Riordan CatSkill.

I was numb before she finished. I'd never really believed I was good enough for. . . I barely digested the details of the catastrophe I'd been asked to stem which was but minutes away.

And she further pushed me, adding to my confusion, "Hurry, child! I know you'll make the right decision."

Had she given me all the details?

Before Riordan had the chance to pull me away from the chamber, I traveled to him.

"Bonnie?"

"We have to go- it's about to happen." I tried to rush from the anteroom.

Zander looked on, oddly, conspicuously, out of sorts. I guessed he was worried about his home, school- whatever this chamber of horrors was.

"We're not going anywhere until you tell me what went on in there."

"There's no time, Riordan," I kept my eyes lowered. "Later, please. The Oracle said it has no bearing on where I place myself, suggested the furthest tip of Sicily. C...can you t...take me there?"

I couldn't bring myself to gaze into his golden eyes. If I did. . . The block still held between us, though fragilely. I wasn't sure if he were powerful enough to take me home without my permission or even if he would really want to.

Every emotion I had was as jumbled as. . . Something I'd known of, but couldn't recall; I was that confused, and covertly, desperately, fighting not to fall apart.

"Hurry, Riordan," I choked. Perhaps he believed my distress was solely due to my task at hand. I wasn't giving him the chance to read me. Did it matter? I was done thinking.

The sea appeared tranquil enough- too much so.

"Feels like a ghost town," Riordan joked, his fingers running up and down my arms.

We were perched upon a fairly flat slab of salt-brined rock, ready or not.

"Notice, no sounds of any wildlife? Just humans who haven't the sense to read their world," he said.

The frequencies were peculiar. The air charged- eerily potent- a harbinger of. . .

Ships sailing on a previously sunny day which had hastily darkened into a sick gray-green shroud, floundered- too late, desperately trying to reach a dock- the closest haven.

As the waters began to roil, the nearest ships spun in circles, out of control, sails dipping in trepidation, and figures aboard flailed for lifesaving handholds.

"I bet the weather service is finally ringing the bell," Riordan attempted levity, sighed, gave up, and grimaced at what was transpiring.

Beneath my feet, I felt the earth's vibrations deep in its core- buckling, tripping, rearing and opening far below us. Riordan's arms held me tightly to him.

"At the first sign of anything out of our control, I'm getting you out of here." His last words to me.

The sky went from nauseous greenish black to jagged, spectral, war-mongering clouds- echoing the convulsions in my stomach. The waters of the Mediterranean blackened with white-capped turbulence, and rose to breech their perimeters. Black- my nemesis.

Repercussions of the earth's violence somewhere under the sea traveled to where we stood. I raised my ring hand without the remotest confidence. Not sure if anything mattered anymore.

I was going to stare down. . .

Suddenly, the ground beneath us tilted and dropped in response to the vehemence of whatever was violating the sea. Earthquakes. . .

'Intend,' Irusan had always told me. 'Intend'.

Silently, I beseeched the ground to still, the waves to calm. My answer consisted of the water agitating even worse- waves ran helter-skelter, rose tower-like- Armageddon in the sea.

Incredibly, Riordan kept us upright on the rollercoaster strip of rock. My hand shook and my ring flashed- the only colors amid the surrounding, boiling blackness.

A lurid wall rose directly before me, and a voice thundered in my head, 'You think to oppose me, foolish, stupid girl?'

'Who are you?' I asked tremulously. Could Riordan hear it?

'These waters are my domain. HOW DARE YOU!'

'Would you destroy the civilizations that ring this sea?'

'And why shouldn't I? They plunge their spoilage into me. There is no more respect, as in the ancient time. There is no more honor.'

'There are some who still care,' I tried to appeal to the riled, definitely male energy confronting me.

'Bah!' The voice shot back, spray hit my face taking my breath away. 'The Oracle promised me a sacrifice if I stay my hand.'

The black wall undulated before me, rising higher and higher. I supposed Riordan thought I had some control over it. He was pouring his strength into me.

'What do you mean, a sa...sacrifice?'

'You. There is something powerful in you. If you come with me willingly, I will not destroy your man. Though, I will bathe the lands around my home. Maybe lightly, depends on you.'

This is what the Oracle meant. Dying for Riordan. The black wall roared and raced to our position- I had the distinct impression of horrid red eyes beyond the black, intent on me. I felt Riordan. . .ready to. . .

Decision time. I'd never really felt myself worthy of Riordan. But worse than that was the cracking inside my chest- my heart torn asunder as I surrendered. Perhaps, the Oracle. . .

"Bonnie!" I screamed aloud. She'd fainted in my arms- dead weight. I gathered her up preparatory to traveling away from this nightmare- the nightmare of Bonnie's sweat lodge experience, I now realized.

More rapid than my rescue attempt, the maelstrom of a giant wave heaved and bore down on us. I tightened my grip, fractions of a second to leave, but too late.

Its power superseded mine in that it was unbelievably faster. Bonnie was torn from my grasp. Why had I waited so long? What were the spirits up to? And damn them for this trial!

The rocky crag beneath us broke into fateful shards. The wall that stole my heart plunged back into its den with my Wife in its grasp, and I. . .

The only animal I could think of to call on. . . I dove into the last sighting of my Bonnie. Her senses were closed to me. Strangely enough, they'd been so since. . .

My body lengthened and slickened as I allowed the dolphin to take me under, deeper and deeper using his supreme swimming capabilities and. . .

Echo-location- I'd learned from my stint as a bat, came to the fore of my senses. I avoided a sinking yacht in the wrathful depths- no thought for the passengers- I had a single pursuit, my own life at stake.

Seaweed, torn from its moors, sought to tangle my body, as if to net fish. I slithered sideways through phalanxes of broken shells, upended sea creatures, some still battling for life, others defeated, oars, engine parts. . .

I avoided what I could, took the brunt of the hits I could not dodge- leaving injuries to my shamanic powers to heal.

Harder and harder I fought to control my loss of control of this horrific situation. Where? Show me spirits!

Just ahead, tumbling in the detritus boiled up by the roiling sea- Bonnie, slowly sinking to the disparaged sand bed.

With a great flick of my tail, I placed myself under her and made to ascend, but something pulled at me- held me- forced me- imprisoning me in the depths.

For the second time in my life, I found myself in a situation beyond my power to influence- shades of Bonnie's coma. I fought the force seeking to jail me, knowing I needed to hurry Bonnie to the light above.

Light. . . Hadn't Bonnie mentioned something about a light?

'Irusan,' I implored. 'I need your help. Send us the light if you can.'

That should rouse him- surely he didn't want us destroyed.

As soon as the word 'light' left my telepathic consciousness, I felt the release. My tail flippers took over, and we surged up, resurrected into a golden light which beckoned us to salvation.

A torrent of curses streamed behind, below.

As my dolphin self, I vaulted from the waters, phasing back into my human body before touching land. Not caring if anyone saw. And who could have survived that maelstrom anyway? Not caring about anything, but the comatose body in my arms.

I probed Bonnie's sodden, dead-white body searching for the slightest sensory feedback. Nothing.

'Great Spirit, help us,' I prayed, clasping and rocking Bonnie to me. Pain inside my chest- a true heart attack.

An anguished, angry roar- and cougars do not roar- broke from my diaphragm- this was the Oracle's doing.

With my lifeless Wife cradled in my arms, I traveled to the Oracle's lair.

"CatSkill, what happened?" Zander's face registered complete shock, and greater, anxious concern.

"Where is she?" I snarled.

"The Oracle? She. . ." The acolyte broke off. He'd been with the devious witch long enough. His eyes widened, catching on to. . .

Why had I left them alone?

'Because the spirits bade you to allow this lesson,' seeped into my brain.

I kicked open the Oracle's chamber door.

"What did you do to her, witch?"

"Now, dearest, darling Catskill, you can see she isn't the one for you. Much too weak, too young. . ."

25

A measure of my distress was that I didn't even feel his presence until, "My son, take her to your palazzo. I will be there momentarily."

"Irusan?" I hesitated, a question rising with my gut-purged bile, but he sent me and the weight in my arms away. Irusan was bent on his own silent rage.

The Oracle's screams echoed on the telepathic air waves as Irusan, in his giant cat body, tore the thousands-of-years-old, scheming Oracle to bits.

"Wake, Daughter. It's time to take your punishment."

Protectively, I dared to stay Irusan's hand with a hiss. He did not reprimand, but instead cast sympathetic eyes at me.

"Most of the punishment will be of your own making, my son. You are distraught right now-rest."

His great cat nose, whiskers quivering, bent over Bonnie's blue-white face and breathed.

I held myself forcefully together as she began to cough up copious amounts of filthy, bile-flecked sea water. A white tipped paw, bigger than Bonnie's entire torso, briefly, softly touched her forehead.

"Go and rest. Call in Grace, but you must rest, and think, and make your peace with the spirits."

Bonnie's choking subsided, and her eyes fluttered as Irusan ultimately demanded that I leave. With every cell of my being refuting my distancing myself from her, I obeyed.

Irusan would not let her die. As for suffering. . .the lesson. . . I felt myself cave in. Bonnie's suffering was my own. The misery in my chest had stopped its anvil-shattering blows at my heart. Quietly, heavily, it waited in limbo. I nodded to the King of the Celtic Cats and left.

I must address the spirits and ask their pardon for my 'damning' them, as well as settle myself and think.

"Grace," my voice croaked, surprised. Grandfather's love, the swallow, the ra. . . Had I died? And something worse occurred to me. . .

Riordan! Great Spirit, please, not Riordan! I tried to rise. Immediately, my head spun like a sick top and my stomach threatened reprisals. My mouth felt parched with the taste of salt and grit and worse.

Grace's hand went to my chest and gently pushed me back to recline against piled pillows.

"Wh…where's Riordan?" My eyes scanned our palazzo bedroom- no sign, not a single feel of his existence.

I called up my senses- no response. I put my full focus into allowing my wild nature, my shamanic powers, into locating my husband- no response. A deadly, silent zone.

How could this be? What. . .? A smattering of panic seeped into me and then poured, drowning me, drowning me in a horrendous fear.

What had I done? Spirit, help me, save me. . .save us. . .

I pitched against Grace's hand- to no avail. I had no strength; baby-helpless, I sunk into the bed. Where were my healing powers? Where was Riordan?

"Riordan?" My scream was a feeble croak.

I couldn't see him, couldn't feel him. Couldn't sense him in anyway. My body began to shake. . .if he were gone. . . Let me die also. . .

"Bonnie, you must rest. Your ordeal. . . You are very weak. This test. . ." Grace's jaw tightened, so unlike her, "was unfair."

Her words flew over my head, not registering an iota.

"Grace, where is R...Riordan?"

Her hand went to her lap as she sat next to me on the bed. Her eyes flitted from mine to her hands and back.

"I don't know," she finally murmured.

My shivers turned to full-blown convulsions. Fruitlessly, I hugged myself, rocking, trying to hold myself together.

"Why can't I feel him? Is he. . .?" The dreaded death word must not be said aloud.

"No, he called me to sit with you."

"Why isn't he here. . .with me?"

She gave me a blank look before coyote answering with a stern tone, "Perhaps you can answer that?"

"Me?" I put my fist in my mouth to stop my teeth from chattering. My straight-A student's brain deciphered the question, but there were no brain cells responding with anything resembling an answer.

"Why did you do it?" Her quiet inquiry was dense with meaning.

"D...do what? Try to stem the flood?"

My stomach heaved and I turned from her, fell over the side of the bed and vomited into a half-full waiting bucket of stench.

Grace helped me back into the bed; her eyes set in disapproval and. . .disappointment?

"I'm waiting, dear."

I thought back. The last thing I remembered was the wall of black, similar to, but not wholly like, the experience I'd had in Grandfather's sweat lodge.

But, before that. . .before. . . When had I blocked Riordan? When had I disregarded all the warnings? When had I cut myself off from the spirits and my heart?

"The Oracle," I whispered.

"What of the Oracle?"

"She. . ." How could I continue?

"I'm waiting, dear," Grace patiently intoned once more.

"Oh, God. . ." I broke, hiccoughed, convulsively sobbed.

"Listen to me," Grace's voice took on a commanding note, such as I'd never heard from her. "Stop your caterwauling and listen."

The violence of my crying subsided into silent tears, compelled by her shamanic skill.

"Shall I reiterate what the Oracle told you? She hit you with every insecurity, every self-esteem issue you've ever had: your childhood loneliness, your mother's leaving you; she besieged you with a young girl's so-called foolish dreams, and deviously dashed them."

"She picked you apart with more cunning thrift than a cotton gin picked apart cotton balls. I'm sure her semantic usage was worthy of Clarence Darrow or any other fanatic courtroom attorney. What would a great shaman like Riordan Catskill want with a silly, teen-age girl?"

Grace mimicked the Oracle so closely I almost slid away from her in fear. "A teen-age girl without a woman's full curves, without a woman's experience of how to keep a man such as Riordan happy, without the thousands of years of power which that wicked Oracle possessed?

How could such a one as you hope to hold a lion such as CatSkill? If, in your dreamy-eyed world, you feel as if you truly love him, then let him go- step away. He doesn't need your clinging; your needs continually stifle him. You keep him from his true calling. He can't leave you for one night. . ."

"Stop, stop it! Please, stop," I broke into raucous sobbing once more- sure that between throwing up and copious tears that my body would completely rid itself of all necessary fluids. Self-embalmment in my self-pity. Dry up and die, except. . .

Something tugged on the outskirts of my memory. I was too weak to recall. . .

'I hope your listening, Riordan,' Grace's voice silently reached me.

I'd gone to hibernate as Irusan had dictated. I'd simply not gone far. In a corner of the portego's high azure ceiling, I'd joined one of Bonnie's 'creepies'- a spider in a web of my own making.

Bonnie had no cognizance of me. Part of that was the huge block I'd put into play. The rest was Irusan's doing.

It was my belief that the King of the Celtic Cats had siphoned off Bonnie's shamanic powers. How? I had no idea, but then he was surely as powerful as the ancient shamans in the cave, and they had stemmed our power.

It certainly was a surefire way to gain attention and make one think. And I would figure it out. . .later.

Before this trip, I would never have believed it possible to interfere with all of her powers, maybe some, but not all. Even in the cave we still communicated telepathically. Irusan had taken care of that, too. My block was therefore unnecessary.

Irusan had given her enough of a healing balm, but still she lay enervated, sickly, physically and mentally spent.

Keeping myself from her had to be the hardest thing I'd ever done, but the lesson was not yet complete. Bonnie had to finish the last page of the test.

26

"You superseded all the warnings. You knew better. You ignored your spirit guide. You conveniently forgot your wild spirit-guided senses- those you share with Riordan. You came here for a good purpose, and you stayed for the wrong reasons. Taking yourself from him because a devious bitch fed you a line- and you believed it!"

Grace interrupted her truthful, hurtful recriminations, offered me a glass of water, held my shaky fingers around the glass and helped me to drink. And she further lambasted me.

"You forgot who you are- what you've become- who you've vowed yourself to. You regressed back into the confused, human 17-year old girl you might have been without Riordan's and the spirits' intervention, and of course your acceptance of them. Only in that guise could the Oracle influence you. Do you understand?"

Teeth chattering, I acknowledged my guilt. I felt worse than death and I deserved to. Maybe I was dying. . . Had she come to save me? And where was Riordan? Had he given up on me? In which case, let me die. . .

Grace pulled the covers up to my chin and around my shoulders.

"I let. . .Riordan down."

Grace scowled, so unlike her- that's how perturbed she was. "Do you think you're the only young girl ever to be duped by an older, so-called femme fatale?"

"He's always saving me. . ."

"Another of the Oracle's arguments- listen to yourself! Dear, you let Riordan down, but you let yourself down first. Do you think he rescued you solely out of the goodness of his heart? Save yourself, Bonnie.

Return to who you were born to be. The whole is greater than its parts. In the human world, to die for someone else is a sign of love. Admirable, but you are no longer simply a human. Your life is tied to his and also to the purpose of the spirits- did you not think to ask him if he were ready to die, too? Did you think to ask the spirits for their approbation?

Not to mention the hair-raising fright you gave Gunne- that knucklehead! The sooner he falls in love with someone else, the better. Honestly!"

Grace gave in to her exasperation. Her eyes suddenly sparked as if she'd just thought of something else. Her chin rose defiantly.

"I'll leave you with this last thought. Who did Riordan CatSkill ask to marry him?" She kissed my forehead. "Good-by, dear." And in an instant she was gone.

I was alone. More alone than I could ever have believed it was possible to feel. A thousand times more alone than my growing up years- I was kidding myself- the growing part never ends.

There was no strength in me to return home, to my friends- the animals, my dad. The emptiness engulfing me. . . I couldn't return home. I had no power, nothing.

Without Riordan, there was no strength in me to get out of this beautiful bed. Had it been only 24 hours since we'd been wondrously happy here?

And now, I couldn't even telepathically talk to him. Where had he gone? Perhaps he didn't want me anymore. . . Had the spirits taken my powers, for good?

Rest, she'd said. Impossible without anyone to answer my questions. Impossible without Riordan.

Her parting query- who had Riordan asked to marry him? Not the Oracle. Not the Oracle. . .

He'd had 150-plus years to find a mate and he'd not asked anyone until. . .me.

I had to find him. Struggling with the covers as if they weighed hundreds of pounds, I wriggled to escape the bed. My body felt completely drained- like a long bout with the flu, only worse. Why?

Why wasn't my body healing itself? For that matter, why hadn't Grace helped?

But, of course, she had. She'd returned me to a semblance of reason. Made me face the truth.

I'd allowed myself- pitiful self- to cave into the Oracle's diatribe. I truly didn't deserve Riordan. I'd allowed myself to. . .

Slowly, I demanded my deaf legs to move out of the bed. Slowly, they did. But upon gaining the floor there was nothing left in them to keep me upright.

The cold of the stone floor, its colors so beautiful, now seemed insidious as I crumpled to the ancient paving and shivered uncontrollably.

I wore a long sleeve shirt and nothing more. Someone must have taken my wet clothes. Who? Never mind. If I couldn't walk, I'd crawl.

Riordan was holding himself away from me because of me. Me and my stupid, asinine, human doubts.

I would find him. With every breath left to me, I would find him. . . Or I would have to become the living dead, for there was no life for me without Riordan.

I watched her crawl across the terrazzo floor. A snail would have out raced her. My body cringed with every move she barely made, for of course, everything she felt, I did, too.

In all her humanity, she defied the loss of her powers and continued determinedly pulling herself along, destroying fingernails seeking to grasp any indentation in stone to creep forward, teeth chattering, stomach recoiling- through the bedroom door, into the portego.

A lesser human would not have made it so far- not after her self-induced ordeal. She collapsed under the chandelier, whimpered and tried to rise again.

Night had descended. Not caring whether it were day or night- what could it matter anymore?- I'd not flicked on the lights.

I did it now.

"Riordan," what remained of her voice called pitifully. She twisted her upper body, rested on a shaky elbow.

"Riordan," her voice took on more volume. Where did she dredge up the strength?

What held me aloft? What kept me from her? She had to know, she had to feel. . . But, no, she couldn't. Irusan had usurped all of her shamanic powers- she was running on strictly human endurance, the resolute perseverance of Bonnie, alone.

"Riordan, Riordan, Riordan," her attempted screams were nothing more than a battered throat could produce.

"Riordan," one last croaking attempt. "Please, please," she collapsed onto the cold stone, shivering, sobbing, curled into a fetal position.

I'd not attempt to reach her silently, she probably couldn't hear that way, yet.

"How do you feel?" My inane opening gambit.

She stifled her cries; one hand clutched her stomach, the other at her mouth.

"R...Riordan?" Through a sodden veil, her eyes blinked, seeking the source of my voice.

"How do you feel?" There was no way to keep the emotion from my voice. I nearly choked on the depth of my feelings.

"W...worse than d...death. Riordan. . ." She valiantly tried to rise once more, but fell back, helpless.

I changed from my spider guise into my human self. I walked toward her, but did not close the gap between our personal spaces.

Perched on my heels, I faced her. Her eyes fell into mine, as they had over a year ago when Bonnie stood from our outdoor lunch at school. Green to gold. A bonding begun- forged between the worlds of human and shaman- at spirits-behest.

If this were an important lesson for Bonnie, it was the utmost test of my endurance.

"Now you know how I felt when. . ." I cringed at the words. "When you took yourself from me."

My eyes, all my senses, were glued to her child-like body.

"Riordan," again she struggled to rise, ended up in a crawling position. Dizzy and drained, this time some inner-tapped strength kept her from collapsing. Her weight rested on shaky hands.

I noticed, felt, the goose bumps of her chilled, bare, pale legs. Slowly, quivering, she tried to reach me- a baby seeking shelter.

"I. . .I w…was wrong. S…so wr…wrong. Please forgive me. I denied everything I should have believed in. I un…understand this now. P…please. . . I'm s…sorry."

"Don't apologize," I raised my voice at her.

As if struck, she crumbled, tear-filled eyes wide.

"Bonnie, listen. Either we are one. . ." I swallowed- the last part of the lesson- the last test question, "either we are one or we are nothing. Do you hear me?"

Her lower lip quavered, vying with her trembling muscles. How did she keep from passing out? If I weren't ardently intent on the final answer, I would have openly marveled at her human tenacity.

"I u…understand, Riordan. I w…will never let a…anything c…come between us again. I will n…never block you again. Everything I am I g…give to you. I want, need to be one with you- as I'd always dreamed, as it's meant to be."

With each word I felt strength coming into her.

"Please, please want me still?"

The spirit's lesson was ended. Great Spirit thank you for never sending this kind of a lesson again!

From experience, I knew lessons were not generally repeated ad infinitum- one either learned or one did not remain with the spirits- hence there was not an overindulgence of shamans. The spirit guide abandoned permanently those who did not learn along their paths- therefore, it was vitally important to listen and act accordingly.

My heart began a regular, peaceful beat. Filled anew. Fueled by my love. The whole exists where the parts are insufficient unto themselves. Before Bonnie, I'd not realized this.

Now, she was more than my life, more than my world. I placed my hand on her heart. Shakily, her hand found mine.

Together we felt the renewed fusion. A great, inviolate solidity. My senses picked up the return of her shamanic powers. Within seconds, her healing subconsciously took over. The shivering ceased, the goose bumps subsided, the queasiness in her stomach disappeared.

Her pale features flushed alive, dull eyes glinted with recognition of our welding.

"Come, Wife, I've a much more comfortable place for us to adjourn to."

27

"How do you feel, Wife?" I'd catnapped on and off 'til the last hour before sunrise. No sleep soothed me as well as the sight of my Bonnie, my Wife.

Her tiny body as close to mine as possible- every one of her cells now completely tied to its reciprocal in my body. In the dark, my cat eyes savored every inch of her features as she slept peacefully. My fingers, of their own accord, gently pushed the hair back from her face.

I remembered the first time I was treated to the sight of her tawny locks hiding her face from me as she slept in class. There would be no more sleepless nights for my Wife.

I inhaled her scent- that tantalizing aroma that drew me to her in a classroom full of hopeful-eyed females. Ah. . .her scent- joyfully, I could attach my nose to her neck all day and night and suck in her addictive, natural, distinctly female, Bonnie scent.

These thoughts were moving me into a more romantic mode when her eyes- deep, laughing, green eyes, fluttered open. Our gazes locked as my eyes rose from counting and loving every freckle across her pert nose.

"How do you feel, Wife?" I repeated, as if I didn't know- our new bond, forged from the ashes of the spirits' most anguishing test of her, gave me firsthand information- very firsthand.

Enticing, pink lips curled up at the corners. She stretched, arched into me kittenish-like.

Her voice bubbled, contrary to just hours ago, "Wonderfully renewed, Riordan, thank you."

Her hands strolled up my bare chest and to my neck. Her thumb rubbed along my jugular vein. My lips descended to hers, when, surprise, surprise. . .

"Riordan, I have a question."

I groaned- how had I missed that?- too intent on. . . Sinking back into the covers, I pulled a pillow over my head.

"Riordan?" She attempted to tickle me.

Might as well get it over with. "We're not going to play 20 questions. I'll answer 2. We've a sunrise to catch."

Her eyes lit up further. How and why were we going to leave this comfortable bed to go and watch a sunrise? Think, CatSkill- has to be a private locale for a bit of. . .as the sun greeted the day.

"One," I urged her.

"I…I forgot to ask about the flood. Did m…many people d…die?" She frowned, duly concerned.

"There was an earthquake in the Mediterranean- sent out several tsunami-type waves. Whether it was coincidental or you were instrumental, damage was slight. Venice did not suffer at all. Casualties were few- mostly boaters, yacht owners who refused to read the signs and get to safety fast enough.

However, there are some new lakes- one in the Sahara, one in Saudia Arabia. . . Two," I didn't give her pause for reflection.

"Th…the Oracle?" Her gaze almost faltered.

I held her chin up. "Look at me," I said, unnecessarily, because she'd recovered herself and did not shrink from me.

"Irusan was beyond livid that her scheming nearly k…injured you. The Oracle, that one anyway, is no more. Reduced to fish food most likely.

Zander is the new Oracle- something different- a male Oracle. With any luck, he's learned from her mistakes. Now, back to more pleasant topics. . ."

I sought her mouth again, which conveniently, quickly turned. Slippery little cat. I'd have to step up my pace. If I weren't so focused on playing professor, I'd have caught her lips before they moved.

"You never mentioned her."

I stared at her. No sense of jealousy- that was good. So I gave her a second to figure it out.

"Because she wasn't important to you. Oh my! Riordan you didn't say it or think it, but. . .I…I heard it."

I chuckled, thrilled with our new closeness and the look of incredulity on her delectable face.

"Soon, we'll never have to speak at all, Wife. On second thought, though, I'd miss the sound of your voice. Speaking is good and singing- I have to sing."

Bonnie giggled, "I love it when you sing."

"You make me sing and your Lorelei call is the only siren song I've ever heard."

"My human side doesn't quite understand," her brows furrowed.

Here we go again, I nearly murmured.

"Riordan, please be patient with me. I'm still learning. I'm so glad you're not disappointed in me or angry. . ."

Hurry up, CatSkill. Got to find that private sunrise spot.

"The situation was not solely of your own making, though you could have reacted differently- you did have the right of choice. The spirits were testing you- to make sure we were indeed one. It's done, over, period.

As for your human thinking, it seems to me I told you, on our first date, in the ice cream parlor, remember? You asked if I'd 'dated' other girls. I'm a guy, Bonnie. No girls before you meant anything to me.

I'd not bore you with my change of clothing styles through the years, why bring up. . .girls? Not a subject to be discussed with one's future Wife. Look into me- you'll know exactly what I'm talking about. Understand?" Less than a few seconds. . .

"Yes, wow!"

"Wow is right. Now. . ."

"No, I meant, wow, that you wouldn't consider 'her' important. She was so beautiful, so compelling. . ."

"Nothing to me. You should feel the surety you're not quite getting yet, my young, young Wife."

I felt her wild senses exploring my inner thoughts which were getting fairly hot. A delightful probe- nothing to hide, ever.

Her blushing response signified her success at completely reading me. This new oneness. . .whew!

Something else was coming, darn it! Hold on, sun.

"Riordan, I heard voices in the wall of water," Bonnie tremulously said.

"Bonnie, you're cheating. Just because you do not phrase a statement in a questionable manner. . . You little sneak."

"Will you tell me. . .who or what was in the water?"

"Do I have a choice?" I grumbled. "The spirit of the ancient waters was affronted that some girl, shaman or no, would travel half-way around the world to tell him his business.

Call him Neptune, Poseidon, whatever. . . He was right to warn you off. We were fortunate that you are loved by spirits greater than his powers. Else, I might have lost you. . . And my own life.

Now, all that's done, over. Not one more word, if you please. The sun will not wait for us, Wife. Come!"

"What do you think?"

"Uh,. . . Where are we, besides up extremely high?" I glanced over the edge of an historic tower. Ant-like boats rocked gently in the placid, mirror waters below.

"The bell tower of San Georgio Maggiore. Neat, huh? Walk around with me."

I placed my fears and fingers in Riordan's hand and let him guide me around the small space poised high above Venezia.

Interesting how a shaman could retain some human fears- namely, my fear of heights. Not as in cabin roof high, but this tower and the roof of the Doge's palace were really. . .

"No one's perfect, Wife, though, I must say you approach perfect in my estimation."

"I'll never be as perfect as you, Riordan." Nothing bothered him, well, maybe my onslaught of questions at times.

Riordan, reading my every thought, rolled his eyes and kissed me giddy. Then turned me to face forward, into the sun.

"Venice is considered the bride of the sea, they even celebrated their union in the old days with a gold ring cast into the waters by the Doge- you are my Venice," his closeness and the tranquil footing allowed me to focus on the view and his love.

And the sun lit up the glorious museum of Venice, laid out in all of its splendor for over a thousand years in St. Mark's basin.

Riordan pointed out several sights we'd passed, but it wasn't until the sun's rays graced the Doge's palace, fired up its pink façade and the domes of St. Mark's cathedral, that I sighed with the beauty of it all and my perfect contentment in my cougar's arms.

"My last suggestion before we head home is a tiny island with a most charming church- maybe the oldest mosaics in Venice. The island, itself, may have been the origin of Venice. Archaeological evidence shows it was used by Romans.

And if we're lucky, Paolo will be busy in the kitchen. Breakfast and lemon sorbet for dessert."

"Sounds great," my stomach rumbled in expectation.

I'd spent a good half hour appreciating the golden mosaic of the Madonna holding her baby Jesus- a lovely, loving rendition. Monumental art consisting of tiny, tiny squares of gold and precious stones' colors. And Riordan had to show me the top of another bell tower.

Afternoon was well upon us as we finished our tour of Torcello, skirting a wedding in the newer church.

The last activity Riordan drew me to, was to watch an artisan glass blower, hard at work, on the island of Murano. The artist placed a gold tipped cat in my hand with a wink at my husband. A cat forged from the fire and sands of Venice- what magic!

"You can tell me how romantic I am now, Wife."

I leaned into his chest, his arms wrapped around me. "Riordan, I'm so blessed."

"As am I. . ." His focus altered.

"What is it?" I knew of his disconcert nearly the same instant he acquired it.

"We have to go- immediately!"

28

"Riordan, what is. . . Not Rick!" My stomach fell as we emerged from shadowed bushes outside Cody Hospital.

"Come, Wife. Grandfather said Rick has asked for me. There was an accident an hour ago. Rick was in a hurry to get home for his father's surprise birthday party. A semi crossed over center line, caught Rick's car. . ."

I found myself knowing everything Riordan told me a split second before he said the words. I felt every single blow to his emotions along with him. I pressed his hand to tell him, but he needed to vocalize what had happened.

Rick had become a good friend to us, and my husband, though calm, felt emotional turmoil. Please, spirits let him be all right, I prayed.

"Riordan," I stopped him outside the hospital door, "they won't let you into ICU- family only."

"Gunne's there," he replied as if that took care of everything. But Gunne was a doctor in the hospital- I had my doubts about. . .

"It's all right, Bonnie. Stay close to me. Don't touch anyone. Don't talk- we're going straight to Rick."

I didn't get a chance to ask, but my question was on the link between us.

'A little trick I picked up over the years," he'd gone silent communication.

I stuck to Riordan as if glued, his hand kept me firmly in his wake, and in wide-eyed disbelief I was towed as we wended our way through classmates keeping a vigil.

Callie and Kristin holding each other as their dates hovered, not knowing where to look or even if they should sit. A sobbing Lil was held in unfamiliar arms. Dear Rick, I'd hoped Lil and he would have the happiness that Riordan and I knew. No time to reflect on that. . .

Not a person registered our advance. Weird!

It was funereal as some of the gathered spoke softly of Rick, his love of basketball, his new-found interest in archery, as if he were already gone. Was it that dire? I glanced at others engaged in silent prayer.

I felt like shouting, 'He's not dead. All of you should be praying, pulling all your thoughts together. Positive energy.'

'Bonnie,' Riordan telepathed a warning.

"What was that?" Someone asked.

"What?"

"I. . . Somebody walked right past me," an older woman, probably an aunt, peered around.

Inadvertently, I'd almost tripped over her suitcase-sized handbag resting at her feet, and I think my arm brushed her hair before Riordan righted me. For a spirit-guided cat I had the most awkward moments at the most untoward times.

I stared back at the waiting room full of relatives and friends- sure I'd entered an Invisible Man movie set, as the elderly woman stared right through me.

"I think Rick passed. I felt him touch me as an angel. He patted my head," she started to cry.

"Ssh," a voice comforted her. A stricken man put his arm around her shoulders.

Others heard her and frantically looked for a doctor, a nurse, someone to answer THE question.

Was it true? Is Rick gone? Questions and more cries followed Riordan and me.

I bumped into Riordan, not attending where he was pulling me. The vigil-keepers were huddled, exchanging condolences and elevated cries.

I allowed my wild senses precedence. I could fathom no death- no scent of our friend's demise.

'In here,' Riordan silently directed me, and we slid through a door as smoothly as if a breeze caused the door's movement.

Dr. Gunne scrutinized our entry. The dragon had no difficulty seeing through Riordan's David Copperfield disappearing act.

Our doctor/shaman friend leaned close to Mrs. Winslow, quietly said a few words to Rick's parents with a gentle hand of solace at her elbow.

The mother, in silent tears, nodded. A stricken Mr. Winslow put a supporting arm about her waist and led her from their son's bedside. Riordan pulled me from the doorway as they exited.

Rick, face as white as his covers but marred also by dark blotches, lay hooked to various machines and fluids. The aura of death hovered, waiting patiently in the wings.

I shivered. This must be what Riordan had seen of me when I was in my coma.

The dragon's jaw clenched and he briefly shook his head.

Riordan's nostrils quivered. Together we checked all vital systems to make our own determination of Rick's condition.

I felt Dr. Gunne's diagnosis and prognosis. Hopeless. But my gut argued the point, and my husband reciprocated my decision.

Riordan released my hand. As if we were of one mind, which we indeed had become, we took our places by Rick's hospital bed.

I went to Rick's left side. Riordan stayed on our friend's right. Perhaps, this was a better job for Grace, but our newly joined strength gave me an invincible feeling. We would stare down the force that sought to take Rick from us.

Our tall friend's eyes fluttered, opened, perhaps he sensed our approach. His face took on that death-blue shade. We heard the rattle in his chest. Riordan put a hand on his arm.

"CatSkill, I...I'm...not r...ready...to d...die," an obstinate whisper barely escaped Rick's broken lips.

The bruises on his face were nearly gainsaid by the threat of death's door creaking open.

I settled my ring hand on Rick's left hand, sent a silent question to Riordan.

Bonnie had fully embraced her lesson. Our decisions would be made together- as one being, from now on.

The normal medical profession's prognosis did not offer life to our friend. Gunne, nor Grace, could intervene- Rick had asked for me, and me included my Wife. I nodded to her.

"Then we suggest you live, Rick," Bonnie encouraged with a smile. "As Dylan Thomas so aptly put it, 'do not go gently into that goodnight'".

We grounded ourselves, sought the spirits indulgence and aid for the success of our channeling healing energies of earth and air. Bonnie's stone shot silent fireworks which filled the room with shimmering, dancing rainbows as she opened the gates of healing. Nothing to do with sunlight- it was night time in Cody. Nothing to do with the ICU unit's lights. Just the magic of the stone from the stars, which worked solely for Bonnie. My strength added my all to it.

Healing frequencies flowed, bounding unleashed from our hands as if bursting from racehorse starting gates into Rick's battered body, swirling through each one of his systems, enlivening every assaulted cell.

Gunne had stepped back to give us space, but his eyes were fixed on us. I felt his healing join with ours.

Slowly, color returned to Rick's face- the blush of life. He'd closed his eyes, completely fatigued upon refusing to give up, and we watched his breathing take on Rick's signature rhythm.

The bruises became horrifically colorful- but only superficial- all below the skin healed, covertly unimpaired. His nose, though, would take on a bit of character that would only add to his charm. Rick's shattered bones knit as my teary-eyed Bonnie smiled fondly upon him. And the rainbows continued their elegant display.

The long lungs of the star basketball player had been punctured by broken ribs in several places. As the ribs returned to wholeness so did the lungs.

His left kidney had been torn from bits of annihilated hip bones. Our combined frequencies sent those bits back to be united in a solid, entirely healed hip. The kidney regenerated itself. Pooled blood and lost blood replenished and regained the correct viaducts. Vertebrae realigned.

Rick failed in his attempt to smile with his cracked lips as he felt the course of healing surge in his body, but lips, not being vital unless you're contemplating a kiss, were not a priority right now. His eyes opened willfully, languidly moved from Bonnie to me, and then flared at the dancing rainbows in teary, astonished gratitude.

Wonder and deep appreciation glowed on his face. His tears flowed; his head slowly moved on his pillow as he realized he could do so. Rick's hands tried to reach for ours.

I got misty-eyed, and Bonnie gave her tears full rein to tumble unchecked. Together we praised the spirits for coming to our aide.

"It is done. You must rest quietly, Rick. Don't think you can get up and locate a basketball right away. Wait a day or two," I joked. "Look me up, then."

"M…Matt was right," Rick managed through his drowning face. "It wasn't Dr. Gunne. You, CatSkill," his face turned to my Wife, "and you, Bonnie."

He blubbered his thanks. I was all for retreating immediately- way too much emotion. What a roller-coaster- the past 24 hours!

"Now, Rick, you mustn't cast aspersions on Dr. Gunne. He is a great doctor."

"Why, thank you, CatSkill." The dragon un-propped his leaning form from a vacant wall space and physically joined us at Rick's bed side.

He went through the unnecessary motions of checking Rick's pulse, actually pulling out a stethoscope, for the love of the spirits! And with all those noisy hospital gauges staring us in the face, save us!

"My Wife and I," Bonnie snuggled under my arm, "are simply specialists." Gunne rolled his eyes.

She raised her relieved face to mine. I kept my kiss. . .well, not too lengthy.

"I think I'm going to be sick," the good doctor's mouth twisted derisively.

"We leave him in your care, Dr. Gunne. Thank you," Bonnie said by way of good-night.

"Yes, do that, please- another miracle I'm supposed to explain," Gunne laughed. "If we're not careful, we'll be starting something akin to Lourdes or Fatima here in the good old, previously wild west. Great to have you here," Gunne offered his hand.

Grinning, I stuck out mine to shake his.

"I'm glad you're well, too, Bonnie," he offered as an aside. To which I applied a little too much pressure in our handshake.

"Take care, Rick. We'll check in on you tomorrow." Rick grinned as much as his slow-to-heal lips allowed. The most important injuries had been dealt with completely- there would be no repercussions.

"Thank you," he mouthed.

In our invisible cloak, which I was positive Bonnie was busy compiling questions about, we strolled through a now jubilant atmosphere in the waiting room, found a janitor's closet.

"Let's pick up our backpacks and get home, Wife."

"You're wonderful, Riordan," she tiptoed up to kiss me.

"I could say the same about you, Lioness," and I pulled her close in order to travel before we got carried away in the tight confines of brooms, mops and stinky cleaning solutions.

29

"Riordan, can you feel. . .?"

His lips twitched as he dipped his head and gazed at me. During our rush to the hospital and our friend's near death experience, I'd not lent focus to anything but Rick. Priorities.

But now, one remarkable eye brow rose above a glittering, gold cat eye.

"You do feel it," I said sheepishly. All of the ramifications of our new closeness had not completely settled in my psyche.

"Everything you feel, see, hear, sense, think. . . Get the picture?"

"Oh, my goodness!" I reflected on a few thoughts I had entertained in the past 24 hours.

"Yes, those thoughts too. I'm absolutely thrilled on how you wa. . ."

"I can't keep anything from you?" I blushed, thinking some things should be private. Like how I looked forward to his looking at me, his touch, the feel of his lips. . .

Oh, dear heaven, I was in trouble!

"I wouldn't exactly call it trouble, Wife," Riordan's loaded smile and glittering eyes feasted on me until I started to tremble.

One little, but promising kiss, and he explained, "To answer your question, unless we mutually agree to a block, a brief shield mind you for private surprises, we're open books for each other."

His nose skimmed my neck. Shivers rick-racked upon my skin as his lips teased along my pulse points.

"I hope I don't get the big head with all of your 'admiring thoughts'," he softly inhaled.

A giggle bubbled through my blushing unease as Riordan's amorous ideas pictured, movie-like, in my brain.

"Too much for you?" He teased me.

"I…I. . ." I fumbled, would have sunk to the ground as my knees gave way.

His soft chuckling stirred my hair. "All right, Wife. Hmmm. . . There is definitely something different in the air. It's good we're home; the crop circle did not designate a time frame, but. . . Let's get to the ranch."

To a normal person, no change in the surrounds would be evident. The sounds of an early Wyoming morning were the same. Birds twittered- leaving nesting sites in search of breakfast.

Hmmm. . .breakfast did sound good.

"Bugs?" Riordan voiced. I shuddered at his teasing suggestion.

The foliage was not in denial, the greens of the tree-lined stream were preening for their short summer stint. Cottonwood leaves stirred in the ubiquitous breezes of my home.

Antelope and mule deer sipped their dawn thirst away before foraging. What is it? What had Riordan and I sensed?

Our alarms were not ringing- whatever it was, it wasn't due, yet. The wildlife didn't seem concerned, yet. . .

"Peace, Bonnie, the spirits will reveal. . ."

"When they are ready," I knew. "Grandfather. . ."

"Yes, we'll ask Grandfather, after you fix breakfast and we should relieve your father of chores," Riordan stated as we walked home, hand in hand.

"Vacation's over," I mocked a response.

"What's the chance of cookies?"

"For breakfast dessert?"

"Or main course, why wait?" Riordan pulled me into his side as we drew near the cabin.

Sticker and Stalker raced to meet us. Barks, neighs, clucks, and the cabin walls didn't begin to hinder the meows from within. Dad burst out the cabin door with a feline retinue effervescently in tow.

"Damn, I'm glad you're home," Jim visibly exhaled by way of hello.

"Dad, you OK?" Bonnie gave her father a hug and studied him intently for signs of anything out of the ordinary.

"I don't know how I am. I guess I forgot how much this place has grown since my bachelor days. Seems I've become a personal valet to a zoo full of critters. And I'm not just talking about the horses."

"Or chickens?" Bonnie added.

"Or dogs?" I thought I'd add my two cents.

"Must mean Amore. . ."

"And her kittens," Bonnie and I fell in step with finishing each other's sentences.

My Wife dropped to the ground and was inundated with the feline contingent, some of which clawed their way up my legs. As head cat, I'd have to do something about these tiny, clawed creatures. Manners, manners.

"Hungry, Dad?"

"You bet I am, honey."

"How's my favorite horse?" I called over to Handsome as Bonnie went to pet his cavorting self. Talk about attention-getters.

Bonnie mused, 'If we get this kind of movement at our first show, we'll blow the judges away.'

'Missing my favorite girl,' the beast shot back at me- my fault for bearing her away.

"Now, be good, and we'll practice later," she assured him.

The black beast rested his muzzle in her neck, gently whuffling.

'Watch it beast, that's my territory,' I warned him. I refrained from hissing- I did owe him something.

'Sharing is a virtue,' the stallion reared his head.

'Handsome, where did you come up with that?'

'Good question, Wife,' I mused. But the stallion remained imperiously mute on that point.

Super, Cali, Fragi, Listic, Expe, Ali and Docious perched on various places that should have been off limits. And Amore regally rested on my dad's lap.

I drew out eggs, bacon, biscuit-makings, and shredded potatoes for hash browns. All with a pert black nose examining every bit of edibles from the balcony of my shoulders.

"Kitten, cookies?"

"Maybe for lunch, Riordan." Disgruntled, he nevertheless kissed my cheek before sliding into a kitchen chair.

The cheeky little Docious picked that moment to steal a slice of bacon, and ran off with her siblings in nosy, noisy, hot pursuit.

"See what I mean. It's a circus around here," my dad quibbled until Amore meowed and rubbed her puss along my dad's jaw line. "Well, maybe not that bad."

Riordan winked at me, 'They're training him well.' I stifled a laugh.

I dished out three plates after filling kitty bowls and joined my dad and Riordan.

"You guys should slow down when you eat- better for the digestion; I'll make more, sheesh!" Dismayed, I watched food disappear at an alarming rate. A biscuit surreptitiously found a convenient pocket.

I managed to snatch the last biscuit from Riordan- a biscuit-hoarder every bit the equal of my dad, slipped another batch of biscuits in the oven and fried more bacon.

"I never realized how smart cats are," my dad managed in between sharing bacon pieces with Amore and dipping biscuits and hash browns in egg yolks.

"You don't say, sir," Riordan bristled.

'Riordan, he didn't mean it that way,' I silently soothed my husband.

"When I was a baby, the doctor told my mother I was allergic to cats, so they were pretty much banned from the ranch, except for a few, mostly feral ones, that kept the mice and rat population under control in the barn.

I guess I've outgrown those allergies, if I ever really had them. My father claimed to hate cats. But, these kittens, I swear. . ."

"Sir, a cat is as close to a wild animal. . ."

"As today's human will allow in their house," I finished for Riordan.

"I can see that." He gave us a puzzled look. "Now, a young dog left on its own- wouldn't give much for its chances, but a young cat. . . I mean these little tykes play hunt and are so agile and curiously into everything."

At that moment, Super gained the counter and was diligently investigating. . .

"Bonnie, any chance of getting some of that bacon before it burns or Super figures out how to use a spatula? See what I mean? If I didn't know better, I'd almost believe these guys are psychic. Not that I can find it anymore, but I don't need my alarm clock. I'm pretty good with my internal alarm going off, but if I'm a second late, all hell breaks loose. A parade of cats races across me. A meowing station opens up in various vocal ranges in true surround sound.

Fragi, I think it is, can even flip on the light switch. Unbelievable," my dad refilled his plate. "How was your camping trip?"

"Fine, Dad."

"Fine, sir," Riordan and I answered together.

My dad paused in his food shuffling and eyed Riordan and me. "What did you two do? Never mind, don't answer that."

He glanced speculatively between Riordan and me, frowned and continued. "You seem different- the same, but different." Confused, he massaged his neck.

Riordan grinned, his eyes caressed me. "You might say, sir. . ."

"That we renewed our vows," I grinned back at Riordan.

My dad's jaws stopped chewing, tried to swallow, choked, coughed, wiped at his mouth and gulped his juice.

"What did I say about eating so fast?" I took his plate away, but his hand shot out and stopped me.

"Renewed your vows? You've only been married. . .not even 6 months?"

"You're right, sir."

"Why wait so long?" I asked.

"Every month," Riordan winked.

"Every day," I winked back.

"Every minute," he rejoined.

"Every second," I was not to be outdone.

"Sorry I said anything," my dad muttered.

Jim entered the barn, hesitated. I gave Bonnie a 'heads up'.

He stared outside, at the sky, the ground, the resting dogs, foraging chickens, placid horses, sniffed the wind. Now this was very interesting. . .

"Kids," he wasn't sure about what he ached to confide. "If you were normal, young people, I'd not broach the subject," his cap came off, dusted against his leg. "I'd not even bring this up with my oldest friends, but. . ."

I was surprised when he bit his lower lip. Laying aside our stall cleaning tools, I took Bonnie's hand and walked closer to my father-in-law, the least nosy human I'd ever met.

"What is it, Jim? I know something is bothering you."

In turn, he studied Bonnie, then me, and reached a decision.

"I've lived here all my life. Always felt part of all this," he waved his hand at the outdoors. "Lately, I get the feeling that. . . I don't know, exactly, but there's a premonition in my gut. It's a big one and I don't like it. That business with the ghosts and all took me completely by surprise. Normally, I've an inkling when things are about to go wrong. The air. . . I sense something, and I don't think it's good."

30

"CatSkill, Bonnie!" A much improved version of our friend, Rick, exited his vehicle and excitedly hurried to us. His long, going-places stride and return-to-normal skin color heralded his well-being.

"Rick, hey!" Hand out, Riordan's graceful, long legs extended to greet his enthusiastic, friendly, first-rate basketball competitor.

I sensed Riordan throwing out his shamanic tentacles- physically, Rick was in great shape. Mentally, his psych exploded with questions. I could certainly relate to that. Riordan winked at me, recognizing our mutual exam of Rick's mental status.

They shook hands. No qualm on Riordan's part, for which I was grateful. We had come so far together and in such a short time. Absolutely remarkable!

"Great to see you up and about, Rick," my husband tapped Rick's shoulder.

Rick's eyes sidled to my Wife. Silently, I gave her the go-ahead. She stepped into his embrace, returned his hug of brotherly affection. Unlike Gunne, who still harbored a painful passion for Bonnie.

"I...I need to talk with you, uh, are you busy?" Rick looked around, nervous and hopeful at the same time.

"Nah, just headed over to Grandfather's. C'mon, let's sit by the creek and catch up."

Rick had never exhibited a nervous moment, not in all his pre-game warm-ups, not in entering our wraith war. . . But something about a near-death experience will make a thinking body stop and really think.

"My parents," he ducked his head, "my parents think I should go into the ministry, be a priest, or something along those lines. Because of. . . They consider my being here a miracle. Becoming a doctor isn't enough, now, as they see it.

I know the miracle part is true. But, the miracle is because of you, Riordan and Bonnie. I can't pretend to know how you did it or even begin to understand that mess back in May. I do feel, with absolute certainty, that my path includes the two of you.

I don't mean to force myself on you. . ."

"Nothing like that, Rick. Don't ever feel that way. We're friends, right? We were simply acting as conduits for the Divine. It wasn't your time to go." Bonnie's hand rested inside my elbow and she cheerily smiled at Rick.

Not entirely convinced, he nodded. "Yeah, I guess so. Since. . .since you helped me. . .uh, I…I see things."

Bonnie leaned into me.

"See things?" I echoed. This came as a surprise. What had we done to Rick besides heal his body?

"I haven't told anyone this. Not even Dr. Gunne, though I feel like I could have told him. I see. . .auras- energy fields. . .around. . .around everyone. Colors, moving. . ." Rick's dark eyes, framed by bare shadows of circles underneath and furrowed brow, waited, hopefully expectant, for our response.

"Colors, Rick?" It was Bonnie's turn to echo. Gave me time to think. As the more experienced of the two of us, I sent out a quick question of my own into the spirit world.

"Sometimes colors, usually an opaque, wavering light. I witnessed the EMT's bringing in a man who had had a heart attack. I saw a light, uh, his spirit, I guess, ascend from his body as they wheeled him into the emergency room. Later, I heard he'd died, before entering the emergency room. I see colors with Dr. Gunne. . .and with you." Rick eyed us speculatively.

'Riordan, what does this mean?'

'Our friend has reached an accord with the spirits. He needs help to determine his future,' I silently replied.

'Shaman?'

'Possibly,' I allowed.

Rick's hands rubbed together. He patted his thighs, preparatory to leaving, thinking we'd written him off.

"Go on, Rick. Tell us all of it." I saw tremendous relief in the slump of his previously rigid shoulders. There are times when a person needs a supportive ear, a non-judgmental one. And if one is lucky, a knowledgeable mentor. Or two as one.

"Dr. Gunne's aura is a pastel rainbow. Not only do I see it, but I…I feel an energy emanating from him."

"Anything else you see in or around Dr. Gunne?" I kept my poker face while my brain cells did jumping jacks in expectation of what was coming. Bonnie's bloodstream raced equally with mine.

Rick's nervous eyes didn't waver this time. He realized he'd encountered the listening souls he needed.

"In the aura surrounding Dr. Gunne, I catch a glimpse of an oriental-style dragon. Not full on, not articulate in all of its parts- just a shifting shape."

Bonnie and I shared our fascination. "And you've not told anyone?"

"Are you kidding? If I asked the minister at our church, I'm sure he'd be sympathetic, tell me to pray and rest, all the while wondering about my sanity. If I told my parents, they'd probably recommend a psychiatrist outright for help in dealing with my 'miracle', and to play it safe, also order my brain tested. I just need. . .I need to have you tell me. . .I know I'm not crazy.

I know you two are very special. I'd hoped you, Riordan, would be able to heal me. Dr. Gunne was attending that night in the emergency room. I begged him to contact you, and in no time you were there. Like angels. . . I don't understand any of this, but I want to. I want to so bad I can hardly stand it.

I really see. . .see that Matt was absolutely right. 'It's the CatSkills,' he said. Both of you." Rick's eyes softened, near tears, looking with beyond normal human sight and extreme yearning at me and Bonnie.

"Rick, what do you see when you look at us?" I felt Bonnie's senses, linked with mine, mindfully studying Rick.

He paused, swallowed hard, and his face lit up with his eyes eagerly 'reading' our otherness.

"A vibrant rainbow of colors, every shading from pale hues to an intense depth of every color of the rainbow and all of those in-between. An entire living spectrum. You're beautiful. And there's no separation between you. When I stepped out of the car, Riordan, you were the first to reach me, but the colors filled the area between you and Bonnie."

"And?" Bonnie further urged as Rick's enthusiasm caused his tongue to fumble in its search for the correctly descriptive words.

"Your shadow animals are. . .cougars. And I catch faint glimpses of other animals with you, especially you, Riordan. Help me to understand this. . .this gift."

"Have you seen animals in other auras?"

"No," Rick raised his head to the sun, breathed deeply. "But, I can see energies around these trees, plants, rocks, water, the animals here. Around every object, whether it's considered alive by science or not."

"Rick, I apologize for not being there after your sweat ceremony. Grandfather said you were pretty quiet, and didn't want to talk. Will you tell me what the spirits' message to you was?"

"'You are where you are supposed to be.' I heard it clearly, from where I don't know. Whether inside of me or out, I couldn't say, but I did hear the voice. I've thought a lot about that. Not sure if I'm supposed to go back to college or stay here. I am sure about the two of you, though."

'I think we have to tell him,' Bonnie sent to me. I agreed.

"Rick, have you ever heard of shamans?"

"Aboriginal healers?" His face was completely open. Luckily, as someone interested in the field of healing, he'd studied holistic-wise, and not with the short-sighted mentality of corporate-backed, so-called western doctors.

My smile got sort of twisted, "That's only part of it. I promise to go into this in-depth the first chance we have, but right now, something else extremely important needs to be addressed."

Rick glanced away, wondering if he was being put off in a nice fashion.

"No, we're not putting you off." That surprised him. I laughed, extremely happy for my friend. "You're not crazy, I promise."

"Rick, can you feel anything different in the air?" Bonnie asked out of curiosity- very cat-like.

Rick inhaled, trying to use powers he'd not yet been fully gifted with or apprised of. "Only the electrical charge between you and Riordan."

'Go ahead, Wife.'

"Riordan and I are shamans, as is Dr. Gunne," she said.

No surprise to Rick in our admission. The ramifications, though, would probably come as a bit of a shocker. But, then again, after the wraith war and what was coming up, maybe not.

'Riordan, we don't have to tell him everything,' Bonnie leaned into me.

"We will answer all your questions, just not right now," I promised.

"Can you tell me, for now, why are Dr. Gunne's colors so pale compared to yours?"

Interesting. Nothing about dragons or cougars, but the vibrancy of colors. Too much for him to handle, as of yet? Or maybe not. . . Something for us to ponder, when time allowed.

"Dr. Gunne is a pacifist. When you asked him to call me to you in the hospital, you effectively tied his hands in so far as healing you. That's all right, you couldn't have known, but the Great Spirit directed you."

Puzzled, Rick frowned, held up his hand, "How could a dragon in his aura be considered pacific?"

"Indeed," I chortled, only to be reprimanded by Bonnie's swift gig in my ribs.

My Wife addressed his question. "Rick, you're thinking along the lines of how westerners view dragons. The east sees the dragon in a completely different light- as a protector and bringer of luck, and in the old days a harbinger of rain." Bonnie's arched brows in my direction caused me to pull her into a satisfying, but all too brief, kiss. Which brought on a beautiful blush.

"Lucky for me he was there in emergency that night," Rick dropped his head into his hands- emotional upheaval at what Gunne's absence might have meant for his longevity.

"Cheer up, Rick. You're in for the ride of your life. Whatever your path is, we'll be there to help. As for Bonnie's and my auras, we're much more territorial and up for battles, so to speak. Not to mention, being in love and married- heavy duty colorations."

'I believe the spirits have brought us a student, Kitten,' I silently informed Bonnie. 'Day after tomorrow, we'll all go to Grandfather's. I think your father should come too.'

Bonnie's protective feelings for her father caused her to begin chewing her lower lip, indecisively.

'Remember, Wife, he now has an inside track, and he feels the change in the air. You can't put him off his scent- he won't let you.' This didn't quite relieve her.

I held her tight, and asked Rick to join us on the day after tomorrow. Meantime, we had to go. Plans.

31

"It seems forever since we've had a good, long run," I stretched up to the sky, bent over backwards and then forward to touch my toes. The flexibility of cats is phenomenal.

"Do I detect a challenge in the lilt of your voice?"

I smiled sweetly and winked at my bare-chested husband. Axe in hand, he was lording it over a hill of freshly split kindling. Promptly, the ax propped against the trunk used to chop wood. Riordan took his time stalking me, flexing various muscles, fervid gold eyes hooded by profuse, black lashes.

"Did you just wink at me, Lioness?"

"And if I did?" Was I being provocative?

"Mmm. . ." he grinned and his hands shot out, pulled me close. A nibble on my ear, a whiff at my neck and a caress of his lips on mine and then. . .

I broke out laughing, as his fingers tickled my sides. No getting away, I was held fast.

"R…R…Riordan," I couldn't catch my breath.

About that time, my dad pulled into the drive. He gave us a wide berth, shaking his head, stopped on the porch to watch.

With an eye on my dad observing us, Riordan made a suggestion. "Maybe, I need to cool you off." One glorious brow rose and he sent me a picture of the horses' watering trough.

By this time, the dogs were jumping about, sensing the fun- Sticker barking and Stalker putting his nose to the best effect. Too much racket transpiring, the peace-loving chickens, under Hector, the boss rooster's guidance, headed for cover. Handsome snorted jealously. Hoss and Lil Joe figured it was business as usual, and kept their muzzles focused in their strewn-about hay.

"Hey kids, before you turn this place completely into Bedlam, how about dinner?"

Saved by my dad's stomach.

'For now,' Riordan leered. 'After dinner it's on, Kitten.'

"Keep close to me tonight."

"Afraid I'll outrun you?"

"In your dreams, Road Runner." Riordan's nose sidled along my jugular vein. "It's where you are in your cycle- stay close. I don't want to have to kick any bear butt defending your honor."

My face fired up with this pronouncement. No semblance of privacy between us, sheesh!

Out of sight and scent of home, Riordan and I slipped into our wild natures- avidly desirous of racing each other. I felt wondrously as much at home in my cougar body, as in my flannel shirt and jeans- long trial of mishaps behind me, thankfully.

Thrilled to the core with my supple elongated frame, I released and scathed claws, gave myself a spate of giggles twitching my tail.

'You were born for this, Wife,' Riordan complimented. 'Uh, if you could hold off on those tail maneuvers for now. . .'

Could a cat blush? Hastily, I stilled my long cat tail. Riordan's heated thoughts- whew!

'It's great to take my love of long distance running into a body that would rather lie patiently, spring suddenly and sprint.'

'A melding of two species' talents,' Riordan's chest rumbled his hearty accord, and he rubbed his whiskered cat muzzle against mine.

In unison, as if an invisible starting shot fired and ushered us on, we spurted from a standstill, headed west.

Skirting the reservoir, clinging to shadows in the cool night, we amicably raced.

'That all you got, Lioness?' Until, Riordan issued the first challenge.

Without a hiss, I put on a burst of speed, felt my lithe cougar's body hug the ground, haunches propelling me, kicking out bits of dirt and rock at the surprised Riordan who was briefly left to eat my dust. Beep! Beep!

My tail flicked his nose right before he gained on me and playfully barreled into my side.

'Cheater!' I howled- oops, wrong word- as he knocked me off stride, and I rolled, coating my tan fur with dust.

In scrambling to right myself, I came up between Riordan's extra-long cougar frame and an ominous snarl cast from above.

Ears flat back, teeth bared, tail thrashing to and fro- my cougar reciprocated, defying the testing stranger- a male cougar.

'Peace,' Riordan's eyes glowered, belying the possibility of the truce indicated in 'peace'; his teeth fastened on the scruff of my neck, and he deftly set me behind him.

That was going to cost him later- I mused on the indignity of being hoisted like a tiny, errant kitten, and I addressed our potential adversary from Riordan's nether region, 'We mean no harm.'

My green cat eyes fastened on his as I peeked around; Riordan's never left off- his male prowess heightened by the anticipation of feline battle. Although he remained temperate, I felt Riordan on guard.

With no further challenge issuing from my cougar, the unknown male stood down, prepared, but patient. His ears perked; he would listen.

'This territory is taken, but I think you knew that,' Riordan offered.

'I had no choice but to come this way. Others are seeking paths out of this place. Something bad is coming. It's impossible not to affront someone's home turf,' the stranger rejoined.

'Why are you on the move? It's past mating season. What is it you sense?'

'I'm not the only one, though the cougars are some of the first to abandon known territories. The slower species are beginning to gather and move. The pronghorn have already left. Their migrating patterns may be the death of them as they refuse to deviate from their age-old routes which have been compromised. All of our wild has been undermined. . .' he grievously broke off.

'It's the change in the air?' I asked the male.

'You are going the wrong way,' he simply sighed.

'Have you felt rumblings from inside the earth?' Riordan asked.

'If I waited to feel such, I'd be as stupid as the two-leggeds. Nature warns those in tune with her ways. Others will pay the price. The dogs, for once, have shown a lick of cat sense. The Hayden valley pack and offshoots are gone. There is no safe direction. Guns await. . . I'm not even sure mileage will provide a true haven, if any of us can find a free path.'

'Have the bison begun to move?'

'Not yet. They are gathering. But, as huge animals that need to walk or run the earth, they have many enemies- no matter which way they turn.'

'Riordan?'

'In a moment, Bonnie.'

'Will you allow me safe passage or do we fight?' The cougar inquired- equally at-ease with either scenario.

'Of course- go with our best wishes, but please refrain from all domestic animals while in our territory.'

The cougar slunk down the boulder-strewn height, his senses open to potential pursuit, and he remained vigilant until well out of sight.

'It's Yellowstone, isn't it? Why are there no signs?'

'Nature is providing the initial warnings- you sensed the change in the air. Remember the tsunami a few years back? The wildlife sought the high ground. . .'

'While the tourists and others. . .' I shivered.

'Yellowstone is the only potentially volatile aspect in our sphere. I'd assumed earthquake or volcano- could be a combination of both. We've got trouble, Wife.'

'Riordan, if the bison try to leave, they'll be shot by those not about to attempt understanding of the situation. Fences won't hold them. . . The ranchers. . .' I tried not to think of a massive buffalo slaughter the likes not seen since the railroads swept through and passengers killed the massive, Lakota-loved Tatanka for fun. Just for the hell of it, for pity's sake!

'Listen, Wife. We have a little time with the buffalo. Right now, it's the pronghorn that must be our priority.'

'The bottlenecks on their migratory paths,' I exclaimed.

'Exactly.' I felt Riordan's inner turmoil- it was my own. His favorite game involved teasing the antelope- he called it antelope tag- sans claws. I hadn't yet been made privy to what the antelope thought of the whole ordeal, I momentarily mused, but felt sure I'd eventually be presented with the opportunity to indulge in the game.

'With the summer tourist traffic and developers. . .'

'They'll not stand a chance. It's bad enough in spring and fall when they move from the Grand Tetons to the upper Green River. Come, Wife. We're going to need help.'

I sent out a calling card- one with a note of emergency. I'd traveled with Bonnie to a knoll at a place called Trapper's Point to wait for a response, knowing it would not take long.

An historical placard explained about the white fur trappers and Nez Perce and Crow peoples who'd gathered at this point to trade during the fur-trapping heyday of boisterous rendezvous. Liquor swilling and unchecked gambling. . .but I digress.

The fast-moving pronghorn had already navigated another bottleneck to the north along their 7000 year-old, 170-mile long migration route which now ended in a natural gas dotted minefield.

As the encountered cougar had said, the pronghorns were wired to one path, right or wrong. Increased development or not, the animals would not be swayed; thus it should have been up to the so-called 'intelligent species' to acquiesce, the earth belonged to all, by virtue of the Great Mystery!

Fast moving tourist traffic, added to the regular inhabitants' driving, made it a real crapshoot for the original denizens, my antelope friends- a carnival game ready to happen. Let's play dodge the cars- if we miss, we die. I felt my bile-flecked ire rise.

Other species also used this corridor, but the pronghorns had a few disadvantages. They relied on keen vision and 60mph speeds to escape predators. Safer forest and willow bottomlands' paths were therefore out of the question. Pronghorn used high, open routes between river and woods. They went under fences- no jumping over. An unhindered snarl issued from my gut.

'Easy, Riordan. They're not here, yet; we need to think. What can we do?' Bonnie's brain whirred seeking an answer a mathematician's brain could not provide.

"CatSkill, old friend."

"Osiris." I sensed another feminine presence near.

"Isis came to watch," my godly friend surveyed the area. Below us, the pronghorns' would-be crossing point lay- a busy, well-used highway.

My calling card had included a succinct description of the problem.

"Thank you for coming," Bonnie welcomed Osiris and Isis.

"We must extend our gratitude to you, also," the God and Goddess replied, but Bonnie ducked their attention.

'Riordan, what can he possibly do?' I laughed at Bonnie's silent question.

Osiris roared, once I interpreted. The girls exchanged looks. I read Bonnie's 'are our men crazy?' thought.

"Ideas, Osiris?" I asked.

My Egyptian friend crossed his arms, "Several- none of which are politically correct, but, what a grand time! Ah, well, to business. Bonnie, I'll need your help. See those sign posts?" Osiris pointed to 2 poles north of the pronghorns intended crossing point.

Bonnie nodded, perplexed, but willing.

"I'll need you to stop the traffic while I create a corridor, otherwise there will be human fatalities."

The way Osiris said the last part, it was pretty obvious human fatalities would not have concerned him overly much.

Osiris grinned, "Non-thinking humans should have solved this problem long before now. I guess I'll have to provide the impetus. May I suggest a well-placed bolt of lightning? Fell those poles on the highway, create a massive bonfire- if seen far enough in the distance, the drivers will at least slow down, maybe even brake if they engage their brains fast enough. We'll need this diversion for the north and south bound lanes."

Osiris, used to being obeyed, did not expect any quibbling from Bonnie. To my surprise, he didn't get any, not a single question. My jaw did the proverbial drop. Not even a hint of 'I'm not sure I can do it.' It seems I needed to take a course from Osiris.

'Don't even think it, Riordan.'

Right. What was I thinking?

"CatSkill, I'll need eyes above the ground. Warn us when there is a break in the traffic flow- give Bonnie a signal."

In a flash, my raven guise soared high. The new traffic reconnaissance-copter- filmed at 11, I cawed.

"Osiris," my acute hearing picked up Isis' silky voice. "They're coming! The pronghorn- they're just over the rise."

"Can you hold them, my love?"

"I'll try."

I felt Bonnie trying to split her job in two directions. Bonnie would be able to stop the pronghorn antelope- they'd listen to her. I didn't know of Isis' qualifications in that department.

'Now, Bonnie!' I telepathed a signal. 'A long break in the southbound lane between a black SUV and a slowing semi. And an even longer break in the northbound lane. No vehicles in sight.'

Intend, Irusan had said. All you need. Intend and ask.

I implored the spirits for the good of all creatures and raised my ring.

I felt my cells sizzle with a force I was only a conduit for. From a cloudless sky a rumble of thunder started out. Muted at first, it drew force, and reached a crescendo as a huge, electrical bolt streaked from the night sky, hurtling at my direction to the base of the electric poles.

The black of night turned day-bright as forks of eye-blinding white gashes gouged the sky, descending, gathering power, pin-pointing telephone poles and sign posts.

The crack of the thunder-announced lightning bearing on the posts assaulted our hearing, and the crash of the poles across the lanes was whisper-soft in comparison.

I breathed my thanks to the Divine, and watched spellbound as an unfueled bonfire soared 30, 50, 90 feet into the night sky- upping the temperature to record heights. No driver could miss the intense red-orange glow igniting the night.

What happened next? Hard to explain. Osiris stepped to the crossing point. I heard the rush of a startled herd of pronghorns. . .

Innately, I sent a quieting essence to the herd- a message they would understand. Isis stood like an angel before them- trying to protectively hold the puzzled antelope, their huge eyes nervously sparking to and fro.

Throwbacks to ancient creatures- the mammals with the longest migrating pattern in the continental US- the beautiful-eyed, harmless, God-given gifts huddled, disoriented.

Slowly, my message soothed them. Slowly, they settled, but their eyes were wary, watching.

My focus returned to Osiris as my calming frequency stayed with the pronghorn. Riordan, with a rush of raven's wings, landed next to me in his human form. His arms encased me.

And Osiris- approximating the biblical parting of the Red Sea. . .

Lit by the bonfire spotlight, the asphalt crossing point rolled in retreat- one lane returned north and the south lane rolled back to the south- giant snakes silently surrendering to an unbelievable force. The in-between section fluidly rose- a perfect, clay path arched bridge to match the preceding dirt trail the antelope occupied. Spellbound, I watched a God at work.

"Release the animals, my love. Bonnie, keep your calming essence in play. You may douse the bonfire some, if you like," he chuckled.

My stone flashed playfully and the tremendous fire banked to a mere 10 feet or so- a soft, lovely light to watch a miracle by.

Traffic backed up in both directions, but eerily, no one laid on their horns. Emergency lights flashed to warn approaching vehicles in the surreal surround.

In droves, people exited their cars, walked calmly to the edge of the broken highway; some climbed atop cars to achieve a better vantage point.

A parade of nature's wonders, bent on escaping the summer range months early because nature had issued a warning, stepped across Osiris' homemade path and continued on their ancient route.

Many humans would never witness anything like this- enraptured, they watched the unprecedented unfolding.

A muffled clapping erupted- applause of amazed approval, it gathered momentum. Discovering their way unimpeded, the pronghorn picked up speed and fled across the new path- hopefully to safety, I prayed.

"CatSkill, my friend, this would be a most appropriate time to fill these humans' heads with helpful hints."

I felt Riordan's hypnotic frequency reach out to penetrate the by-standers brains. The message: you can do more to appreciate and help wildlife- learn. Do not dither or remain idle.

"I love to watch my husband in action," Isis whispered to me as she took Osiris' arm.

"I know exactly how she feels, Riordan." This earned me a kiss.

32

"So this is your wild west, CatSkill- land of Buffalo Bill, fast gunslingers, Washakie. . ."

"Let's not dwell on the past, shall we?" I appreciated Osiris empathizing with my home turf even as I cut short his memory-spew; after all, he'd been around much longer than I had and consequently seen lots more, too. "Actually, I prefer your take on the 'wild west'."

The four of us, couple to couple, hidden by shadows, stared at Osiris' destructed construct.

"I especially like how you raised the pronghorns' path," I admired the lithe animals traipsing across their brand new, inviolate track- part of me itched to play tag. Priorities, priorities. . .

"The news agencies' explanation of this will be very interesting," Isis leaned her head into Osiris' black silk clad chest.

"Do you think they'll get the message?" Bonnie asked of no one in particular.

The antelope, previously hesitant, accepted Bonnie's auspicious assurance and merrily made use of their ancient, renewed migrating corridor, incongruously seeking protection in a natural gas minefield. What a travesty so-called civilization had wrought!

"They'll get the message eventually. Repetition works wonders. And I do not shrink from reminding even the most deaf and blind of humans," Osiris promised.

"My husband is such a perfectionist- notice how the road's lanes are rolled back like artisan, cinnamon rolls. Not a crumb out of place," Isis proudly proclaimed.

"It seems the appreciative audience is in no hurry," I mused.

Folk in conversational cliques idly watched-many with silly grins of wonder on their faces. Amazingly, no one expressed perturbation at the delay of their vacation or homeward drives. No one exhibited distress at the implacable lack of continuous road. No one gave it a thought about how they were going to get wherever they were going.

"There is hope for the human who can still feel awe," Osiris sighed.

"Did someone say something about cinnamon rolls?"

"Riordan!" Bonnie chided me. "You just ate!"

"That was hours ago, Wife. You didn't perchance pack a sandwich for my suffering stomach, did you?"

"Or cookies?" Osiris cut in.

"Oh brother," Bonnie and Isis rolled their eyes and chorused together.

"Let's seek nourishment for my raven lookout. I think a sandwich sounds like a good idea," Osiris sided with me.

"Like a double date?" Bonnie got all 17-year old, girly excited.

'What's wrong with that?' she telepathed.

'Nothing, not a thing. I didn't say anything.'

'No, but you thought it,' she silently quibbled.

This kind of togetherness was going to get me in trouble, I could see it now.

We located a mom and pop hamburger shop- standing room only. After one bite we all understood why.

"Homemade hamburgers- in a restaurant of all places."

"With long slices of dill pickles."

"Real cheese and real hamburger- no fillers!"

"Tomatoes that taste like tomatoes."

Finishing my third burger, I had to go for dessert. I couldn't decide between ice cream floats and pie, so I had one of each. Bottomless pit- that's me. Bonnie was used to my appetite, but Osiris and Isis chortled, Isis cradled in his arms.

I had a question I couldn't wait to ask, but felt silly asking.

"What is it, Kitten?"

I blushed as Osiris and Isis smiled at our reading each other's thoughts. The striking God and Goddess sat in a simple restaurant booth, surrealistically out-of-place, yet it seemed the restaurant customers didn't see them as I did.

Osiris with his perfect profile, black, flashing eyes, long black hair, immaculate goatee and mustache. Isis, dressed in dark blue, with her silver-blonde hair, black brows and blue-green chameleon eyes.

"First things first. I believe our friends have a glamour about them- not the glamor of Hollywood stars, but sort of a lens cloak that makes them more ordinary looking, keeps them from standing out."

Riordan's explanation stirred my curiosity, but I had something pressing, niggling at me.

"I…I've never attempted using several skills at once."

Osiris looked blank. Riordan's lips twitched, and he playfully ruffled my already mussed-up hair.

"I couldn't hold the entire herd of antelope," Isis admitted ruefully. "I've only ever worked with one or two animals at a time. Bonnie felt the herd's distress and. . ."

"Talked to them in antelope," Riordan added.

"I…it seemed natural to call on lightning, and talk to the pronghorn at the same time. Like my energies were going where they were needed without hindering my focus in either direction. It's just that. . .I was surprised, and I don't understand how. . .how it all worked."

"The spirits work in their own way, Kitten," Riordan offered.

"You were wonderful, Bonnie. I know we will be good friends," Isis' congenial gaze supportively graced me. I reveled in the import of her statement. Her offer of friendship, her innate acceptance, came from a childhood as bereft of human friends as mine had been.

My husband broached the burgeoning frisson with a suggestion. "Osiris, had enough amusement for one night?"

"By all means, let's continue. Lead on, CatSkill."

"Riordan?"

"I'm sure Osiris can deal with another bottleneck in the pronghorn's migratory path and after that. . ."

"The buffalo!"

Riordan nodded, "Osiris, we believe we have our own imminent cataclysm to deal with."

Osiris sat quietly, inquisitive, communing with. . . I couldn't say who, other Egyptian Gods?

"Your Yellowstone Park is really a caldera- the remains of a super volcano," the God interpreted. "Cataclysm, indeed," he looked at me intently, until I felt Riordan's chest rumble a warning.

"Can you help guide the buffalo from the park when they're ready to leave, whether quietly or stampeding?" I distracted Riordan by tickling his full belly. Trying to tickle- his taught muscles didn't give me a chance for success.

"You're speaking to an animal guide par excellent," Osiris bragged. "Seeing how we work so well together, let's attend to this funnel you spoke of, and then, a brief overlook at possible buffalo routes."

Environmentalists and newscasters alike would have a field day with the continuation of Osiris' artistry.

A portion of the pronghorn's route was less than 200 yards wide, and developers were besieging the territory around this section.

"Simple fix," Osiris grinned, scrutinizing the over-wrought ground.

Isis and I tended several injured, stranded antelope which had got tangled in orange, caution fence at the dig site. Not that the developers were concerned a whit, but no one could have foreseen the antelope precipitously abandoning their summer range in hopes of outrunning whatever they'd sensed was imminent.

It was probably slated by the developers that the site would have offered a clear path of sorts in the fall, but it was a sure bet it would not be the most appropriate one for the animals.

Civilization only regarded the monetarily-endowed as worthy- wild animals and their homes were so far down the list as not to exist.

After we sent the recovered antelope off to join their kith and kin, Osiris dealt the landscape a remodeling job- Green Man style. Everything: heavy equipment, port-o-lets, fences, generators, construction office trailer etc. was sundered into sweep-able pieces with a single deep breath. At which point, Osiris motioned with his hands as if using a broom, and all and sundry bits of metal and detritus were moved back, way back, out of the way, creating a huge dump pile.

To top off the unsavory sight, Osiris' hands rose form his sides and trees- I'm not fibbing- surged from the new pyramid and leafed as they soared.

One hand rose and the cleared ground lifted higher and higher and extended itself, widening and lining up with the migratory corridor on both sides of the bottleneck.

"That should just about do it," Osiris chuckled as Isis clapped her hands in appreciation of his special 'resurrection' technique. "Any vile substances have been- uh, disbanded, and sent to the nearest black hole containment," he assured us of the inviolability of the new pristine layout he'd engendered.

I was thinking thoughts I couldn't voice as my jaw was locked open, in astonishment, with what I had just witnessed. Within seconds, Osiris had silently, comprehensively, rearranged the developers' site.

Come to think of it, the only sounds of his previous redecoration had been the thunder and lightning I'd called in and maybe a few protesting brakes. No one would recognize the area, and I giggled thinking of the construction crew and head honchos' expressions when they showed up for work. How wonderful! Talk about powerful friends!

Riordan was amused by my being dumbstruck. This didn't happen often. He laughed, head turned to the sky almost as if he were ready to howl with delight.

"I could do that, you know," he winked at me. "But you, who can call lightning, stop floods, talk to animals and who knows what all else, are struck dumb by this?" He pulled me into his arms.

"Bonnie wants to know what will stop the developers from returning and undoing your lovely handiwork?" Riordan had gleaned my rising concern before I had time to put it to words.

"I've put convenient fractures in as preventative measures. The weight of the pronghorn herd will be acknowledged and accepted by this ground. Anything else- machinery, for instance, will cause an earthquake of sorts that will decimate developers' dreams," Osiris' eyes gleamed.

"I'm speaking literally as well as figuratively. I've made this so very clear that a high school geology student will understand the ramifications of any developers' incursions. And if they dare to brook my fail-safes, I will be immediately apprised. The antelope will not suffer, as their path will spontaneously regenerate as needed, and I will assiduously hunt down the malefactors- nowhere to hide, eh, CatSkill? "

"Call me if you wish a bloodhound companion. Off to Yellowstone?" Riordan's lips twitched.

"Oh no," I groaned as he kicked up his heels, scarecrow-fashion and sang about following the yellow brick road. The Wizard of Oz would have been proud- of all of us, I imagined.

"With Osiris' power why did they ask me to go to the Mediterranean? Surely he could have. . ."

"He was told to stand down by his father, Ra. Why, I don't know, but the spirits are in control. Osiris' specialty is his affinity with the earth and all beleaguered species, not humans. He's the original Green Man of mythology. I'm sure he hoped his birthplace might survive, hence their coming to us, and the spirits providing the opportunity for your test, Wife."

Poor Bonnie, she didn't want to be reminded of that last test. She wasn't at all proud of her grade. I didn't care to recall the test, either. But, it had led to an unparalleled togetherness.

"Bonnie, Wife, we're here together. Your learning merits you the highest grade- life, our life." My thumbs stroked away the frown lines between her brows and my lips teased hers until a smile dawned.

"Why can Osiris change into a wolf, but Isis cannot?"

"Different talents," I shrugged. "But their love and togetherness is irrefutable."

'As is ours,' we telepathed simultaneously. And that got the kisses going. The fire inside me combusted with a life of its own. Bonnie, Bonnie. . .

Hold up, CatSkill, there's more to speak of. I forced myself from Bonnie's sweet mouth.

"Osiris has a familiarity with Yellowstone, now. He's tuned to the buffalo's mindset. Don't worry about them. They could not be in better hands," I tried to reassure her.

"Osiris has the power to prevent the volcano, doesn't he?"

I opened my thoughts to her on this front, hoping she'd understand.

"I see, Riordan. It's not his responsibility. The circle in the cave. . . I hope. . ."

"Bonnie, remember, the spirits know all. As above, so below. We are where we are supposed to be, Wife. You're not alone." I kissed her worries, well not exactly away, but at least she responded which made my blood roar. Until she pulled back and her eyes pinned me.

"It's really going to happen, isn't it?" The quaver in Bonnie's question had me pulling her tightly to my chest. "Everything is happening so fast, Riordan. The animals moving. . ."

The bison were definitely edgy, nearly set to leave their erstwhile safe Yellowstone Park home. It wouldn't take much to launch them on a stampede the likes of which hadn't been seen for well over a hundred years- bar DANCES WITH WOLVES, which I'd rather enjoyed for its true-to-life portrayal.

For a second, I wasn't sure who had the hardest task- Osiris with a bunch of unruly, huge creatures barreling out of control or our circle with Bonnie central, us as helper-guardians, to deal with the coming fiasco.

"The ranchers won't allow the buffalo near their herds. Brucellosis. . ."

"Bonnie, look!" We were lying on the cabin's roof. The Pink Lady and her colorful cohorts blinked as if reprimanding us for ignoring them for too long.

I felt Bonnie's focus, our focus, on the light show. Light. . . Something about light. . .

"It's as if she's trying to tell us."

"Maybe, she's offering hope," I gently squeezed Bonnie's hand resting in mine.

33

"That seals it!" We found my dad on his cell phone, bird-watching by Handsome's corral. He pocketed his phone, scratched the back of his head, scanned the home-site, and eyed Riordan and me with fretful, tight lipped mien.

"Dad?"

"Bonnie, I've seen one too many birds flying in the wrong direction lately," he grimly acknowledged.

I followed his eyes, admiring the huge wings of a Trumpeter Swan. I would have loved to converse with him and his mate, but there was a large convoy behind him, they seemed to be in concentrated haste, and my dad was about to make an important announcement.

"I've just been on the phone with the Gregors, honey. I'm loading up as many of the animals as I can and heading east. Right now. No argument. Give me a hand. Hey, Rick!"

Riordan had greeted our tall friend while my dad and I had been speculating on swans and company. My husband and Rick strolled over.

"What's up, Mr. Lance?"

"Notice anything strange lately, Rick?"

"Uh, Dad," I tried to forestall Rick's answer as Riordan turned his head to hide a grin. Talk about loaded questions.

My dad looked sheepish for all of two seconds, briefly recounting the events with Chac and Rick's near death experience, but then he turned serious and began tossing out orders.

"Riordan, throw together a makeshift chicken coop, if you would? Bonnie, gather the kittens and a litter box. God, don't forget the litter box. The cats can stay up in the goose-neck on my bedding. . ."

My dad was moving fast as he issued orders. Rick cast an appraising eye at him, looked puzzled, but amicably joined Riordan. Hammers and chicken wire went to work, noisily and hurriedly.

Silently I warned Grandfather we would definitely be late. 'Sorry, Grandfather.'

His silent rejoinder of 'It's alright, Granddaughter, come as soon as you can,' slightly alleviated my worries.

In the cabin, my dad hastily shoved a few articles of clothing into a duffel bag, opened and closed the refrigerator countless times as if he couldn't make up his mind about something.

"Dad," I touched his arm.

"Honey, I'm running on a gut feeling. It's always served me well in the past. I hope I'm wrong. The newscasters have barely touched on the animals shifting at Yellowstone. I guess if a damned scientist doesn't come up with the appropriate readings on some godforsaken machine. . ."

"Dad, I understand." I'd only seen my dad's face this anxious once- coming out of my amnesia.

"I feel it too. Something is happening." I was my father's daughter, after all. Perhaps some of my talents were actually inherited. I'd explore that later. If there was a later.

"If the news ran on intuition. . . Hopefully they'll catch on. . .before. . ."

How long before? During our whirlwind tour of the park last night, the dwindling of the resident wildlife was plain to see. What were the park rangers thinking? High season or not, they had to be on tenterhooks, wondering when word from 'on high' was forthcoming. Worried for the safety of animals, tourists and themselves.

As of yet, the mass exodus of, say the bison, hadn't begun. How could Osiris control a buffalo stampede? I wished I might see. . . What was I thinking? I hoped none of this was necessary.

I handed my dad the litter box, extra cat litter, a bag of cat food, some cans.

"Take these, Dad. I'll make you a few sandwiches. Oh, and grab Sticker's and Stalker's food, too."

I called for Amore. No response. Not too unusual, but. . .

"Super, Cali, Fragi, Listic, Expe, Ali, Docious!" Seven little bodies lined up. I played top cat and they followed me out to the horse trailer and eagerly jumped into the new, mysterious opening.

"Kittens corralled. I can't find Amore," I searched around, trying to sense where she was hiding. Worry fluttered in my gut.

"It's alright, honey. She can take care of herself." But I knew better- if what we surmised was about to happen, how might any creature survive? "I'll take the broodmares and. . ."

My intuition kicked in, "Take Hoss, too."

"I should be back by nightfall. Gather your things. . ." My dad's eyes lingered on our cabin home. "When I return we'll load Handsome, Lil Joe and. . ."

I nodded, biting my tongue to keep back fears and tears, and walked into his embrace. His arms tightened around me and he kissed the top of my head.

The dogs had tuned into the gravity of the currents swirling about, and patiently sat, waiting for their cue.

'Bonnie, talk to these chickens,' my frustrated Riordan silently beseeched.

Rick uncharacteristically stumbled about, hands out, bent over from the waist, trying to herd or grab Hector and/or one of his harem girls. With absolutely no luck, as the critters clucked, dodged and swooped with great dexterity to avoid his fruitless, basketball-skilled endeavors.

"Boy doesn't know much about chickens," my dad shook his head as he watched Rick nearly topple, long legs playing Twister, and end up with a single iridescent feather to show for his effort. At another time this would have been hilarious, 6'8" Rick trying to catch chickens that did not want to be caught.

I addressed the Houdini Hector. The brightly colored rooster craned his neck, flapped his wings, and his girls immediately changed the tune of their clucks and came together. Hector ushered them into what would have to suffice for a traveling cage. Riordan winked at me, and hoisted the chicken carrier into the bed of the pickup. Rick exhaled in relief and swiped at his sweaty brow.

Handsome nickered as the mares calmly walked into the trailer. Hoss balked, not used to being parted from Lil Joe. He let his angst be known, stomping and neighing frantically.

"Git up," my dad slapped his haunch and he reluctantly walked aboard the new three-horse slant load rig.

"Here are sandwiches, Dad."

"Sheesh, Bonnie! How many sandwiches did you make? This must weigh 7 pounds," he hefted the brown bag.

"You can share with Sticker and Stalker," I replied to the dogs' anticipatory, grinning muzzles.

I speculated on why I couldn't find Amore. It wasn't like her to have no essence of a response, not even a whisper.

'Don't worry, Wife. She's a cat. She knows what she is doing,' Riordan attempted to placate me.

My dad pulled me into his arms again. I felt my eyes brim.

"Riordan, whatever it takes," odd choice of words he used to address my husband.

Did my dad know more than I thought?

"Whatever it takes, you keep my girl safe, understand?"

I felt the intensity of Riordan's vow, "My life on it, sir."

"See you later, honey," lunch bag in hand, my dad opened the cab door and waved a final good-by.

The dogs jumped in the passenger side after licking my hand, and with the skill of years of practice, my dad routed the rig out the drive.

An exodus of birds intently squabbling above, the answering clucks of Hector and his harem, Handsome oddly silent, Lil Joe bellowing for Hoss. . .

Please, please let everything be all right, I prayed.

34

"Let's take Old Reliable, it sits up higher." 'Just in case,' Riordan silently added.

'You don't think. . .'

'Wife, I'm just engaging in the fine art of preparedness.'

"Rick, I'm sorry, but we'll have to put off our talk." Rick had already sensed that whatever was going on was heavy-duty.

"Don't worry about me. I saw the flash of strong colors in your father's aura, Bonnie; I know he's extremely worried. I…I'd like to come along, help if I can," he solicitously offered.

Flash of colors in my dad's aura, hmmm. But there was no time to ponder that now. Rick, Riordan and I piled into the old jeep- Riordan boosted me up. Just like. . .was it less than three years ago?

To a normal person, other than the skies teeming with birds, it would seem a perfectly lovely, Wyoming summer day. Although the sun refused to be bandied about by the wind, the clouds were more than happy to comply and shifted shapes continuously at the behest of stirring breezes.

But Riordan's and my senses, being in tune with our wild natures, clamored alarm. Grandfather, our visionary, had called an emergency meeting.

We were quiet the short distance to the cabin. The jeep, however, was not, as it bucked and groaned down Grandfather's pitted drive.

"Rick, I'm sure after today your questions will triple. For now, I ask you to hold your horses." Our tall friend solemnly nodded.

A driveway empty of vehicles, except for Grace's, belied my sense of a cabin full of disparate energies, all patiently waiting. Riordan winked at me before holding open the cabin door.

"Good heavens, where did all these people come from?" Rick whispered, craning his neck around.

He couldn't help himself. Bodies were crammed together peacefully inside. Bodies from many different shamanic cultures- all in their native regalia, all eyeing me with curiosity, and regarding Rick with exception- politely refraining from frowning at his ill-mannered-from-ignorance query.

The old Bonnie would have balked at being literally put on the spot, blushed and clammed up at the intensity of the speculation directed at her.

As it was, I did blush. Riordan's hand rested at my waist and I could hear his admiring chuckle as I stood without fear, taking my place among my 'compatriots'.

Rick's initiation into auras was about to turn into a major fireworks display, for the cacophony of colors before him was absolutely mind-boggling.

Riordan and I felt every single energy as a wild creature must comprehend his surroundings. Rick stood, absolutely floored, slightly trembling with the sensory overload in the room.

I felt Cloud's recently gained shamanic energy. He nodded, "Lady Shaman," in Lakota.

I responded in his language, "Won't you call me Bonnie?"

Cloud's face remained impassive, "No, Girl as Cat."

'Wife, it's a matter of respect for you and for me,' Riordan telepathed.

"Thank you, Cloud." I felt Rick staring at us as we spoke in a language unknown to him, and then suddenly, he seemed to relax and carefully take it all in, as an industrious, enthralled student would. I wanted to say something to him, but my attention was redirected.

An Inuit man cloaked in sealskin with a sun-wrinkled face and glittering, black eyes, nodded respectfully.

I met pairs of eyes after pairs of eyes. An aborigine on walkabout from the Outback, barefoot, standing on one leg, hair grayed from his native dust and interesting markings on his face. A long spear in his hands acted as an unnecessary support. I felt his spirit pleased to meet mine.

African shamans- tribesmen sporting everything from loin cloths of leather, animal pelts, feathers and paint to sneakers and cut-off jeans, stood implacable. Some wore masks and carried spears and rattles made of various animal parts. All were marked with paint or ritual scarring. My eyes hesitated in leaving sight of them; there were so many others to see.

Grandfather cut into my reverie. "I'm sorry Granddaughter, there's not enough time to enjoy all the social niceties."

I turned to his voice. Dr. Gunne, Grace, Cloud and Grandfather stood together.

A quiver of anticipation, not a happy one, raced up my spine. Riordan's hand gently rubbed my tingling goose-bumps, bolstering my sinking intrepidity.

"It's going to happen, isn't it, Grandfather? And v...very soon?" His serious black eyes indicated affirmation.

My brain picked up an unfamiliar language from one of the shamans. Immediately, my shamanic talents translated.

"An eruption of this magnitude will affect all of our homelands. Many thousands of years in the past an event upset the balance, causing black rain for days and days. The earth cracked open, fire burst, waters tore through villages. Many deaths and great loss of knowledge. Weather patterns changed within minutes. Cold, much cold. The possibility of another Ice Age or something worse. . . We've come to offer you our support, our prayers. We have been told by the spirits of your abilities. Your coming to this moment was known by ancient shamans. Though physically we are powerless to prevent or ameliorate the volcano, all that we are in energy, with the spirits, will be with you."

The others innately understood the Mayan shaman's words. If only the United Nations members could understand all different peoples' languages and be as truly supportive of each other and in such close confines.

"Th...thank you," I stuttered. I didn't know what else to say. My gut churned at the tremendous expectations they had of me. And I was yet ignorant of how I was supposed to do whatever it was I was supposed to do.

The shamans studied Riordan and me with intense, open curiosity, without a hint of rudeness. Riordan and I were the only couple, and the youngest among this illustrious gathering.

Grace and I were the only females. I'd save my questions about a 'man's world' for later. Later. Would there be a later?

'Yes, Wife- know it will be so,' Riordan cut in on my rambling. My husband had something up his sleeve. Unfortunately, it was something not fully formed in his head or I would be privileged to it.

'Later,' he silently quelled my questing. I felt his lips twitch. Please, don't let him break into song right now, rang in my brain.

My head spun with the import of what was calculated as my purpose in the shamanic realm when Wolf Walker, bare-chested, long, black hair loose, sidled easily through the throng, his eyes completely focused on me. Riordan's chest began to rumble, until Wolf Walker stopped, ceased his profound perusal of me and nodded respectfully to him.

The ring of a cell phone rudely, momentarily, shattered the peaceful equilibrium of the shamans. Frowns of annoyance flitted across several countenances.

"Uh, s…sorry, sorry about that," Rick mumbled. He'd actually jumped when his cell went off, his head easily grazing Grandfather's wood-beam ceiling.

Checking the number, Rick blushed, "Uh, it's my mom, I have to. . ." Riordan ushered the floundering, embarrassed Rick outside.

"Girl as Cat, White Buffalo Heart, all of us are believing in you. Remember, you have a special connection- the source of your greatest power- you will have to call on. . ." Wolf Walker's voice died as he sensed my confusion.

"You must acknowledge. . ." he tried again.

Special connection? Other than with Riordan, other than with these brother-shamans. . .

I didn't know what he meant. All of them expected something great from me. . . Did they really think I could stop. . .the volcano?

Misgivings now replaced curiosity on the shamans' faces. Had they all ventured here thinking I could perform a miracle? And I. . . Was I too young yet, too inexperienced to meet their expectations? Why had they believed my powers could do what they couldn't? Why couldn't I find the answers?

Attempt the impossible? Even Osiris had. . .

'Bonnie, Osiris can create a cataclysm to aid, but not to forestall the earth's own ideas,' Riordan was again at my side, his arms around me. 'The spirits have their own agenda.'

To Riordan's ears alone, I quailed, 'And I'm supposed to do this? How?'

"Grandfather," I sought his insight as my husband was his usual too calm self, and I did not want to disintegrate in the illustrious assembly gathered within, but I was beginning to feel the black, the darkness. . .my nemesis.

"Granddaughter, I don't know, but the volcano is ready to speak. The circle is with you, as are all of these shamans. We must believe the spirits will direct us- direct you, when they will."

Rick had rejoined us, caught the word volcano.

"You all think Yellowstone is going to erupt?" Rick couldn't contain himself. "That's impossible! The scientists, seismologists would have warned us!"

Every eye in the place, except for the original circle, Wolf Walker and Cloud, chastised poor Rick. If the eyes had been weapons, he would have been flayed alive and suffer physically as well as psychically. I knew his chagrin.

Rick wilted under the foreign contemplation. Only two others matched his height- reminded me of Zulu warriors, and they were especially disdainful at our tall friend's outburst.

"As you are a fellow warrior," Wolf Walker addressed Rick, "I will explain. The spirits issue warnings to those who are in tune with them. Maybe you've noticed the birds leaving their quarters?" The Blackfoot patiently spoke.

"Uh," Rick hastily scouted the room. "Please forgive me," he whispered into the hushed environs.

The dearth of cars outside, the costume party-like selection of clothing, the aura colors meshing, the conversing in foreign languages. . . It had finally dawned on Rick that Never Neverland might be real.

"Riordan?"

My husband shook his head, "Not now, Rick. Later, I promise."

Wolf Walker shot me a last meaningful glance, "You are the White Buffalo Heart, remember."

My Wife did have a special connection- her elemental powers for sure, but there was something more, I just didn't have my finger on it, yet, and the spirits were holding their own, in the closet it seemed.

Though Bonnie had used fire, water and air, I felt sure earth was also within her repertoire and that 'something' else.

For the volcano, she'd need every one of her talents. I had no doubts about it. And the backing of our original circle and these shamans.

As for the source of the mysterious connection. . .something flitted in my mind. Ah well, in their own sweet time. . .

Rick's cell rang again. Telephones, the bane of humans- couldn't just ignore them, or God forbid, turn them off or leave them at home, or my idea- stomp on them, rather like my mammoth boogie atop Chac.

The shamans muttered again as I shoved Rick out the door.

"My Wife and the circle of protectors are ready in an instant to do whatever we can. Your prayers and energies sent our way are vital and much appreciated."

"If you fail. . . Our world will be cast into darkness," one of the shamans spoke with deep remorse.

"Fail is a word that is not in my vocabulary," I supposed this might be considered bragging, but I believed in my Lioness and myself and the erstwhile silent spirits.

Bonnie sank against my chest, stunned as all of these proceedings pounded home. I closed my arms tightly about her.

One by one the shamans approached, inclined masked, feathered and/or painted/scarred heads to me and my Wife, and travelled back to their homelands, leaving behind a vibrant bastion of energies which would stay with us in our impending endeavor- come what may.

I tried to soothe Bonnie, stem her growing apprehension. 'Wife, don't doubt yourself. The spirits are not always precipitate in providing simple things like relevant details. Besides, it's fun to do the impossible.'

I heard her ruminate about my probably joking at the end of the world. I felt her heart tremble as she pleaded with the spirits for this not to be the end. Time to pull one of the aces out of my sleeve- not to say I cheat, you understand.

'Bonnie, Osiris once asked me how it felt to be married to the most powerful shaman of all.' I kept up the silent communiqué.

'I don't understand, Riordan.' I was perceptive to Bonnie's senses struggling to catch up with mine.

'Did you not wonder why a God and Goddess, legends and an Oracle seeking to destroy you, all called on you? I told Osiris that as you and I are one, there is no question of who is most powerful.' I believed in equality, just ask me.

'That's what Irusan meant when he first spoke with me. My mate would be the most self-assured shaman.'

'And you would complete me?' I knew where this was going.

'We complete each other,' Bonnie's smile dispatched the chewing of her lower lip.

'These shamans all came here because of you.'

'Because of us,' her lips twitched in dawning serenity as our strengths merged, nullifying her fears, and I couldn't resist, I kissed her delicious mouth.

'Are you up for saving the world, Lioness?' I grinned as my mouth reluctantly released hers.

"Bonnie, Riordan," Rick rushed in, stared at the relatively empty cabin, his jaw agape in horrified disbelief.

"What is it, Rick?" Bonnie and I simultaneously asked. I caught Gunne rolling his eyes, and I smirked at him.

"Th…they've closed Yellowstone. They're evacuating everyone around. . ."

That announcement was endorsed with a great earthly vibration. Party time!

35

"Rick, I suggest you get the hell out of Dodge. Take the jeep," I'd just issued an old time warning when darned if Rick's cell rang yet again.

"My cousin says the traffic out of Cody is crazy backing up!"

"Oh no! My dad!" I felt a rush like a loosed arrow piercing my chest as it did my Wife's. The Sisyphean ball was rolling out of control in multiple directions.

"Bonnie, don't lose it Kitten. Your dad got away in time," I qualified as I ushered her to the jeep.

"But, Handsome and Lil Joe. . ."

"Get in the jeep! C'mon Rick, move it!" I hoisted Bonnie inside, leaving Rick in the lurch as I floored Old Reliable home. Somewhat slow on the uptake, his right leg was left hanging out- poor guy had to hang on to the open door for dear life. Reminded me of the old joke about when is a door not a door. . . Bonnie gigged me to return to the program. And Rick, might as well get used to it- comes with the territory.

'Grandson, we must go,' Grandfather's silent advisory hit the telepathic hotline.

I replied, 'Grandfather, Bonnie and I have to take care of a few things first.'

'Hurry, Grandson- not much time,' prefaced another harbinger vibration from the earth.

The jeep bucked abnormally, and threw us around inside the cab- not all due to my driving. At present speed, I wondered if the old jalopy would hold together in our mad dash melee (old jalopy- I almost burst out laughing at the catastrophic mess we could not escape), and if we'd get Rick back in one piece.

Four inches taller than I, his head was first to hit the roof; rubbing his riled crown, Rick hunched his lengthy frame for the sake of continued consciousness while bopping around in the crazed vehicle. Luckily he was able to finally shut the door after it banged his leg a few times.

The earth's upheaving and the car-defying pot holes had me in full comprehension of what it must feel like to be popcorn.

"Riordan, I…I've got your back. I'd rather stay with you, help any way you need me."

Rick's concerned offer tossed into the palpable tension did set me to laughing, "I don't think you can help with this."

My mind raced- options, options, ah. . .

With a spray of gravel I didn't think the old jeep capable of, I fishtailed into our drive, braked hard, hoisted Bonnie down.

"Rick, can you ride?"

"Horses? Sure, I was born out here." In spite of all that our tall friend had been through lately, he displayed remarkable aplomb. His usual before-competition, take-it-in-stride relaxed semblance, held sway- the kind of person you wanted around in an emergency. And boy howdy did this qualify as the mother lode of emergencies.

"Riordan, what are you. . . Ooh," Bonnie saw my plan forming.

"Rick, I'm not talking just ride. Can you stay on no matter what?"

His eyes blinked between Bonnie and me.

"Whatever you need me to do, I will do," he uttered with the utmost resolve.

As one, Bonnie, Rick and I raced for the barn. The skies were darkening their ominous forewarning at an alarming rate- a barrage of sickening hues.

The black beast, mindful of the charged atmosphere, had his ears operating like satellite disks, turning every which-away. He'd flung his head, snorted and pranced. I heard him calling to Bonnie, worry for her paramount in his soul.

Lil Joe was in a state, especially without Hoss, the calm one, to influence him and assure him everything would be all right. His corral churned up, his body was lathered in anguished sweat over being left behind and to his way of thinking, all alone. The stallion did not count in his book.

Bonnie slid through the fence rails, spoke telepathically to Lil Joe. She sent a message to Handsome as she soothed the gelding. As her words began to sink in, Lil Joe settled and stood motionless, neck arched, waiting, although a shiver raced across his wet coat.

As I slung a western saddle on his back, a meow greeted us. That's Amore was tight-rope walking the top fence rail, tail held high.

"There you are," Bonnie gathered the all-too-calm cat in her arms as Rick bridled Lil Joe.

Her nose snuggled into Amore's huge white collar. She kissed the upturned puss and with glittering eyes. . .

"Rick, That's Amore will guide you. Follow her directions absolutely- no deviating, even if you think you know better. Are you OK with that?"

Rick's tongue flicked his lips. I know if I'd been him, I'd come up with a suitable rejoinder about being led by a cat, but I am not solely a human, and Cats are King in my book.

"I...I guess so. If you want me to stay on this horse and follow a cat. . ."

"Hold her in your lap, pay attention to her and she'll point the way," Bonnie finished her instructions.

I guess the serious expression on Bonnie's face confirmed to our question-suffering friend that he had, in truth, not entered the funny farm, and the tornado of the WIZARD OF OZ had already been unleashed- no bicycle with basket for him.

That he was willing to stick it out spoke volumes of his incredible loyalty as a friend, his wealth of inner fortitude, great psychic transformation, and his supra-natural education was just beginning.

He had the temerity to grin, truly a man after my own heart. "Whatever you say," he agreeably shrugged.

"And you'll have to hold Handsome's lead, too."

"Why not? The more, the merrier," Rick's grin widened.

"Now, that's the spirit, Rick," I high-fived my favorite basketball competition.

As hell winged its way for an impromptu visit, Bonnie spent a full minute remonstrating with the black beast. He was not happy about leaving his girl and being pawned off on a relative stranger.

I leaned against a fence rail, considered hollering over something about taking your time, but Bonnie actually scowled at me. Rick superseded me with a madcap comment on the weather, and we collapsed, laughing, as if it were just another day.

Easy to detect the patience in Bonnie's telepathic tete-a-tete with the disenchanted, balking stallion; I knew a comment on mules would not be taken lightly- maybe another time.

'Amore's not a stranger; you have to be the brave one for everybody. You know Lil Joe is really scared and Rick needs your help.'

That would do it. Appeal to his manhood. Got us guys every time.

"C'mon, Bonnie! We have to go."

That's Amore ensconced in lap, astride Lil Joe, Rick accepted the dancing Handsome's lead line.

Bonnie kissed Handsome's and Lil Joe's muzzles, told them to be good for Rick (he'd received a hug before mounting) and stepped back, sending them on their way, eyes all a brim with torrential, emotional tears barely held in check.

I ran after the quickly departing Rick, handed him wire-cutters, told him not to be afraid to use them- a brief return to a better time when the range was free.

"Rick, look for a red-tailed hawk. It'll be like the dove out of Noah's ark signaling it's all right to come home."

"CatSkill, whatever you and Bonnie are up to. . .well, good-luck and Godspeed," he managed to blurt out. Nodding, I tapped Lil Joe's haunch, gave Handsome a thumbs-up and hurried to Bonnie who watched them, teary-eyed, lower lip quivering, out of sight.

The ominously still air- so dissentient of Wyoming's typical aura, had its charged frequencies palpably pummeling our bodies- reminiscent of a stormy ocean striking shore. And then a familiar sizzle broke into the ranks- Osiris' calling card.

Previous to the earth's first tremor, the buffalo had taken to exiting Yellowstone- rather peacefully, but purposefully, without stopping to graze. Osiris had kept them on a protected corridor, using all of his wiles to stave off any overly destructive encounters. What were a few downed fences if no one was around to protest?

But various ranchers had been watching, and were up in arms at the huge herd shuffling near their lands. Somehow, Osiris had stifled the occurrence of any impetuous shootings- I would've loved to have seen that. And now the ranchers had more important things to do- like evacuating their families.

'CatSkill,' Osiris called, 'the buffalo are stampeding, out-of-control; I'm barely able to keep a vacant corridor open. Praise Ra, what powerful animals!'

'Sorry, Osiris, can't help,' I shot back.

'Any advice?' I heard his admiration mixed with frustration- must be one hell of a sight live- I was so very young when I'd last seen the tremendous herds running free, unencumbered, except for the hunger of my people.

Osiris had concerns for the buffalo's safety- didn't he know they could tear through most anything? Talk about tanks. But then, he was a perfectionist and probably didn't want streams or a single tree to be harmed- must be a great trial of his ingenuity.

'Can you sing Home on the Range?' I advised.

Osiris' answering guffaw and Bonnie's quirky lip-twitch had me shrugging my shoulders.

'You know, in those old westerns, box canyons came in handy. . .'

'Now that is something I can use,' Osiris chortled. I heard a bull bellow in the background rush.

'Yippee ki yay, Osiris! Ride 'em, cowboy! We're off to see about a volcano!' I couldn't help it.

My lips were twitching. I grabbed Bonnie, ready to transport to Yellowstone. To Grandfather, the dragon, Grace- all waiting. And to whatever the blow-up had in store for us.

"We're off to see the volcano. . .," I sang to the tune of WE'RE OFF TO SEE THE WIZARD. Surprised the heck out of me when Bonnie joined in.

36

A nauseous hue had defeated the morning's blue sky. The happily bantered clouds were gone, replaced by a sickly, eerie complexion. An ominous stillness tried its best to suffocate us. Although I'd put up a brave front for Riordan, he felt the cumbrous air- as heavy as my heart.

"Don't worry, Wife. We're together, no matter what. Come, you were born here, I believe, for this specific purpose as well as. . . Come," Riordan softly caressed my back as I took a long, emotional last?- no I'd not think that- survey of our home.

Could I do this? What exactly was I expected to do? Stop a volcano before it erupted? Contain it if it did? How? In ancient times, religious personnel threw helpless virgins into the fire, hoping to stop destruction. . .

"And the damned thing went off anyway, right? Good thing no false priests are around. Or any virgins, either, come to think of it," he teasingly tugged my ear. I nearly smiled. Had I really been singing mere seconds ago?

"You're not alone, Lioness, come." The urgency in Riordan's voice and the further darkening of the sky. . .

I melted into his embrace and let him guide us to our pre-ordained meeting spot. Grandfather and Grace awaited us on a rise overlooking Yellowstone Lake.

Sulfur-ridden gases gurgled from the lake waters. Trying to steal our breath. The stench, a portent of the hell to come.

"Yuck!" Riordan snorted. "What an obnoxious stew!" A vibration in the ground pitched us as if we'd been tossed on a rough sea- without a ship.

"Best get our sea legs on," he read me while gently keeping me upright- where were my cat balancing legs?

No animals, no birds, no humans, no RV's. . . Ooh, the fish! My eyes watered as much from the gases as for the fish bodies floating in the bubbling lake.

I clung to Riordan as his embrace and calming energies pierced my sadness. Get ahold of yourself, I mentally kicked myself, to Riordan's amusement. He actually grunted as if I'd kicked him.

"You did kick me! Those blasted paddock boots!"

"Sorry, Riordan. Where's Dr. Gunne?" I asked, perplexed by his absence. Grace and Grandfather had no answer. The lake's response- a sulphurous belch.

"Probably gathering aloe," Riordan offered, tongue-in-cheek. I swear my husband would be laughing during Armageddon. But maybe this was. . .

At that moment, Dr. Gunne appeared. "Don't knock aloe. It's one of the few plants as good for the inside of a body as the outside," the dragon smirked.

The sibling-like antagonism sparked between Dr. Gunne and Riordan. I thought, hoped, they'd outgrown all of that- especially in light of circumstances. No such luck.

The dragon smiled at me with enough affection to make my husband hiss.

"Please, you two! Sheesh, this is hard enough," I stomped my foot. Riordan, reading my intent in time, removed his foot from the danger zone.

We turned to form our circle as Dr. Gunne winked at me behind Riordan's back, "Sorry."

Our formation mirrored the ancient cave art. I faced Riordan, my chin up to hold his gaze, my hands rested in his. Grace, Grandfather and Dr. Gunne took up their precarious positions, arduously balancing on the shifting earth.

I sensed waves issuing out from and swirling about our circle- not only my protectors' energies, but the prayers and frequencies of so many different shamans from around the world. I could only pray their confidence in me was not unwarranted.

A thought flitted through my near numb brain. "Riordan, it's…it's like the picture burnt into the ground. The colors represented not only our group, but the variety of people worldwide. You see. . .feel them?"

Grandfather, Grace and the dragon agreed.

"You're right, Wife. All the shamans of every culture are with us in spirit- the diplomats of the world, praying for their tribes- no separation. The burnt out section in the midst of the colored circumference would represent Yellowstone. . ."

"Riordan, are we set to fail?" My voice quivered.

Riordan scanned the lake, tested the frequencies in the atmosphere, eyed Grandfather, our visionary. But, he'd not gleaned any vision of success or. . .

"Or failure, Granddaughter. Take heed," he cautioned me. "Remember, you were placed here by the spirits."

"You, sweet Wife, are the only shaman of the white race. . ."

"I beg to differ," Irusan's throaty voice interrupted.

The very sound of him lightened my soul. If I were powerful, he must be more so. Hadn't Riordan told me Irusan had destroyed the Oracle and appropriated my powers until I recognized my lesson?

"Greetings, Daughter! Your lineage is of the Tuatha d' DaNaan- spirits revered by ancient Celts; they love this earth. Of course, you're the only true, living human Druid, er, shaman, but the might of the Celts and Tuatha is behind you. Have you discerned the connection? You're about to need it."

The lake began a more rigorous bubbling which increased until turning into a full rolling boil- like a witch's cauldron formulating a potion, and hot spew shot around us causing us not only to try to remain standing but play dodge the hot stuff, too.

"Irusan, tell me please," I didn't know what he referred to. It can't all end because of my ignorance. Surely, he. . .

"Look to the stone. Remember your friends. Don't disappoint me." And that was all. Irusan was gone. Gone!

My head swung around to my friends, looking for clues, but their blank faces were of no help.

Buck up, you weakling, I remonstrated with myself. I wouldn't have been put here if I were as helpless as I seemed.

This unsought role, this battle. . . If we came out of this. . .

'We will, Wife,' Riordan silently broke into my teeter-totter reverie.

'Then I want to go on vacation!' I startled myself. Riordan was indeed part of me, I thought, if I could come up with this lunatic tidbit amidst the current turmoil.

He threw back his head gleefully. 'That's my Lioness! Wherever you wish to go, I'll take you, Wife.'

The others had to be wondering about my sanity.

Suddenly, the boiling lake waters began to rise- the volcano making its stinky, noisy entrance, spewing multitudes of missiles. Fiery lava rocks, glowing orange and hissing to black as they hit the cool air, hurtled upon us. The earth bucked worse than Bodacious, the rodeo bull, at his best gyrations, doing its utmost to send us sprawling.

"Bonnie, Baby. . ."

"Don't ever address my Wife as 'Baby'," Riordan snarled.

We dodged the rock-fire rain. I couldn't conceive of what to do. The circle tried to keep its position, but I'm sure we looked like castaways being tossed on some malevolent carnival ride from hell.

My senses seemed to be on stand-by, but for what? Waiting for the blow-up to blow us to kingdom come?

Weaving and avoiding bits of fire, Grandfather remained expressionless. I felt Grace's worry for all of us and the dragon. . .

"Why is it my wardrobe always suffers whenever I'm with you two?" Dr. Gunne, unsteady on the bucking ground, brushed off several smoldering embers from his previously immaculate polo shirt. "I want an all-expenses-paid buying spree, courtesy of Riordan CatSkill."

Dismayed, he gave up on the non-existent probability of his polo shirt's survival, let alone the five of us. "See, aloe would come in handy, if it weren't for my own healing powers," he sighed.

"That GQ look is outdated, Dragon," Riordan offered his sartorial opinion as hand-in-hand we danced a dance with no beat and no beauty.

"I suppose you'd prefer it if I wore a loin cloth?"

"Please, no," I rapidly shot back.

"I outgrew playground games like dodge ball years ago," Dr. Gunne grumbled, eyeing his holy shirt and speculating on his Dockers as he lifted a leg to avoid a hurtling-in-his-direction spate of fire.

"Du du duuu, du du du duuu. . . SMOKE ON THE WATER. . ." Riordan's lip-twitching was a dead giveaway. This had to be a dream- no one could be so blasé with a volcano erupting under our feet.

"FIRE. . ." I was completely floored when Dr. Gunne joined in. "Damn, CatSkill! I knew there had to be something I liked about you, other than your charming wife."

The two traded back and forth with the old rock song lyrics while I gathered my scattered wits and Grace looked stunned and utterly set to knock heads- totally unlike her. Grandfather remained impassive, as always.

The lake waters burst and slithered from the tower which surged higher in its midst. The volcano imperiously took over with ferocious zeal, spitting and raining continuous fiery lava fireworks.

And Dr. Gunne began playing an imaginary lead guitar. Had the volcano already erupted and left us in a version of hot rock and roll hell? This was nothing but a nightmare?

"Is it only me or does anyone else see we have a problem here? A minor Armageddon?" I shouted to be heard over the singing and the environmental disaster.

The song continued.

"Children!" I screamed. Contrite, the dragon and the cougar abruptly shut up.

I felt as if I'd become the leader of this expedition. I didn't want to be the leader. If it were all up to me. . . I felt no inclination- had no idea what to do- pitiful me!

'Riordan, help me, I'm lost,' I cried.

"Bonnie, look at me, Wife." Through my agony of tears, I fastened on his eyes, those glorious golden cat eyes, the beauty I'd dived into at our first eye-to-eye meeting at lunch, outside, at school.

"The stone came from. . ."

"The stars," I filled in, and. . .I paused.

His eyebrows rose and when I scrunched my nose, he looked to the heavens, which were now streaking with lightening. Strobes of violent red, green, even purple shattered over our heads.

The colors. . . Something was coming to me.

"Remember your sweat lodge message, Granddaughter."

And it hit me. As the volcano rumbled, ready to disgorge the center of the earth. . .

37

Black had ceased to haunt my nights. My dreams were peaceful, except for when Riordan stirred my senses. My cougar kept me safe. His hands held mine, and the flow of his strength into me gave me courage. And now, on the edge of a potential worldwide catastrophe, oddly enough, black no longer existed for me in any way shape or form. I saw only colors about me.

"The light! Ask the light. . ." My entire body thrilled with. . .an innate, but heretofore unrecognized knowledge. It didn't really surprise me, only, like, finally realizing you're capable of something you'd not thought of before.

Riordan mirrored my smile- he wasn't at all surprised. Maybe we came to the recognition together, but maybe not- he wasn't saying.

I took my ring hand from Riordan's hand. I was here because I was the conduit, the liaison between my world and the world of. . .

As a child, I'd seen in the heavens what even my father couldn't. Only when Riordan had joined me on the roof that night after dinner, the night he kissed me for the first time, did I find another pair of eyes that truly fathomed the wonder I knew- what a revelation!

The Stars- the Tuatha d' DaNaan- the pre-Celtic 'peoples'- spirits from the Stars? Irusan had intimated such.

It had to be. I saw them because of my heritage. Riordan saw them because he was one with all; as above so below- so he'd told me.

And I was also one with all, through him, and also because of my own shamanic destiny. The Stars, my friends, for as long as I could remember!

"Lady, excuse me for calling you Pink Lady, but I...we need you. Please?" I sought the aid of the Stars, those I'd admired for all my growing up years.

A burst of sweet, vibrant pink starlight rent the horrid, flashing strobes of color. So brightly did it descend, that the black, lightning streaked skies bowed to the more powerful divinity. A minor star always salaams to the major Star.

"Daughter, I thought you'd never ask," our group heard a chiming that translated inside our brains.

The stream of pink starlight, the Pink Lady, was joined by her art deco cohorts. Mr. Blue, Mr. Green and many others. Together their lights surrounded us with a living, dancing aurora borealis.

Rainbow colors flashed, mirrored and bounced off the stone in my ring as I held it high, the stone a piece of the stars, meant for me.

The lights fused and honed, like a lighthouse beacon, directed to the volcano spewing its heralding horror of molten lava. Hisses of disgruntled water fogged our surrounds as the fire hit the cold lake. The stench of sulfur gagged us and tried to inveigle our focus.

Our circle was jerked terrifically as the ground voraciously ripped open. Our cat-like grace had Riordan and me prancing to stay afoot. Grandfather hovered above the ground as did Grace. The dragon was a different story.

"She'd going to blow!" His body was hurled to the ground; he scrambled to get up only to be thrown again. Dr. Gunne gave a direful cry, bellowing over the violent crash of the soaring tower of destruction bursting from the lake and its wake of hissing, rancorous steam subjecting him to biblical hell.

The overflowing crown of the volcano, a fiery cauldron, a sight I might consider magnificent if I were elsewhere, but not at this close range, gave me a fleeting idea of what the Pompeians had succumbed to.

Riordan gave Dr. Gunne a hand up while continuing to support me.

"Thanks, CatSkill," the heaving dragon managed.

"Bend at the knees, works better. Think yoyo," Riordan advised.

And the dragon desperately tried- I nearly giggled- slap happy are we. . . Riordan's raised brow stifled my inappropriate behavior.

'Not to be a party-pooper, but keep that image in mind for later,' he winked.

The volcanic crown cannoned into the sky with supernatural force; streams of lava disgorged from the mountainous tower.

Talk about home-run potential. Fiery red-orange vied with the Stars' lights' beacon as the heat of the lava scorched the air. A sign of the shamans' and Stars' protection about us was that we were not incinerated or even scorched, except for Dr. Gunne's attire.

"Bonnie, ready?" Riordan calmly asked- his serenity flowing full force through me.

"Daughter, decide what you wish to do with this giant fire-beam. Be artistic," we heard the Pink Lady's chiming, heartening suggestion.

With an earsplitting belch, the Hades stench redoubled, and a daunting wall of fire shot up and up, miles into the sky- a seemingly endless river- an earthly version of Hiroshima at hand.

I called to the earth to slow its fiery fuel and it momentarily suspended the horrific rush of fired lava. The Stars' lights held the flow on a straight road, heaven-ward.

Not a single rock escaped the starlight-held cordon. Lucky for the remainder of Dr. Gunne's clothing- I personally did not want to see him stripped.

"Riordan, help me! Where would water do the most good?"

"How about a little ice up north, as in the North Pole?" I felt his grin take over my lips.

I waved my ring hand from south to north, asking for the winds aid and the magma stream broke from its road to heaven and swept to the Arctic, turning to innumerable ice crystals as it broke from the volcano's blast and blew north. An inundation of ice and snow would make for very happy polar bears and Inuit who grew up knowing how to live with the isolation of the Arctic cold.

But there was more, much, much more. The inside of the earth kept up its vomit of fire.

"Riordan?" I hurriedly cried as I began to feel overwhelmed. What to do with all of this? The north could only hold so much.

"The Antarctic, Lioness," my cougar laughed.

I swept my ring hand from north to south, calling on the winds again and on my congenial relationship with water. This greater distance to sweep ice and snow had me begging the Wyoming draughts to hold their lengthy course while my elemental powers changed the fire to frozen water.

A blizzard changed course from northward bound to southward.

My Star friends continued their powerful, entwined, colored beams, lending me all the strength I needed.

The lava belching from the earth's core began to slow and I continued to ask it to turn to snow upon its ascent. How long had I been at it? It felt like a long, long endeavor, but in reality I supposed only minutes had passed.

Snowflakes on my nose and eyelashes- wasn't that a song?- Riordan joyfully hooted. I took a deep breath, relieved and pleased.

Riordan had believed in my rapport with earth. He'd accepted that my elemental powers included all of the elements, no great surprise to him.

But I marveled at the whole scenario and was grateful beyond words and pleased I'd come through and not disappointed the spirits, the Stars, the shamans and the earth. . .

"Rambling, Lioness?" I swallowed snowflakes in a gasp of wonder.

Through the fall of huge snowflakes, I saw Grandfather, Grace and Dr. Gunne being turned into living snow people, but they stayed with the circle, adding their efforts to those lent by the shared energies of shamans worldwide.

The earth had ceased its bucking, stilled all vibrations, and we stood in awe and jubilation as heavy snow danced and whitewashed everything.

"Riordan, don't you dare start singing FROSTY, THE SNOWMAN," I felt his twitching lips and his urge to dance.

"If I only had that magic silk hat," he mused. I couldn't help it, in tremendous relief I burst out laughing.

"Please, spare me," Dr. Gunne harrumphed, brushing snow from his shoulders, shaking his white-wigged head and stomping his bedaubed boat shoes. "I need snow shoes and. . ."

"Riordan, don't make me lose concentration," I chided, ignoring the dragon's ever-present complaints.

For we weren't finished. The lava still emerged from the earth's core and continued to be transformed into snow crystals- a veritable blizzard.

"Granddaughter, the west needs its water tables refilled."

As of their own accord both of my arms swirled as if I were painting, water-coloring the sky.

Winds bandied with the slowing stream of fire as it shifted into ice and huge snowflakes made a snow globe of our circle.

The Stars' lights' colors created diamond-like flashes among the ice crystals. Multitudes of rainbows! Absolutely, breath-takingly beautiful!

I beseeched the winds to settle the snow where it would do the most good. My elemental talent urged the earth to slow its disgorge even more.

Fascinated, I realized instead of feeling enervated as I usually did after employing these energies, I thrilled with harmonious exhilaration.

The Pink Lady was right- be artistic. There is artistry in being one with all, and nature had taught the greatest artists of all time- look closely at crystals, flowers, shells. . .

I felt Riordan's exuberant chuckling, reveling in how much fun I was having. And the best part, he didn't feel threatened by my talent!

"Granddaughter, can you put into play a temporary freeze that will keep the snow and ice from melting too soon?"

A great suggestion, I didn't need any more flash floods to redirect. But could I affect a sort of freeze?

I summoned my rapport with the elements, backed by the strengths of all my friends and my cougar-husband and my ring and asked. A supreme assurance vibrated throughout my body.

And then, a slightly weary feeling began to seep into my muscles as the volcano suddenly imploded, sinking into itself, and the waters of Yellowstone Lake rushed to fill the vacuum and extinguish the remaining fiery coals.

The hissing and the stench of sulfur slowly dissipated- to an overwhelming silence.

Still standing! We all were. The earth fancifully quiet as if nothing the least out of the ordinary had occurred. Other than the tremendous amount of snowfall in the dead of summer, it might have all been a dream.

Briefly, I wondered how Osiris was making out- I mean how often do Egyptians get snowed on?

A wink from above and the Pink Lady and her entourage bowed out, returning to their heaven.

"Watch for me, Daughter," I heard the words as my mind translated her wind chime voice.

"Thank you with all my heart, spirits of the Stars," I saluted my gratitude.

The heavenly colors had helped save the colors of the earth. I felt the relief of shamans worldwide and their thanks accompanied mine.

Quiet descended along with the silent snow, as the skies no longer fought the battle of lightning bolts and nauseous shades.

The volcano slumbered, for now, and the gaseous gurgling in the lake whispered until drowned out completely by stilling snow-flecked waters.

With the continued shrouding of lace-like patterned snowflakes upon us, we had turned into living snow-shamans, wearing crowns at least a foot high made of snow.

"I wonder how long the snowfall will last."

"If you consider the thousands of feet of ash that these snowflakes might have been. . ." Grandfather intimated.

"Who's going to shovel my driveway?" Dr. Gunne grumped, to no one's commiseration.

"Wonderful! Bonnie, you were able to call your elemental powers into play and turn the fire to snow. This may be your greatest painting yet. And your friendship with the Stars- I didn't know," Grace licked snow from her lips to speak. The snow promptly conspired to re-cover her mouth.

"And extinguish the blasted volcano, too," Dr. Gunne finally left off complaining and spitting snow, congratulated us. "I don't believe Yellowstone is ready for that kind of a forest fire. We knew you could do it, sweetheart."

"Watch it, Gunne," Riordan snarled, although the strength of his remonstrance lost something due to the snow filter.

"I'm going home, take a long, hot, uh, shower, open a bottle of wine, change into some decent clothes," and indeed, his Dockers and polo shirt were full of holes which had allowed snow easy access. "I'm wet all through. . ."

The elation and wonder of what we'd staved off. . .

A sensuous whiff of weariness slowly seeped into me- the sort that accompanied a job well done- home sounded good.

"I assume we're done for today?" The dragon asked.

"Are you staying in Cody, Dragon?"

"Of course, CatSkill. We haven't finished our song, and I'll always be at your beck and call," he winked at me. "You're not getting rid of me, CatSkill," Dr. Gunne snorted snowflakes.

Riordan bristled, but acquiesced, and I think he smirked, but visibility was difficult so I may have only interpreted a smirk from feeling his mouth move.

"We'll see you at home, Grandson, Granddaughter," and Grace and Grandfather followed the dragon in disappearing.

'Grandfather,' Riordan sent a silent communiqué. 'If you would find Rick? He's looking for a red tail hawk to advise him to come home- might have to swoop rather low,' he suggested.

Riordan and I were alone. I felt my lips beginning to twitch. The enormous snowflakes basted us. No, could it be true? I was actually going to beat him to it. . .

"Oh, the weather. . .," I blew out snowflakes and began that old, pop song- LET IT SNOW, LET IT SNOW, LET IT SNOW.

"Bonnie, Kitten!" Riordan's glorious, black brows cast aside snow as they rose in elated surprise and he shook his over-laden mane.

"Something about a fire," I struggled with the words, but continued without a hope of imitating Riordan's perfect singing voice. "And as long as you love. . ."

"Care to tango, Wife?" Riordan held out his hand.

"Lions tango?" I smiled as I stepped into his embrace, into the alluring warmth of my dream.

Recalling our first tango and how I wanted him to. . .

Every sense I possessed vibrated with Riordan's touch, every cell sizzled, as always.

Ah, tango- the sexiest of all dances. That would melt our snow clothes!

"No, Wife, CatSkills Tango." His lips licked the snow from mine and lingered.

And we chorused as we danced, closer than human bodies allowed and with ballet-like, cat grace. "LET IT SNOW! LET IT SNOW! LET IT SNOW!"

EPILOGUE

Hank Winch had remained sober for quite some time and having joined AA- the congratulatory coins marking his stages of success jingled in his pocket as constant reminders- he was lucky enough to be sponsored by a VIP who providentially aided in Hank's reinstatement at his old job, a Yellowstone Park Ranger.

But he began to wonder what the diner waitress had put in his coffee as once more his eyes found something which defied all reason.

What were those two kids doing in the snow storm at Yellowstone Lake? Didn't they realize the danger? A volcano was supposed to go off, for God's sake!

The area, he thought, was supposed to be empty. Heck, he'd done the evacuating himself. Hadn't he? He put his gloved hand to his mouth and sniffed his breath.

"What are you two doing?" He barked in his best authoritative ranger tone.

Sheesh! They didn't even have coats on under all the snow falling from their moving bodies!

Two startled pairs of eyes turned in his direction as he struggled through the hip-deep snow.

"Why sir, I thought it was patently obvious- the tango." I refrained from dissolving in laughter, and danced my Wife- our eyes locked in love on each other, atop the new-fallen snow and traveled home.

Bonnie's flagrant swish of an impermeable snow shield covered our exit- easy to lose things in a blizzard. No sense in putting the hard-at-work fellow back into the bottle.

Bonnie anxiously picked up the phone in the kitchen and dialed her father's cell phone number. I cautioned her about reception and finagled the frequencies to aid her. A sigh of relief indicated she'd reached Jim.

I also reminded her about slowing or directing the snowfall so Jim might have a snowball's chance, so to speak, of getting home.

Of course, I could also escort her along his route and cheer her to play snow-shoveler extraordinaire. . .

Checking in with Grandfather, I received a picture of Rick astride Lil Joe plowing deep snow and shivering with the cold, despite That's Amore draped across his shoulders with her immense tail tucked around his neck.

I was pleased to see Handsome minding his manners, for a change. Easy to see Rick would be compiling a question list upon thawing, and as our prospective student, well, at least I'd been down that road before. Maybe I'd leave the questions to my Wife.

Bonnie spent a second deciding on how best to clear corridors for Rick's and her father's return. Her artistic tendencies with snow and ice, having been practiced, would come in handy, although not quite as exciting as what I'd pictured.

I'd bolster her waning strength as she opened paths and then- a nice, long cat nap was in order. After a little petting, or a lot. . .

I picked her up, carried her to our room and a king-size bed all to ourselves, at least for a short while.

"A vacation, Wife? Where would you like to go, Lioness?"

"Anywhere in your arms, Riordan- as long as I am in your arms," her smile stoked the fire inside of me faster than any old volcano.

Prolonging the suspense as my mouth hovered over hers- I felt the shivers ride an invisible escalator up and down her spine and mine. Eyes delving into the eyes of the greatest, sweetest surprise of my life- thank the spirits!

A blessed glow embraced us as I kissed my Kitten.

"Riordan?"

Here it comes. I rather enjoyed the fact she'd overlooked that she, by virtue of our union, had access to all my knowledge. I would gladly remain Bonnie's private Google source- ask away, Wife.

"What took you so long, Wife?"

"What is the best way to spend a euro?"

A Note

The plight of the antelope with their age-old migratory patterns, the treeing of cougars to be shot, as well as the beleaguered status of the WILD worldwide is a sad commentary on the so-called intelligent species.

The Lakota say MITAKUYE OYASIN- WE ARE ALL RELATED. This does not pertain solely to humans. There should be room for all.

A TOAST TO ALL CATSKILL AFFICIONADOS!!- Many thanks for sharing your time with me and for asking- when is the next one coming out?!!

To computer guru- BRIAN, for his invaluable help!

To my greatest fan- my SWIM!

To Lover Cat, the inspiration! And to the wondrous creative energies that fascinate my life!

Please check out the CatSkill Trilogy Facebook page- many thanks for sharing and liking!

And stay tuned. . .!!

Correspondents welcome at:
lisaannettepowell@gmail.com

Following is a reading list for the curious:

LISTENING TO COUGAR by Marc Bekoff and Cara Blessley Lowe

THE COUGAR by Paula Wild

All Lakota history and spirituality books by Ed McGaa- EAGLEMAN, a Lakota author

THE LAKOTA WAY books by Joseph M. Marshall III, a Lakota author

SPIRIT TALKERS by William S. Lyon

THE MIND IN THE CAVE by David Lewis-Williams

THE CAVE PAINTERS by Gregory Curtis

THE QUEST FOR THE SHAMAN by Miranda & Steve Aldhouse-Green

DICTIONARY OF CELTIC MYTH AND LEGEND by Miranda Green

LAKOTA STAR KNOWLEDGE by Ronald Goodman

TIPI Home of the Nomadic Buffalo Hunters by Paul Globe
Just for Starters!!

Celeste said I should include a picture of myself.
Here goes, Celeste!